THE DRAGON'S SAINT
THE SAINT GEORGE CHRONICLES
VOLUME ONE

M.L. EADEN

Print ISBN: 978-1-962655-02-6 – Douglas Illusions

eBook ISBN: 978-1-962655-01-9 – Douglas Illusions

Book Cover by Joanne Kwan: linktr.ee/dashalutris

Dragon and Iconography designs by Martin Whitmore: martinwhitmore.com

Edited by Victoria Flickinger: flickeringwords.com

Ed. 2 edition 2023 – Previously titled: The Saint George Chronicles

"I'm a Bad Idea" T-shirt/image referenced in this book is the property of Meghan Murphy and used with permission. murphypop.com

Content warnings **can be found on the** author's **website at mleaden.com.**

THE DRAGON'S SAINT

Reader's Note

The universe you are entering is contemporary, with magic, myths, and legends living and working alongside each other. There are many sentient and varied species. Some of them are out in the open, while others are not. However, everyone knows they existed, knows there's magic in the world, and knows that whether something walks in the light or goes bump in the night, it's as real as the sunrise and sunset.

It's a world where science and magic work hand-in-hand, creating advanced technology and building a day-to-day life where you could easily meet a dragon astronaut, an orc mage specializing in medicine, or a fae working as a tailor. Moonbases exist, sustainable living is a reality, and promises which seem to be mere figments of imagination are woven into the fabric.

Enjoy!

CONTENTS

HEADQUARTERS

GREGOR

Lockers clattered in the changing room as one shift transitioned into the next. While I had fond memories of the days when I'd worn the white-and-green public safety patrol uniform, holding the rank of detective fulfilled my need to serve the public and help individuals find justice.

I noticed a new guy a few lockers down from mine when I came back from the showers. Decently built, he was slightly shorter than my six-foot self, with a smattering of freckles across his tan skin. When he bent over, I couldn't help but approve of the view.

"First day?" The least I could do was be polite.

He looked in my direction and smiled. Dressed casually in a V-neck T-shirt, jeans, and sneakers, I tried not to ogle. In truth, I was a tiny bit upset with myself for looking. Besides, he was a new coworker, and I was already in a relationship.

"Yeah." He straightened and stuck out his hand. "Xavior Brantley. Nice to meet you."

His short, red-brown hair was well-kept, as was his mustache and the hair on his chin that wasn't quite a goatee, but it suited him. What put a slight hitch in my breath were his unnaturally bright green eyes. He was definitely someone with magic. I had no idea what he was beyond the visage he presented. With the variety of species and individuals with magic that lived in San Francisco, he could be anything.

"Gregor Lyndon, likewise." I shook his hand while barely keeping my gaze in check.

Xavior moved back to his locker and continued to unpack. I tried to dress and sneak looks at the same time and noticed he had a projectile safety vest, some restraints, and a few packs of the bluish-gray magical restraining gel that most of us call stop-goo. I didn't see a uniform, but when he pulled out a silver shield and hung it around his neck, I knew why.

"Ah, so you're the new dick," I said with a smirk as I finished buttoning my shirt. I pulled my badge from the locker shelf and clipped it onto my belt.

"Uh, yeah." He looked at me and laughed. "Guess so."

"Where were you last?"

"Nob Hill."

"That's pretty cushy." I closed my locker and pressed my thumb to the lock to secure it. "Why transfer to Jefferson?"

"Thought it might be nice to be more active instead of sitting around an office all day responding to missing familiars and the occasional prank magic trick by the local teens."

The Jefferson subdivision definitely wasn't the sprawling estates of Nob Hill. It contained a cross-section of beings tightly packed in apartment buildings, walk-ups, and shoulder-to-shoulder houses, most of which weren't up to code for the powers, types of magic, or species that lived there. The public safety patrols helped with mundane things, like parking violations or magical interference complaints. Detective divisions coordinated with them to investigate occurrences outside the patrol's day-to-day purview.

"Are you assigned to General Support?"

"Yeah." Xavior shut and secured his locker. "Figured it was the best fit, since I wasn't looking for a spot on either violent crimes or destructive magic."

I shrugged. "Fair." I checked my phone. "The GS division briefing is in five minutes. I'll see you there."

"Okay." Xavior smiled, and I nodded back as I escaped to grab some caffeine with a side of self-control. Most guys I worked with didn't turn my head like that, especially since I started dating Keith.

Keith and I met when we both worked the same accident scene about five years ago. He was in Jefferson's paramedic division, usually assigned to a bus working twenty-four-hour shift rotations. It made it difficult to spend time together, but we managed.

Coffee in hand, I took a seat in the briefing room at the back. Xavior sat near the front, and I caught myself glancing at him as Captain Lang walked in. Lang smoothed his suit jacket before he started the briefing.

"Alright, a few notes before I hand out assignments." Lang's brown eyes scanned the room to register our attention. "There's a new drug called Dreamweaver on the market. While most folks experimenting with it are staying indoors, some become disoriented enough to wander into traffic or think they can fly even if they don't have wings.

"Signs that someone might be on Dreamweaver include general confusion along with a light show in their irises. Talk them down if you can or herd them back to a safe location. Use stop-goo if you think the individual might be in a dangerous situation. We don't know how stop-goo magic interacts with this stuff yet, so use caution. There will be medical training in the next few weeks on how to counter the magical effects during high-risk situations. Please sign up as time slots become available."

Lang cleared his throat. "On a lighter note, we have a new individual starting today. Detective Xavior Brantley." Lang pointed at Xavior, who stood up and gave a small wave. "He comes to us with an extensive background in investigative research and has training as a CSI. His previous post was Nob Hill. Nice to have you here, Brantley."

As the captain gave out assignments, working pairs left the meeting room. The detectives around Brantley gave him the usual department greetings as they left. Eventually, Xavior and I were the only ones left in the room, which meant I was the lucky one on training duty.

The captain was chatting with Xavior and motioned for me to join them. "Lyndon, have you met Brantley yet?"

"Yeah, just before the meeting." I acknowledged him with a nod.

"Excellent. I'd like you to work together. Get Brantley up-to-speed with the division, the department, and your current caseload. We'll do an eval in thirty days."

I gave Lang a reassuring smile. "No problem, Captain."

"Good," Lang said, then turned to Xavior. "If you need anything, let me know. Lyndon is one of our seniors, so you'll be in expert hands."

"Thanks, Captain," Xavior said. Lang walked out, leaving us in the briefing room to get better acquainted.

"So we're working together." I smiled as I rocked on my heels a little. I opened my mouth to give a quick rundown on my current cases when Xavior stepped a little closer and whispered.

"While I'm flattered—and the feeling is mutual, by the way—if we'd met under different circumstances, I'd certainly be interested, but it's my first day, hmm? Maybe we should take things slow."

I blinked. The sound of his voice traveled down my spine while his words tumbled around in my brain. "What?"

"I've had the scent of your attraction in my nose since the locker room. Like I said, I'm flattered, but since we have to work together, we should probably try to keep it professional."

It surprised me how fast his words reduced me to monosyllabic replies. "Scent?" The word rang between my ears while everything else turned to sludge. I smelled like attraction?

"Dragons can scent pheromones that relate to emotions. Though overall we have a pretty good sense of smell too. Most shifters do," Xavior said.

That snapped me out of my daze. "Oh, no." I upgraded to two-syllable responses as I took a couple of steps back.

"Oh, yes." Xavior had a slightly amused expression.

My slight panic and tension fought with my need to explain our dangerous predicament to him. "No, you don't understand. This," I said as I pointed between us, "won't work."

"Why not? Are you a speciesist?" His mood shifted from flirtatious to irritated.

His irritated look drew my gaze to his emerald-green eyes and the line of his lips. "No, absolutely not." I swallowed to clear the knot in my throat and tried not to think about anything else he might pick up from my scent.

"Look, you'll have to take my word for it. It's not safe for you to work with me." I could tell he didn't buy it. In the entire decade I've been a public safety officer, not one dragon had crossed my path, that I knew of anyway.

If Xavior and I worked together, I would have to tell him and the captain or risk flushing my career down the drain when they found out about my power. I'd be back on patrol duty within the week for withholding information, and that was if they let me keep my job.

"Not safe?" That got his attention. "I'm a dragon. We're practically indestructible." I could tell by the way his eyes narrowed and his head tilted that a thought had occurred to him. "There's only one family of humans that have the ability to kill a dragon outright. Last I knew, they lived in Europe."

"There is a small branch of that family in Oregon." I let him read between the lines.

"You're a Saint George Knight?" Xavior's voice held a note of surprise.

I nodded. "Now, do you understand why this is a bad idea?"

"Not really." Xavior shrugged and crossed his arms.

His movement drew my eyes to his chest for a split second before my confusion at what he said surfaced in the proper location of my brain. I lifted my gaze to his face, but that didn't help. I knew I had a type, but I never expected it to show up in the form of a dragon that I shouldn't be within ten kilometers of, let alone half a meter. The fact that he still wanted to work with me was completely baffling. Did this dragon have a death wish? "Of course it is. The last thing I'd want is for anything to happen to you because of me."

"So you do like me." A smirk appeared, which prompted me to glance at his lips before he took a step toward me. "I was worried for a minute that I'd been completely off about that or that you hadn't realized you were attracted to me, which would have been more awkward." His lack of self-preservation did not help the situation, nor did his cocky charm.

I backed away with my hands up and tried to ward off the handsome apex predator. "First of all, latent attraction aside, I have a partner." I couldn't believe I'd admitted it out loud, but I pushed through my mild embarrassment. I waved a hand between us. "This won't happen. Second, I have a magical ability that can lethally harm dragons. It would border on criminal negligence for us to work together." I needed to get out of this room and find Captain Lang immediately. Never mind my career; being brought up on charges for harming a magical being was way worse. I slowly turned and headed for the exit when my name on his lips brought me to a standstill.

"Gregor." It had a wistfulness to it I used to hear in Keith's voice, but it had been a while.

"What?" I wanted to be irritated. Instead, my reply was more of a discontented sigh. I wanted to kick myself for not leaving fast enough.

"I'm three-hundred-seventy-three years old. Unless you have some pointy object nearby or some compulsion to harm dragons, I think we'll be fine. Besides, what's life without a little spice?"

I didn't know if he thought "spice" was my lack of control over my libido or him not caring that I was the one thing that could cause him legitimate harm. By his expression, my guess was both. "I'm stating now that I think this is a bad idea," I said as I turned to look at him.

"And I'm telling you, unless you're planning on telling Lang what you just told me, I accept the risk," Xavior said. "So, partner," he walked over and slapped my shoulder, "let's get to work."

I watched as he opened the door and walked past me into the office area. It was the closest I'd ever come to a dragon in real life. I desperately wanted to protect him from harm, and myself from everything he made me feel.

SMALL SPACES

XAVIOR

Greg had a secret. The sleeve of tattoos on his left arm, covered by his light blue button-down shirt I watched him put on, made more sense now. The tats were of fictional detectives and crime fighters. Most of those fictional characters had secrets to keep or hidden identities, and they were obsessed with justice. From the histories I knew, the Saint George Knights were not that high-minded. The tattoos made me think Greg was looking for justice or redemption. I'd bet they meant something more to him, or he could be a fan. I was curious to find out.

As we walked out of the briefing room, I followed Greg toward the detective's area. I watched as he ran his fingers through his black crewcut. A nervous gesture. He could be a threat, but he certainly didn't smell like one. Not with the protectiveness and attraction that surrounded him like a storm cloud. Humans were absolutely horrible at hiding their emotions, especially ones they thought were private.

"I'm assuming Nob Hill has a similar interface and reporting system?" Greg asked as he sat at what must be his desk. He pressed his thumb into the right corner, then pulled his badge from his belt and set it on a recessed spot on the surface. The slick display immediately lit up with files associated with his badge number as he picked up a stylus. He made a couple of taps to open the first file.

"Ah, yeah, somewhat. We didn't have physical desks, just holo displays and the latest haptic gloves. You know, the kind that gives sensory feedback directly to your fingertips." I wiggled my fingers, and Greg's light tan face went from neutral to slightly annoyed, and so did his scent. "Yes, it's similar enough."

"When they finish uploading your work profile, you'll be able to choose a biometric, then use your badge to access files and central data."

"Cool. One of my coworkers used their nose print. . ." The nostrils of Greg's slim nose widened, and his shoulders inched toward his ears as his ample lips thinned. Apparently, he'd switched to business mode. That was frustrating. He was much more relaxed in the locker room. "Sorry, please continue."

He made a couple more taps with the stylus while I pulled a chair from the empty desk across from him and took a seat. He didn't hesitate as he jumped into the details of the first case file.

"A chain of small corner stores are being robbed about every two weeks at the same time of night. The owners have taken precautions, but the individual somehow scares the shit out of the clerks. So much so, the clerks can't describe them, and none of the countermeasures available activated. The shop's imagers haven't caught anything either."

"Interesting," I replied as I looked over the information.

Greg let out a frustrated breath, then continued. "Yeah, you could say that." Out of the corner of my eye, I watched Greg absently scratch his face, which was framed by a trimmed goatee the same color as his hair. He made another tap and opened the folder of interviews and surveillance footage.

"The interviews describe the same experience. One minute everything's fine, the next, they all report having fear and anxiety so bad they remember nothing even after the individual has left the scene. The footage from all the different shop imagers showed fuzzy smudges, and the spectral analysis was inconclusive. There's only a vague reference to where the individual was in the room. By the size and shape of the missing data, it looks like one individual, but I haven't ruled out a cooperative group."

"You think it could be one or multiple individuals with abilities working together?"

"That's plausible. The lack of magical trace elements suggests it. What's interesting is that they take the same thing every time: whatever is in the till, about a dozen or so lottery tickets, and a pack of gum."

"Gum?" I chuckled. "Why gum?"

"Fresh breath? Who knows?" Greg shrugged, and I caught the faintest hint of a smile.

I liked that he kept an open mind. That was good. I could work with that. As I reviewed the information, details leapt out at me. "All the shops have the same name, or a variation of it. Are they all local?"

"Good question." Greg shrugged. "Don't know. Let me make a data request from central. They can put a cross-reference together for regional associations."

I watched as he opened a tab on his desk and sent the request. Even though Jefferson didn't have the latest interactive holovids, apparently they had a central technomage group. That was exceptionally more valuable to any case work than upgraded interfaces.

"How long will the request take?"

"Five minutes at most."

"That fast?" I was even more impressed.

"I'll have to take you to see their setup sometime. They are more wired down there than some government agencies."

"I'd like that." We glanced at each other, and for one moment that glance held the promise of friendship, at least, but maybe more. The poly-membrane surface of his desk pinged with the requested data, and Greg cleared his throat as we turned back to the case at hand.

The regional request didn't turn up anything new, so Greg loaded a map of the robbery locations, which were all locally owned by one family in the Bay Area. "Based on the pattern and lack of any similar thefts regionally, I'm confident the clerks recognize the thief or thieves," he said.

"What makes you think that?"

"They never use the counter measures, nor make any attempt to stop the theft. My theory is that they know who they are dealing with and try to talk them out of it."

"That's a decent theory based on the information. So, what were you thinking?" I sat back a little and observed his body language.

"Undercover work. Have a few officers work with clerks as new hires. See if we catch a break that way."

"Sounds like a plan. Do you need help with the requisition forms?" Greg liked to lead. His whole body relaxed when I didn't push back. He even laughed a little.

"Glad you volunteered. Here." Greg pulled a tablet from the side of the desk and moved the forms to the temporary workstation. "If you can fill these out, then call the owners; I can work on requisitions for personnel and extra tech."

After we had all the requests and forms filed, Greg and I went over the rest of his case files. One was about bike thefts. Another was a property dispute between the tenants and a landlord. There was an injunction in place so they didn't evict people for complaining about the lapse in building upkeep or the code requirements for magical tenants.

By the time we'd reviewed everything, it was early evening.

"Not a bad day's work," Greg said.

"Given our rocky start this morning, I wasn't sure how today would go."

Greg looked at me and made a dismissive noise. "Thanks for the vote of confidence."

"You have to admit," I leaned closer, "you didn't think we would work quite so well together."

"I don't have to admit anything." He gave me a pointed look with his attractive brown eyes. "I'll set up your access to the case files tonight. Your desk should be ready by tomorrow's shift."

I took the hint. "Okay, then, see you tomorrow, Lyndon."

"Night, Brantley." His tone was neutral, if not optimistic. I could work with that too.

When I transferred to Jefferson, I bought a brownstone within a short walking distance of headquarters. Figured it was easier than trying to commute over an hour home.

To celebrate my successful first day at a new division, I picked up dinner from the Chinese takeaway place between work and my house. As I unpacked my food, I realized I'd ordered more than usual. I briefly entertained the thought of calling the office to invite Greg over.

No, Xavior, get a fucking grip. You're new; he's in a relationship; you're work partners. Complicating shit is not a good idea. You even told him that!

I sat on the lone stool at my kitchen island and ate. The quiet of my empty house bothered me. So I pulled out my phone and checked Omni-Personal—the dating app for anyone into everyone—to see who was available. I set my status to available and immediately had five requests for various activities and two for dates. Options enough to take my mind off my new, admittedly attractive, prickly coworker.

STAKEOUT

GREGOR

Three weeks of surveillance and we hadn't managed one lead. Nor had the extra imagers or patrols turned up anything. Either we'd spooked the individual, or they weren't interested anymore. Without a new lead, the likelihood that we would solve this case wasn't high. We had one week left to make progress on the case before Lang pulled the entire staff and resources assigned to the effort.

I tossed back the last of my coffee as I watched Xavior work with his assigned clerk. We had three pairs of detectives, including us, rotate through twenty-five shops owned by the Kim family. Tonight, we were at a shop somewhat north of headquarters. When the shop finally closed for the evening, I let out a frustrated sigh as I kept my eyes on Xavior and the clerk as they locked up.

Xavior had to know I was still watching as he unbuttoned his store logo shirt and walked across the street toward our unmarked vehicle. The T-shirt under it was plastered to his form and showed off a decently toned body most non-humans had with little effort.

I schooled my face into something less slack-jawed as he opened the vehicle door and tossed the shirt at me. He got in as I scoffed at his antics and threw the shirt in the back with the rest of our gear. "Gross," I said with feigned annoyance.

"How did surveillance go?" Xavior asked as he turned his seat around to dig a container of water out of the portable cooling unit.

I cleared my throat and tried to unobtrusively adjust myself. "Nothing here or at any of the other stores we had teams at tonight." I started the vehicle with a touch to the control panel, thinking that the sooner we went back to headquarters, the quicker I could head home. Being hyped up on caffeine for the last eight hours didn't help with my frustration.

Xavior tempted me in another direction. "Wanna go some-place for a beer?"

The question made me think. Keith wasn't home, we didn't have a surveillance shift tomorrow, and maybe if I could learn more about Xavior I'd get over whatever it was I found attractive. "Sure. I know a place that is pretty quiet at this time of night." I waited until Xavior secured his safety webbing before I gave the vehicle directions to Jackie's.

It was a hole-in-the-wall place that didn't mind anyone as long as you had money and didn't start shit. It had a pub feel to it, with plenty of bar space, including small tables and booths scattered around lining the walls. This late into the evening, most of the sports crowd had moved on, and those left were regulars, off-duty professionals, or folks looking for a quiet spot after dancing most of the night.

We took a couple spots at the bar and ordered two drafts. After a few sips, the quiet stretched into awkwardness. I finally spoke.

"Lang mentioned you trained as a CSI. What's the story there?"

"Nob Hill was pretty quiet, so I took classes, got a degree, and then did my certification training at the downtown head-quarters," he said. "I figured a better understanding of forensic science would help me solve more cases." He gave a little shrug and grinned. "What it did was present more information and statistical noise to my casework than was relevant, though it paid off sometimes."

I chuckled. "Oh? What happened?"

"I was working a murder scene one night," he said with a sigh. "I was so methodical in collecting evidence that it took a week to catalog it all correctly. It pissed off everybody in the lab until this tiny fingernail clipping I collected turned up enough DNA evidence to not only put the individual-of-interest at the scene, it tied her to the deceased. It was trace evidence, but it was enough to obtain a provisional warrant to search the I.O.I's residence. From that, we found enough evidence to take her into custody."

"Why didn't you transfer to downtown? It sounds like they could have used a good CSI." I took another drink, wondering why he thought Jefferson was a better fit.

"Honestly, I was a bit more obsessed than my coworkers about it, and I hoarded as much evidence as possible for every case I ran. While it worked out in one instance, it didn't work well for others. I got my certification, but they didn't ask me to stay, so I went back to Nob Hill."

"Ouch." I felt a pang of embarrassment for him. "All because you were thorough? That seems like a mistake." He obviously enjoyed working forensics. It seemed wrong that they pushed him out.

Xavior shrugged and fidgeted with his beer glass. "There are only so many hours in the day to process evidence. If you treat a random theft the same as murder, because you get caught up in the mystery of it, you slow the investigation down and your department with you." His shoulders were hunched as he stared into his beer glass. "While it's easier to collect and process evidence these days, it still costs time, money, and coworker relationships." He shrugged.

Something he said interested me. "'The mystery of it?'" I repeated. "Is that your obsession?" Xavior gave me a huge grin that lit up my insides, but when I remembered why, it took everything I had not to frown.

He nodded. "After I took a break from traveling, I got involved with public safety work. It let me help people and figure out little mysteries here and there." He turned toward me. "I'm lucky that I am not so obsessed that I have to keep driving for bigger and bigger mysteries or stay stuck on ones that are nearly impossible to solve."

"It's pretty unusual for a dragon to have that kind of self-control." I glanced at him, then inwardly winced. I hadn't meant to let on how much I actually knew about dragons.

"How do you know that? Did you grow up learning everything you could about dragons?"

I could tell Xavior meant it as a joke by how relaxed he was and the way his emerald eyes held a kind of mirth. He seemed amused that anyone would take that much interest in his species. When I didn't answer, I watched as he quickly made the connection, and the carefree attitude I'd enjoyed a moment earlier died as he swallowed, took a deep breath, and answered his own question.

"That makes sense, given your family history, I suppose." To his credit, his mood shifted as he realized the opportunity I'd presented. His eyes lit with a green spark as his curiosity kicked in. If he needed a mystery, from his perspective, my family history was a large one.

"What exactly did they teach you?" He leaned in. It was oddly comforting how interested he was, given the topic. Besides my parents and the Order itself, no one knew about my ability or my history with the Americas branch of the Saint George Knights. Not even Keith.

I took a long drink. What the hell. "Uh, well, my siblings and I were homeschooled, but the focus was all things Draconis varium. Name a subject or topic and our tutors would relate it to dragons somehow. Besides that, we had instructors for weapons and magical item use."

Xavior blinked with his inner eyelids, then blinked with the outer ones. "That's intense."

"Yeah, you could say that." I took another sip, then dared to shift the subject slightly. "Back at the office, when you asked if I was a speciesist... have you dealt with that a lot?"

He took a deep breath and let it out. "Sometimes. Mostly on the job, working with the public. Being called a skin suit isn't the worst thing, but it stings." That particular slang was thrown at shifters a lot. While the Magical Species Pact kept an enforced tolerance between most species, it did little to squash the history individual species had between each other. "I remember when I was younger, my parents talked about how other species treated us and to be careful. Then I met a shepherd on the road, and he invited me to his house for a meal after I told him what I was. He and his wife were very nice to me. I thought maybe my parents were wrong. Though that was during the Renaissance period. Everyone seemed more open to all kinds of things."

"How's it different now?" Xavior didn't look like he was over three hundred years old. He looked like he was about my age, somewhere in his mid-thirties.

"It's not, not really. Or, well, with so many now having cross-species backgrounds, there's more understanding. Most of the time." He took another drink of his beer. "Like you, for instance. When I was a whelp, we used to hear horror stories about the Knights and their campaigns against dragons all the time. But here you are, asking questions, reserving judgment."

"It wasn't like they taught me to do that. They kicked me out." I hadn't meant to say that. The beer and my mild exhaustion were working against me. His slowly forming smile and narrowed eyes told me he would not let it go, so I gave in. "I held too many contradictory beliefs from my family and the Order. One of the biggest was being queer, specifically liking men."

"You didn't plan to tell me that." He tapped his nose when I frowned at him. "Your regret tickled my nose."

I shrugged and cleared my throat. "It's much easier telling an attractive woman I'm not interested than explaining anything about the Order."

"Understandable, considering." He gave me a slight grin.

"Considering what?" I asked and quickly realized I shouldn't have.

Xavior laughed. "Lyndon, you have a distinct lack of self-awareness. I imagine very few people haven't conjured up fantasies of a dark-haired, dark-eyed, brooding type such as yourself."

I gasped a little as I nearly choked on my drink. Once I could breathe again, I fought off my mild embarrassment and groped for another subject. "You know, you're the first dragon I've ever met," I said, adding another confession to my list. Why was it so easy to talk with him about things I never spoke about with anyone?

"Really? You don't have some sixth sense around dragons? Isn't that part of your magical ability?" His tone was playful, even though he was fishing for more information.

"No. They taught us to deal with dragons in their natural forms, mostly. Though, a dragon's shifting abilities were discussed from time to time." I didn't expand on that point. I'd already said too much.

"So then, all your magical ability does is kill a dragon?"

"Isn't that enough?"

"It's weirdly specific, that's all. Why dragons? I know the legend of the knight saving a princess from a dragon, but there were knights that did all kinds of things in the Middle Ages. Killing dragons was only one of them."

I was silent. Xavior made excellent points, and I didn't have answers. They taught the legend like it was the catalyst that gave Knights our ability. But Xavior was right. It was weirdly specific, and it was passed down genetically. They tested every family member for the marker at birth. They taught us it was a blessing bestowed on sainted Knights, since the genetic marker never mutated. Personally, I thought it was a curse.

Xavior finished his beer and set the empty glass back on the bar, then changed the subject. "Did you know that the character Sherlock Holmes was based on a dragon obsessed with mysteries and solving riddles?"

"Seriously?" I wondered if he brought that up because he saw my tattoo. One of them was a bloodhound with a deerstalker hat.

"Totally true. I met Doyle once. I have a signed first edition of one of his books somewhere." Xavior waved off the bartender when they motioned toward the glass. I glanced up at the analog clock above the bar as I finished my beer. When the bill showed up, I thumbed for the tab.

"Thanks. I'll pay next time," Xavior said as he scratched his nose.

I gave him a nod and left it at that. It gave me no small amount of anxiety, wondering what his nose had picked up. The voice in the back of my head, from years of training at my mother's direction, berated me for betraying myself to a predator. I'd been telling that voice to fuck off for years, and tonight was no different.

As we walked toward our vehicle, I made one more confession. "I exercise in the morning before my shift starts if you want to join me."

"Sounds entertaining," Xavior said in a mockingly cheerful voice. "I might take you up on it."

"Hey, not all of us can auto-magically maintain ourselves."

I unlocked the vehicle and got in. Xavior slid into the passenger seat. "Duly noted."

We were quiet as I drove back to headquarters to drop him off, change vehicles, and then headed home. I cleaned up, then went to bed alone with mixed feelings about what I'd told Xavior, thoughts of mystery writers, and a vision of a dragon with bright green eyes.

A GRANDMOTHER'S SURPRISE

XAVIOR

With less than a week left of our special surveillance operation, we caught a break.

I saw a flash of magic even though the external imagers hadn't picked up anything. It looked like the shop's stop-goo device was triggered. I sprinted from my vehicle to the front door with another stop-goo pack in hand. What I saw suspended in the goo was definitely new. That alone made the transfer to Jefferson headquarters worth it, I thought, as I looked at the individual encased from the neck down.

The small individual jabbered while they held the bag of stolen goods in one hand and a knobby stick in the other. They were barely taller than a ten-year-old human; their skin was a pale green, and they had a black, pencil-thin mustache that extended past their rather predominate chin. While I didn't understand everything they said, the context indicated they were upset, to put it mildly.

"Lyndon? Mr. Kim?" I asked, while the chatty figure in the stop-goo continued. "Is everyone alright?"

"We're fine, Brantley," Greg said in a shaky voice. "We're behind the counter."

I walked around the corner to see Greg and Mr. Kim hugging each other, shaking. "You don't look fine. I'm calling for EMS." I pulled out my phone and called central.

"Brantley," Greg said with a tone of warning.

"Lyndon. You both look like you're a few shivers away from shock. The paramedics will have something they can use to counter whatever they did."

"The stop-goo worked?"

"Yeah. I'm looking at them right now. They sound upset based on what little Korean I know. Mr. Kim, do you know what they're saying?" I hoped so, or it was going to be a long night with a linguistic witch.

Mr. Kim nodded, still holding onto Greg. "More or less. Grandmother had a little ritual she would do once a month and said it was for her little helper, that they brought good luck. We thought she did it out of habit, just something she learned as a child, but I guess it was more than that. That's a Dokkaebi."

The small person went quiet. Mr. Kim frowned as they glanced in the being's direction, even though they couldn't see them from behind the counter. I shook my head and asked, "What's a Dokkaebi?"

"A kind of spirit, I guess. A little like a goblin, maybe. There are all kinds, but some cause mischief if you don't do a ritual to keep them happy. As long as you keep them happy, they bring blessings and good fortune, so the stories go." Mr. Kim took a big breath, then shivered.

"Can we contact your grandmother to see if she can help?" I would be upset too if something stopped me from doing what was in my nature to do, especially if it was because of a particular family. It reminded me of Greg's predicament a little.

"No, unfortunately, she's not with us any longer," Mr. Kim sounded like his teeth were clacking together as he tried to speak. "And I don't know the ritual myself. My mother might, if grandmother told her."

When EMS showed up, Mr. Kim and Greg were treated for their symptoms while I coordinated with the other two patrol units and a linguistics witch. The stop-goo would not hold for much longer, so I dissolved it with a neutralizer and asked the Dokkaebi to wait. If their face was anything to go by, my Korean was horrible.

Mr. Kim called a local family friend who had experience dealing with spirits. After an hour with a linguistics spell and the friend, Mr. Kim had the basics for the ritual requested by Hyun-Shik, the Dokkaebi.

Since the Dokkaebi's activity was localized to only the family and the stores they owned, we agreed to release Hyun-Shik into Mr. Kim's care. We scheduled a health and wellness follow-up later to see if they needed anything else.

When the paramedics released Greg, I helped him into our vehicle and drove us back to the station. Greg headed to the locker room while I went to my desk to write reports and file forms. The forms could have waited, but I didn't want to leave him alone while he looked so unsteady. About thirty minutes into the various write-ups and requests I needed to fill out, Greg appeared with wet hair and clean clothes.

"Feel better?" I looked up from my tablet to watch as he sank into the chair next to my desk.

"Yes." He was quiet for a moment. "I don't understand how, but the fear I felt was unlike anything I could have imagined." He ran his hand through his hair, and I had a weird urge to do the same thing. I cleared my throat instead.

"He likely has some ability that targets the amygdala of a brain. No one we interviewed had lasting effects." Greg nodded. "It's the first time I've ever come across a Dokkaebi." I smiled, but I tried to keep my enthusiasm in check. I didn't need to wallow in my obsession while Greg looked haunted by the experience.

"You have anything like a Dokkaebi back home?" Greg asked, as he gave me a curious look.

"No. European goblins are like huge parrots. They mimic words sometimes, but they rarely carry on conversations like the Dokkaebi."

I organized a few more things in the case file and started another form to cover expenses and log the use of the stop-goo. "If you give me about twenty more minutes to finish up, I can drive you home."

"Nah, that's okay. I can get myself home if you're doing all the forms for the case." Greg stood and ran his hand through his hair again. I ventured a tiny whiff. The smell of his soap and undertones of longing made me curious, but I didn't try to distinguish more. Maybe he simply wanted to go home. That would be fair after tonight's experience.

"You sure? It wouldn't be a problem, or I can call your partner to pick you up," I offered.

"You are my partner."

Even though I questioned whether Greg was actually alright based on that statement, I rephrased my offer. "Your other partner. The one you go home to."

"Oh." He thought about it for a moment, then shook his head. "Keith is on duty tonight. I don't want to pull him away from work."

"Are you sure? I mean—"

Greg cut me off, which was probably good considering I was about to say, if I was your partner. . .

"Brantley, thanks, but I'll be fine."

We nodded at each other, then Greg tapped on his desk. "Send over anything you need me to sign, and I'll file it in the morning."

"Sure thing," I said to Greg's back as he started walking toward the door. "Night, Lyndon."

He waved without looking back. "Night, Brantley."

When I finally went home, all I could think of were Greg's dark brown eyes full of fear and how he and Mr. Kim were huddled on the floor as if something were prepared to eat them. I hadn't seen fear like that in a human's eyes in a long time. It took me back to my early traveling days. Sometimes fear was an effective tool for survival. When I was young, I scared my fair share of individuals because I was afraid of them and what they could do to me. It was ignorant, but thankfully I learned other ways to deal with threats.

It wasn't the only time I saw fear in Greg's eyes tonight. When he mentioned Keith, there was something there. Why would Greg not want to tell someone he loves he needed help?

An icy shiver crawled down my spine, and I suddenly missed the hot tub back at my estate. I sighed and settled for the scalding shower at my brownstone. I hadn't been scared into near paralysis, but I understood fear all too well, and I tried to let the scalding water wash it away.

OTHER HALF

GREGOR

It's often said that success generates more work. Given our caseload now, I would say that was certainly true. Since the Dokkaebi, Lang and the staff sergeants had moved several other cases with odd circumstances into our queue.

One dealt with a small neighborhood that used sentient ghost lights, but they were flickering, which meant that the ghosts were displaced. A check with the technomages who sifted through neighborhood data told us it was localized to that neighborhood, thankfully. We suspected a siphon of some kind, but we were waiting on equipment to confirm it.

Another case was about off-season fireworks sales. It was likely stock left over after all the New Year celebrations and someone hoping to unload the inventory. As magical fireworks and devices became cheaper, more popular, and safer for the environment, fireworks sales declined. A citation and help to find a suitable storage location were enough to have them wait until the next season.

Our ongoing bike theft case continued to be perplexing. While most of the bikes that disappeared were free to the public, some privately owned ones were also taken. Both physical and magical trackers failed to locate the missing bicycles. It was as if they had dropped into a black hole.

I promised Xavior I'd pick up the next tab at beer night when I left him to handle the late additions to our list of bike thefts. I tried not to work late on Wednesdays since it was the only weeknight Keith had off.

We'd have dates at a local Vietnamese restaurant sometimes, share spring rolls and chat about our day. Lately, we've stayed in. I picked up our favorite pho and an order of spring rolls, eager to spend time with him.

The last few weeks of the corner store case and Keith's twenty-four-hour rotations as a paramedic meant we hadn't spent time with each other lately. Now that our schedules were back to normal, I wanted to make more time for us.

When I arrived home, either Keith wasn't home or wasn't awake. I set the takeout on the kitchen counter and walked back to our bedroom. He was sprawled out in bed, still dressed in his uniform. I dumped the contents of my pockets onto the dresser, kicked off my shoes, and got into bed beside him. His shift must have ended much later than usual for him to still have his uniform on.

Keith's muscular body hadn't moved a centimeter as I settled next to him. It was a testament to his exhaustion. I itched to run my fingers through his brownish-red hair, but instead, I touched his beige skin where it wasn't covered by his uniform. We'd sometimes play this game with each other, teasing with small touches while the other was sleeping.

I traced his shoulder with my fingertips and smiled as it elicited a quiet moan. Like magnets, we came together until we were a tangle of limbs. It was peaceful, and some days I wished this was how we were all the time.

"Hey, beautiful," I whispered in his ear. Keith turned a little and planted a soft kiss on my cheek. "I brought dinner. Are you interested?" I pulled back enough to see the hint of a smile drift across his lips. I watched as his light-blue eyes fluttered open, then closed again.

"Maybe," he said in a rough, sleepy voice as he tightened his arms around me. I pressed kisses into his lips and forehead and continued until a low rumble of laughter came from him. He rolled me onto my back and straddled my hips as he laced his fingers with mine. He had a libidinous look on his face that I interrupted with a question.

"When did you get home?"

"Around noon. We had a tough call before dawn with a group of yearling vamps that were starving. They'd resorted to feeding off each other to keep themselves going." He let go of me and rubbed his face as if to wipe away the visual.

Yearling vampires were vamps that were less than twenty years into their new life and yet to be accepted by a coven. "They didn't go to a donor location?"

"They were too weak to make it there regularly." He sighed, and I could feel him tense from his frustration. "They really should start making the covens pay for new vampire welfare."

"Probably. Or make them pay blood banks for the upkeep." The conversation wasn't new. Keith often expressed his frustrations with vampire initiation cruelty. Each fresh horror he endured as a paramedic was added to his conviction that the covens were one of society's greatest failures.

"One of them was fifty when they turned him. He said it was the only option he had to survive cancer after all the treatments failed." Keith shook his head. "It was bad, Gregie. How many people like that end up in vampire flophouses hoping they make it through their first twenty years?"

"You helped and did what you could. That's all you can do." I pulled him down and wrapped my arms around him until he relaxed.

He kissed me gently as his hands tugged at my shirt to reach bare skin. "Dinner's going to be cold," I warned.

"That's what heat spells are for," Keith said as we separated long enough to work our shirts off so we could press our bodies back together. He kissed me as my hands drifted to his ass and urged him to move and press closer.

I choked off a whimper as I nearly came from our grinding and kissing. Keith chuckled and pulled away to grab lube and condoms from the nightstand and take off his work slacks. I undid my pants and pushed them off, along with my boxers.

Keith came back to bed and kissed down my torso to settle between my legs.

He worked quickly. "Babe," I panted. "Fuck, Keith. I'm close." I felt him moan and make a deep-throated laugh around my cock, and it went straight to my balls. "Christ, Keith." He kept going, and I reached down to put a hand on his head and thrust my hips a little. His sounds were more enthusiastic, and I went with them. He plunged me all the way to the back of his throat, and I lost myself, spilling my load into him with a groan that rattled in my chest.

I thought I could enjoy the afterglow, but I was wrong. Keith grabbed the bedsheets and expertly rolled me onto my stomach. It was a trick he learned from work. He knew it made me laugh every time he did it.

My laughter drifted into a moan as he dribbled cold lube onto my ass. I blew out a breath to relax and rested my chin on my folded arms as one questing finger was quickly followed by another. Soon enough, his fingers had me floating somewhere between the familiar burning sensation and post-orgasm bliss, until he tried to insert a third one a little too quickly.

"Hey, hey," I reached behind me to grab his hand, only to have him push it away. "Where's the emergency, Elliot?"

"I can't help it if you make me want to drill your hairy ass into next week." He pressed kisses into my lower back and said hairy ass, which made me chuckle.

Most nights, we didn't get beyond mutual satisfaction with our hands or mouths. While we were in an open relationship, condoms were a requirement. Lube was a must for me, but Keith could take it or leave it.

I put my hand back to keep him from slamming into me. I couldn't handle that tonight. He took the clue and worked himself into me slowly, then lay on top of me. It took little to catch my fading orgasm. Our combined movements had me leaking on the bed as Keith panted and groaned above me.

His chest pressed into my back as he thrust his cock into me. "You feel so good, baby, so hot." I wanted to believe what tumbled from Keith's mouth. With a few more thrusts, he unloaded into the condom. His breath felt hot on my back as he panted from his exertions.

After cleaning up, we stood in the kitchen in our underwear and ate reheated pho bowls with chopsticks. As I shoved a wad of noodles into my mouth, Keith caught me entirely off guard.

"I hear your new partner is really hot," Keith said in a coy voice. "What's his name?"

I spat out half a mouthful of noodles. "Where did you hear that from?" I was already annoyed, wondering why he needed to ask.

"The grapevine. You know how everyone talks. Larson was on the bus that showed up at your corner store case." Keith liked to tease unmercifully. He slurped more noodles from his bowl, and I braced myself for what else Larson must have told him. "I'm surprised you were so scared of a goblin that you pissed yourself."

Anger bubbled as I threw down my bowl and pointed at him. "Fuck you. You have no idea how terrifying that was. And it's not a goblin. It's a Dokkaebi. They induce fear as a defense mechanism."

"Aww, babe," Keith said with mock sympathy and a chuckle. "What are you scared of?"

"I'm not fucking telling you. Not now." He kept teasing as he put down his bowl and moved toward me. I tried to move away, but there wasn't much room in our small kitchen. Eventually, I let him hug me as he reassured me with soft apologies and murmured affection.

I hugged him back and thought he'd dropped the topic when he quietly said, "It's okay, Gregie. I still love you, even though you pissed your pants."

"Oh, fuck you." I clenched my fists and gritted my teeth as I pushed him away. I hated when he did shit like that. Escaping to the living room, I took my dinner with me. When he sat next to me on the couch, I purposefully ignored him.

"Seriously though, your new partner, what's the deal?" I gave Keith a sideways glance and narrowed my eyes. I didn't want to talk unless he was done teasing. He held up his hands in surrender.

"His name is Xavior Brantley. He transferred from Nob Hill. We're up for a thirty-day eval at the end of the week. So far, it's going pretty well."

Xavior hadn't made fun of me or said anything about what happened. The paramedics gave us pants to change into, and that was it. Once we were back at headquarters, he still hadn't brought it up, and he hadn't mentioned it in the official reports. The paramedics obviously weren't as kind.

I finished my noodles and set my bowl down on the coffee table. As I turned toward Keith, I noticed his clenched jaw and his narrowed eyes. He pointed at me and said, with a bit of venom in his voice, "You like him."

Whatever he saw in my aura was probably not to his liking. I forget Keith was a hedge witch at the most inconvenient times. I flung my hands up, frustrated with his prodding. "Of course. He's easy to get along with, and he's a good coworker." I tried to be calm, though I felt a flutter in my stomach. I knew exactly what he meant. Keith's words irritated me because they were too close to the truth.

"Yeah, you say that, but I think you like him, like him." Keith's tone was acerbic.

"Really? Are you fucking twelve?" I put my feet on the coffee table to annoy him. Keith got up from the couch, grumbling something under his breath, and went to the kitchen as I made a hand motion to turn on the holo. When he returned with his own dinner, he nudged my legs none too gently before he sat down. I glared at him as I took my feet off the coffee table, then went back browsing on the holo with angry swiping gestures the sensor sometimes failed to catch.

He finished his noodles as I stopped on a comedy show we both liked. When he finally spoke, his request didn't surprise me. "I want to meet him, see for myself what the big deal is."

"He's not a big deal." My words tasted like a lie. Keith didn't know I was a Saint George Knight, nor that Xavior was a dragon —not that him being a dragon was a department secret, but the fact was, I was elated to meet one finally, let alone work with one. That, tied in with whatever latent attraction we had between us and the fact that I could probably kill him with my chopsticks, didn't help.

"You had Gina over all the time. I haven't seen your new partner once since you started working with him. I want to meet him and find out who's protecting your backside besides me."

My lips twitched at the small joke. My annoyance toward Keith melted like ice as he leaned into me, and I wrapped an arm around his shoulders. "Okay, fine." I sighed as I kissed his temple. "I'll see if he wants to go to dinner with us next Wednesday. Does that work?"

"Perfectly," he said, preening. I groaned, and he laughed. I started the comedy show, shifting our focus to something else and hopefully getting back to enjoying our night off.

FAVOR

XAVIOR

I followed Greg by his unique scent and the mix of anxiety I smelled as I left headquarters. It made me wonder what caused it. Greg never struck me as anxious about anything. Once I found him, I slowed to his jogging pace. "Good morning."

"Morning," Greg replied. A half-mile into his morning jog, and he was still tense.

I picked up my pace and ran circles around him, literally, as we continued. Usually he'd call me a showoff and banter, but his mind was obviously on other things. "What's got you so worked up on this fine Thursday?"

"Our evaluation and the bicycle case. All the leads are coming up empty. Lang can't spare any more surveillance resources because they're low-value items. If it doesn't matter, why are we looking in the first place?"

"Maybe someone's hoping there's a simple explanation. Some things are worth looking into, even if they don't seem all that important." The universe appeared to mock us as we rounded a corner, and someone pedaled by us on a free city bicycle. A thought occurred to me. "Or whoever took them had a pocket dimension, used the bikes, then forgot to bring them back."

"The only way we could prove that is if whoever took the bikes eventually brings one back." Greg slowed, then stopped. "That's it." He blinked and waved his hands. "We've only been looking for the missing ones when they go missing. We haven't seen if any of them come back. Central Tech could write a program to see if a bike tries to re-register to the system after it's removed."

"That's not a bad idea." It was actually pretty brilliant, but the idea hadn't eased Greg's anxiousness, so it wasn't really related to the case. I nudged us into a walk, hoping he'd keep talking. "We work pretty well together. So, the eval shouldn't be a problem." Greg winced. "Will it?"

I took a deep breath and sighed. Maybe I had read him wrong, and he was still worried about the whole dragon-sainted knight thing. I wasn't. Though I suppose it was an issue between us, even if I downplayed it. "Lyndon, talk with me. What's eating at you?"

He smirked at that. The subtle shift in his smell toward attraction was better than the sour anxiety from a few moments before. "My partner, Keith, wants to meet you. Invite you out for drinks or dinner. It seems the emergency services crew from the corner store incident talked. He thinks I'm hiding you from him for some reason."

"What?" Greg was honest and embarrassed. That mixed with his attraction was kind of endearing.

"He thinks. . ." Greg paused. His embarrassment increased. "Well, I'm not sure what he thinks." He sighed. "I'm questioning if us working together is a good idea for a host of reasons, not the least of which is Keith."

The first thought I had, which was the wrong one, gave me a strong desire to throttle Keith, then give him a reason to be a jealous, whiny asshole. Greg was about as close to the romanticized knight in shining armor I'd ever seen, and I'd met real knights. They were horrific people mostly, but Greg was the epitome of loyalty, with a leadership quality others would envy. At the corner store, Greg was a mess, but still insisted Mr. Kim was seen to first. He dealt with the public with patience. He used his blinker when he changed lanes and gave pep talks to the other detectives, even the staff sergeant, when they weren't having a good day. I'd seen all that in the last thirty days of working with him. Greg had a remarkable kindness. If there were any part of him that was selfish, it would surprise me.

"Look. I'm not losing you as a partner. We'll have dinner; I'll bring a date. Keith can see that we have a good working relationship, and that's all." I put a hand on his shoulder. "No one should dictate your career choices, Lyndon."

I watched as he took a deep breath and let it out. The relief he felt was evident to my nose. It all but replaced the smell of his subtle attraction toward me. Although I had to admit; I looked forward to it any time I was near him. Given this recent development, I'd need to work harder to keep my own desires in check.

It wasn't a new situation for me to deal with unrecognized attraction. But this wasn't unrecognized; it was being actively ignored. We were able to do that because we liked each other beyond that attraction, plus Greg was in a relationship. If Greg needed his partner to trust him, then I would support him.

I patted his shoulder a couple of times and stopped before my conflicted thoughts sorted themselves out at the wrong moment.

"Race you back to the building?" Greg asked with a grin on his face.

"You're on."

Greg took off, and I stared at his backside for a few moments before I noticed how far he was ahead of me. "Oh, shit!" I shouted as I pushed to catch up. At the same time, I pondered calling Vanessa to see if she was available for a dinner date.

JUST DESSERTS

GREGOR

After Gina left the department to move to Dallas with her partner and their two kids, I'd worried about being assigned another partner. Gina and I had worked well together. Our families knew each other. That kind of partnership didn't happen overnight. It was mostly a formality, but I had to admit, it felt pretty good when Xavior and I were cleared to work together after our evaluation.

Our passing the thirty-day eval also reinforced the fact that Xavior was right. No one should dictate my career decisions. Xavior and I worked well together, and we had several closed cases to prove it. Keith's need to size Xavior up was another thing entirely.

Keith and I had boundaries in our relationship. Most people with open relationships had them. I don't think he'd mind if I was seeing someone else, but after his slip-up, we had discussed what lines were not acceptable to cross, including hiding sexual activities with other people or bringing someone into our house for more than a friendly visit. I could see why he might be worried about Xavior.

Sure, I was attracted to Xavior on some level, but that wasn't as important as our working relationship. That's what mattered to me, and I'm sure Keith would see that once he met him.

When I met Keith, he was upfront with me about the fact that he was a hedge witch and that their group practice involved sex. I didn't understand it, but I made space for it. The fact that he came home to me, he used protection, and kept details to himself, worked. While I thought Keith would be okay if I saw someone else, I didn't see the need. Between our relationship and our work schedules, it was hard enough to find time for each other.

So I was cautiously optimistic that dinner with Xavior would put things to rest for Keith. Then he would see that all this envy over my new partnership would be for nothing.

When Xavior offered to make the reservation for us, I probably should have told him that anything low-key or casual would have worked. It surprised me he was able to make reservations for a new upscale restaurant downtown. When we arrived, there was a valet service, which informed us that Xavior had already paid for our vehicle. Keith and I exchanged glances. We were both wearing nice clothes, but nothing too formal. When someone opened the door for us as if it were their job, that's when I knew this would be anything but a casual dinner.

"Good evening," a woman in a stunning-yet-professional black dress said from behind a podium. "Do you have a reservation?" Her manner and tone questioned our credibility. Keith was staring at the lavish dining room, grinning like a little kid. That made me smile, and I couldn't care less what the woman thought about who we were and what we were doing in a place like this.

"Our reservation is under Xavior Brantley," I replied.

Her eyes went wide. I wasn't sure what that meant, but I hoped we wouldn't be kicked out. She leaned toward me. "Normally, we require guests to wear more formal attire to dine with us, but seeing as you're with Mr. Brantley, we'll make an exception." I nodded. Shit, did he own the place? She straightened. "Can you follow me, please?"

I reached for Keith's elbow, and he acknowledged me with that playful smirk I loved. I smiled back and subtly nodded toward the woman. "She wants us to follow her."

"Did you tell her you're gay?" he said as I led him into the main dining area.

"I don't think she meant that kind of follow," I chuckled.

"As expensive as this place is, that kind of 'follow' has to be somewhere on the menu. These crown mouldings alone cost more than our house."

Keith loved interior design. He claimed that if he ever gave up being a paramedic, he'd go back to school full-time to learn more. Part of me hoped he would, so we could have a serious conversation about starting a family. With our schedules right now, that discussion was on hold, or if I was honest, non-existent.

The host walked to the back of the seating area and through double doors into what turned out to be a very busy central kitchen. Keith got excited, turned slightly, and tapped me on the chest. "Gregie, we're going to the chef's table," he gasped with excitement. "The fucking chef's table, in a place like this. Xavior must be loaded."

I instantly regretted letting Xavior make the reservations. "I guess so," I said to Keith, as if that explained everything. Keith and I couldn't afford a dinner this extravagant with our salaries. My light mood shifted to one of trepidation. What was Xavior thinking when he picked this place?

The host held open another door. It was the entrance to a private room with one table in the center, floor-to-ceiling wine racks on two walls, and next to the door we just walked through, a smaller version of the full kitchen with a cook already hard at work along with a member of the waitstaff. They were serving Xavior and a very gorgeous woman a bottle of wine. "I hope you enjoy your meal," the host said. The noises from the main kitchen disappeared as she closed the door. Keith and I didn't move an inch until Xavior noticed us.

"Welcome! I'm glad you could both make it." Xavior stood and walked over to us. "I might have picked something a little more low-key, but Vanessa wanted to be spoiled." He nodded in her direction and gave her a big smile.

I didn't know if I was happy to see him with someone else, for Keith's sake, or if I was ready to puke. It felt a little like whiplash. I hadn't thought about being confronted by the image of Xavior with someone else, which was an extremely foolish notion considering, well, everything. He said he'd bring a date. That had been part of the plan.

Vanessa was stunning. She wore a burgundy cocktail dress that had a flare to one side and cream heels. Her dark natural hair was loosely styled to frame her dark amber face, which featured makeup that accentuated her dark brown eyes. I couldn't help but stare and maybe be a little envious.

It took Keith nudging me in the ribs to bring me out of my daze. He looked at me as if expecting something, and I realized I had frozen up. I tore my eyes away from Vanessa and introduced my partners to each other. "Right." I cleared my throat. "Xavior Brantley, this is my partner, Keith Elliot." They shook hands. Then we walked over to the well-appointed table where Vanessa waited.

Vanessa stood, and Xavior returned to her side. As he did so, he took her hand and kissed it. She blushed and gave him an affectionate look. The entire scene put me firmly in the nauseous category, though I couldn't pinpoint exactly why. It absolutely shouldn't bother me that he was affectionate with someone else, but it did. That alone sparked a thread of guilt I tried to snip away, but it proved elusive. That's when Xavior saved me from my corrosive thoughts with introductions.

"Greg, Keith, this is my lovely date for this evening, Vanessa Singleton. She's a partner at a local law firm." Keith and I both shook her hand.

Xavior helped Vanessa back into her chair, and then we sat. I was across from Vanessa, and Keith was across from Xavior. It reminded me of table protocol at my mother's house. It felt odd how easily the habit came back to me, even though I hadn't been to a formal dinner since I was nineteen.

"This was unexpected. I mean, we didn't expect this." As the server poured more wine for everyone, I held back a sigh of frustration. I didn't want to ask if he owned the place, or how in the hell Keith and I would pay for our half of the meal.

"Like I said, blame it on Vanessa. She has certain preferences." Xavior leaned toward her and kissed her temple.

"As if I had to beg. You like this place as much as I do," Vanessa replied as she leaned into Xavior's kiss while she sipped her wine.

My thoughts circled like buzzards over a carcass. What the hell is wrong with me? Am I seriously jealous of Xavior's date? This was supposed to be a simple dinner, not some peacocking event. Am I sweating? Why the fuck am I sweating?

Of course, Keith, being Keith, decided it was a great time to comment on my emotional state, which I'm sure Xavior had already picked up on.

"You, okay, babe? Your aura looks like shit." He reached under the table and squeezed my hand. I pressed mine into his and took a deep breath.

"It's all overwhelming." That was mostly the truth. I didn't try to claim otherwise because Keith and Xavior would have picked up on it, and who knows what abilities Vanessa had. Places like this cost a ton, which I knew because of my mother. My resolve about where Xavior and I stood suddenly seemed flimsy. While my brain said one thing, my guts were clearly pointing at something else I'd blatantly ignored for significant reasons, such as my career and relationship.

I was saved from further explanation when the server arrived and explained what we were having for dinner, the wine pairings with each course, and followed by asking for allergies and preferences. After that, the discussion focused on the meal. Topics ranged from where ingredients were sourced to the cultural significance of the dish, even portion size and plate design. We headed back into dangerous waters when we reached dessert.

"Xavior, have you and Vanessa dated for long?" Keith asked before he took a bite of an elaborate deconstruction of a chocolate cheesecake.

"Oh, off and on for a while. Vanessa and I enjoy each other's company. It's nothing serious like the two of you." Xavior nodded toward us with a tip of his wineglass, as if to celebrate. I took another bite of sorbet and kept quiet. Vanessa filled the silence.

"We met at a party, a fundraiser or something, about ten years ago. I can barely keep up with his social calendar, let alone stay on it. The Royal Ballet one week, Irish dancers the next, Sumo wrestlers, fae Shakespeare troupes. . .who haven't you had sex with, Xavior?" she quipped.

"Well, you tonight, for one. But we'll see," he said, in a dead-pan voice.

We laughed, but I fought to keep a smirk off my face at the subtle rebuke. Xavior wasn't shy, but he clearly hadn't liked Vanessa's jab about his experience. It surprised me a little.

Vanessa went on, undeterred. "Xavior throws these parties every couple of months. The themes are amazing. His guests are some of the most A-list people barely seen in public, along with some of the most laid-back, salt-of-the-earth folks you could imagine. It's like the United Nations, but with food, booze, and sex. Wait. . ." Vanessa turned toward him. "Maybe it is the UN, honey."

Xavior only smiled at the implication Vanessa was making.

"Really?" Keith asked, excited about everything Vanessa mentioned.

"Absolutely. Xavior has solved more diplomatic disputes at his estate than most diplomats throughout their entire career," Vanessa boasted.

"That's pretty amazing, Brantley," I said, because it was re-markable. I'd worked with him long enough to know that he enjoyed solving problems as much as mysteries. He excelled at fostering cooperation, so it didn't surprise me he facilitated conversations between people who truly needed to talk.

"All in a day's work." Xavior played it off, but I could tell he was a little proud.

"I bet," Keith said with a grin. "Tell me more," he prompted, his wineglass toward Vanessa.

Xavior stayed quiet while Keith and Vanessa prattled on about parties and orgies until Vanessa said something about Xavior's tongue that had me lift my head so fast I nearly missed my last bite of sorbet.

"That's enough, Vanessa. They don't need the sordid details," Xavior said.

"Are you sure about that?" she teased.

"Yeah, Xavior, you sure? Maybe we need a demonstration," Keith said.

"Oh! I'd be up for that," Vanessa seconded, with a purr in her voice.

"Maybe that's a line we shouldn't cross," I said. "I have to see him tomorrow at work. Thank you very much." I looked at Keith, and he shrugged with a smile. They all had a bit of wine. I stuck to one glass so I could drive home. "Speaking of, it's getting late."

Xavior nodded and wiped his mouth with his napkin. "You're right. Early day at work tomorrow." Xavior stood, and the server swooped in to clear the plates. Xavior thanked the chef personally while another server returned Vanessa's coat and Xavior's jacket.

I didn't want to ask, but I felt like I had to, if only so he wouldn't think I was assuming things. I left Keith and Vanessa to chat as he helped with her coat and walked over to Xavior. "Brantley, what about the bill?"

He shook his head. "I own the place, Lyndon. You're fine." I tried not to seem ungrateful, inferior, or shocked as Xavior handed Vanessa the clutch she had left on the table. Then he turned toward Keith and offered his hand. "Pleasure to meet you, Keith."

If one thought solidified for me the entire night, it was that Xavior and I weren't only different species; we're from different worlds. Never mind that we were trying to convince Keith that we weren't up to anything. The idea seemed preposterous to me now, no matter what thoughts or emotions I pretended to avoid entertaining.

"Likewise, Xavior. Hope we get to do this again soon," Keith said. Xavior smiled and walked toward the door, which a server opened. He led us through the kitchen and dining room, people staring as we passed.

The valet brought our vehicle first, and I put Keith in and drove away before we saw Xavior's ride. I didn't want to know what he drove.

Keith was gushing about the night and handsy the entire drive home, which continued once we got into our bedroom. I didn't mind. Once he passed out, I lay in bed and tried to relax.

To see Xavior with Vanessa hurt like he'd rejected me, which made no sense whatsoever. He was clearly in a whole different stratosphere of lifestyle. One I no longer participated in since my mother rejected me and I abandoned her teachings about the Order. It all added up to me being an emotional wreck. Maybe it wasn't Keith I was trying to convince. I resolved to keep my dealings with Xavior professional. We were work partners, nothing more. I needed to pay more attention to my relationship with Keith.

When I finally slept, I dreamed about Xavior's tongue touching places it had never been.

SEEING RED

XAVIOR

We got a call about a break-in right after Greg and I logged in at work Thursday morning. The location turned out to be a blood bank, and it wasn't pretty. The patrol on the scene reported that half the blood products were destroyed or stolen. When we arrived, we discovered an overnight guard with his head bashed in and the place entirely trashed. There was ruined equipment and blood splattered everywhere, leaving a gory trail all the way to the back alley.

As Greg and I moved into the building, I lobbed an imager into the air so it would follow us to record evidence. It kept track of who was on-site, and where collected evidence was found. It also recorded distances and dimensions of rooms, along with any spectrographic analysis the device performed.

I noticed inconsistencies in evidence collection, which annoyed me. No one else had thought to start an imager before Greg and I arrived, and with all the trace evidence being ignored, I made Greg put on a protective suit. I didn't want us to contaminate it any more than the others. I ordered everyone who wasn't wearing PPE out and told the patrol staff still on the scene not to let anyone in without it.

As we walked through the scene, I could tell Greg was tense about something. Frankly, I wanted to punch his boyfriend, but I didn't think telling him that would earn me any favors.

The dinner had been going well until we got to dessert. At that point, I somewhat wished I hadn't talked Vanessa into being my date. She began telling stories, and as the stories got more explicit, Keith became more interested while Greg zoned out.

I looked around the scene and took a whiff of the room. Even with a mask on, I could usually distinguish between things, but I only smelled blood. I tried to concentrate, but my thoughts drifted to last night's conversation.

"Um, Xavior, what would it take to be invited to one of these infamous parties of yours?" Keith asked. Of course, Keith wanted an invitation. He had Greg's smell on him, but I could detect hints of other people. It might have been from his job as a paramedic, but I doubted it. You wouldn't pick up someone else's pheromones by caring for them, especially if you wore gloves.

"Know someone that's invited, I guess," I said.

"Oh, well, that seems like a done deal." Keith grinned as he finished another glass of wine.

"Totally worth it," Vanessa said. "Xavior's good about sharing, aren't you, babe? How about you and Greg? Do you like to share?"

"Oh, I'm more of a sharer than Gregie is. He doesn't mind sometimes, but he's shy. . ." Keith touched Greg, who shrugged in response while he ate his sorbet.

Shy my ass. "'Gregie.' Ugh, what a stupid nickname," I mumbled to myself.

Greg walked into my field of view and waved a hand in front of me. "Earth to Brantley, hey. . . you paying attention? They have a print and a partial here on the cold storage case. They're asking for you and the imager," Greg said.

"Yeah, yeah, I've got it." I moved toward the area indicated and motioned for the imager to zoom in and pick up the details before the techs lifted the prints. After that, I went outside to clear my sinuses and try to regain some focus.

Last night was not what I had expected, and it was still bothering me. When Greg joined me in the alley, I took off my mask and tried to smile, but his all-business attitude ground that to a halt pretty quickly.

"The imager is still scanning. Are you good with that?" Greg asked with a sharpness in his tone that made me bristle.

"Yeah, I'm good," I bit out, annoyed at the implication that I wasn't doing my job. It was then that I decided I'd had enough of both of us being pissed about whatever wasn't being said. I was determined to have it out rather than let it fester, and got in Greg's face. "What's up with you?"

He backed away a few steps. "Me? What about you? You've ordered people around all morning like you're cranky."

"Cranky?" I said, confused.

"Yeah, cranky, like someone didn't..." He cut himself off, but I would hazard a guess as to what he could have said. "Never mind. I'm going back inside," he said.

I shook my head and stayed in the alley with my thoughts as I replayed what had happened after dinner. Despite what Greg had implied, I had gotten laid, but the interaction hadn't provided the satisfaction I usually enjoyed.

Vanessa had made some snide comment about me slumming it in my brownstone as I unlocked the front door. I hadn't appreciated it, but we were in the middle of taking our clothes off, and I was hard enough to cut glass, so I didn't care.

When we got to my bedroom, I pushed her onto the bed, and while she giggled and bounced, I grabbed a condom from the nightstand. A few seconds later, I was inside her, losing myself. As she made noises, I covered her mouth, which only made her moan more. We'd played a little rough before, so it was all consensual, but she wasn't exactly happy when we were done.

As we lay in bed, it was clear she had something on her mind. "Where did you go?" she asked. I looked at her as she turned toward me, her head propped on her hand, her arm bent at her elbow, which made a pretty line that accentuated her breasts.

"What do you mean?" I said as I reached out to trace a finger along her arm, then her shoulder, across her breast to one of her beautifully taut nipples.

She made an amused noise, but it didn't match the sing-song words as they came out of her mouth. "I was here, fucking you, but you were somewhere else." I made a harsh noise, and Vanessa continued. "You've never done that before, Xavior. I know we aren't overly emotional with each other, but you've always fucked me. Tonight you were somewhere else."

"Vanessa," I groaned, annoyed, and stopped touching her.

"Don't 'Vanessa' me. You were making eyes at Greg most of the night. Do you like him?"

"Of course I like him. I work with him. If I didn't, it would suck."

"Yeah, but this is more. You looked like you wanted to pop Keith's head off at one point."

I vaguely remembered what she referred to and felt a smug satisfaction at the idea.

"Oh, I know that look. If I didn't know any better, I'd say you're jealous. Which is odd because I don't think I've ever seen you jealous, babe."

I wiped my hands over my face. "Fuck, Vinny, I don't know." She made a sympathetic noise and pulled me into her arms.

"Aww, sweetie. It's a little cute and a lot pathetic at the same time. How hung up are you on this guy?"

"Enough to see red where his boyfriend's concerned. It would be one thing if they were in an open relationship, but the whole point of the dinner was to convince Keith that Greg and I weren't fucking around. Turns out, Keith's the one seeing other people."

"Wow. You picked that up from his smell?" she asked.

I nodded. "I'm sorry, Vinny. You're right. It's not fair to you." I nuzzled into her chest and found a small bit of comfort in her calm heartbeat.

"Promise me I get one last fuck before you go all monogamous. Something to remember you by." She laughed softly into my ear and kissed my forehead.

"It's not going to get that far, Vinny. I care because he's my partner, and his so-called partner is treating him like crap. I just need to get my shit under control, and maybe never meet his boyfriend in a dark alley." She laughed and kissed my cheek. I sighed softly and realized I felt better for the conversation. I looked up at her. "Let me make it up to you," I whispered.

She perked up. "Are you going to do the tongue thing?" Her eyes were bright with anticipation and desire.

"Sure. Is that what you want?"

"Is the sky blue? Fuck yes, that's what I want." She laughed. I laughed with her, then eased down her naked torso to settle between her legs.

Greg snapped his fingers in front of my face. Fuck. I looked at him. I hadn't realized he had returned. He backed away, and I pushed myself off the wall. "What, Lyndon?"

"Brantley, what the hell is going on with you?" Greg asked.

"I could ask you the same thing," I said.

"Look. If you're upset about last night, I'm sorry. Keith was a bit much. He's not usually like that. But after a couple of glasses, he gets chatty."

It wasn't the chattiness that Greg was apologizing for; it was Keith wanting to know every bit of my life, and Vanessa indulging him. Why Greg was making excuses for Keith, I would never understand. It made me want to throttle him now, too. "Usually," I growled. "Somehow, I don't believe that."

Greg looked away. I'd hit a nerve, and guilt bubbled up inside me. It wasn't his fault. He couldn't control Keith's actions. While Greg and I might not be having an affair, I was pretty sure Keith was, and fuck if I was going to tell Greg that.

"Let's finish the scene so we can go back to HQ and log everything. All this blood is messing with my sense of smell." I implied that was the reason I was moody, or cranky, as Greg put it. He nodded. It took two more hours before we were done and on our way back to headquarters.

The ride back was as if someone had declared radio silence. When Greg pulled over a few blocks from the garage and parked with the engine still running, I wondered why. Before I had a chance to ask, he swiveled his chair toward me with a determined look on his face.

"What's your deal today?" he asked.

"My deal?" That pissed me off. "You ask me for a favor. We have dinner with your... boyfriend, and then you make excuses for him. I don't get you. You were miserable last night. Why are you even with him?"

Greg's body language was as intense as his smell. Pure anger came off him in waves. When Greg spoke again, it was in a quiet, controlled way. "You don't like my partner, and I don't like yours. Let's leave it at that."

"I never said Vanessa was my partner."

He narrowed his eyes. "That's not what I saw." Was that a whiff of jealousy I smelled? It caught me by surprise as much as his words.

"By all the elements," I swore. "I've known Vanessa for ten years. She's a dear friend, and we enjoy each other's company. She's practically married to her career. You've got some nerve, since the whole thing was your idea."

"Are you fucking kidding me? I asked for something simple, and we ended up at one of your side projects. How is this my fault?" Greg raised his voice slightly as his anger slipped its leash a little.

"Are you that blind?" I grit my teeth. "I saw the way he acted last night, as if you didn't exist until you opened your mouth," I said, fighting to keep my voice even. "You did this all for him, and he couldn't care less. It's not right. You deserve. . ."

"What? What do I deserve? You barely know me, and you know nothing about our relationship." Silence settled in the vehicle. For several minutes, the only sound was the engine cycling through a recharging phase, with the stifling smells of anger and guilt between us.

I squeezed my hands into fists, then relaxed them. "You're right. I don't." I wrapped all my conflicting feelings up tight and tried to rein myself in. "I'm sorry about showing off. I thought it would help."

He sighed. "It's complicated. And not your fault, not really. If I'd known, I would have said something." He shook his head. "Truth is, the whole evening had me off balance."

"How so?" I was curious, since I'd sensed a lot of emotions from him, but thought it was more about Keith than anything else.

"I didn't expect Vanessa, for one."

"Really? I said I'd bring a date."

"I realize that, but I thought. . ." He shook his head again.

"Thought what?"

"You wouldn't be with a woman," Greg said quietly.

That was an odd statement. I would bet anything it was more than that, since the answer didn't really have the same emotional smell as when we talked about partners. "Oh? Why would that be a problem? I know we didn't talk about it, but I figured you knew."

"Knew what?"

"Most dragons are omnisexual," I said with a shrug.

"So Vanessa wasn't joking?"

I shook my head. "She's experienced my parties firsthand." I chuckled. "I have a ton of stories, and she doesn't even know half of them. Like one time, I had the fortune of meeting a selkie couple. They were artists too. We did some nude canvas paintings together..."

"Okay, okay." He chuckled. "I get it. I made an assumption."

"Well, that makes two of us, then. I assumed you knew." I watched him relax a little as he gave me a strange smile. "Are we cool?" I asked.

"Yeah," he said as he took a deep breath. "Let's get this case written up and logged so we can go have a beer."

"Sounds good." We settled into our easy cadence to finish up work. When we got to our usual hangout, we talked about sports, entertainment, and bets on the next office pool. Underneath all that, our subtle attraction to each other bubbled along. I wanted to tell Greg what I knew about Keith, but if I did, I'd be responsible for whatever he did about it, and he wouldn't like me for it. So I kept my mouth shut, drank a couple of beers, and yelled at the FIFA games like everyone else in the bar.

HEALTH CHECK

XAVIOR

Things ticked along for Greg and me. The dinner seemed like a distant memory after a few weeks. While the tech department worked on our data project for the bicycle case, we took other interesting calls. I think the staff sergeant enjoyed giving us the more interesting cases to see what we'd do with them.

According to the interweb and his recording company, Franklin Gibson was a hotshot recording artist no one had heard from him in over a month. He was supposed to be recording at a local studio, but he never showed up. All attempts by anyone Gibson knew to reach him had been thwarted. That's when his executive producer called and requested a health check.

We decided to walk since Gibson's residence was not that far from headquarters. "You up to anything interesting with your three-day weekend?" I was curious since I knew Saturday was Greg's birthday.

"The usual weekend trip to my parents' place."

"How far out is that?"

"About an hour."

"That's not too horrible. What do you do all weekend out there, anyway?"

Greg gave me an odd look but indulged my curiosity. "We have family dinner. My mom, Jennifer, picks the recipe. Then my dad, Philip, and I help her with it, or we stay out of her way depending on what it is, and work in my dad's wood shop." He hadn't mentioned Keith. I was curious about whether Keith would go with him. It was on the tip of my tongue to ask.

Instead, I satisfied a different curiosity. "I assume this isn't the family that kicked you out?"

"Oh, hell no." He chuckled. "Jennifer is my stepmother. I haven't spoken with Narissa since I was nineteen. She remarried, and I have four half-siblings. I only talk with one of them sometimes."

"Why's that?"

"They kicked her out of the Order for the same reason as me." Greg shrugged, and I nodded.

"I couldn't imagine my parents abandoning my siblings for something of that nature. Dragons don't assign any importance to gender and sex. We weren't always shifters, either. Cross-species matings and evolution gave us some things dragons didn't have originally, like being able to shift between our dragon and a bipedal form, nipples, and glands that create pleasure depending on what form we take."

Greg's wide eyes were comically wide, then shifted to focus on the building next to us. "We're here."

He looked around while I knocked on the front door, which triggered an automated notification system. It sounded like someone was home, but that wasn't proof it was Gibson.

After several minutes, with the notification system still chiming, someone opened the door. Based on the information we had, I was somewhat surprised anyone had answered. "Is Franklin Gibson here?" I asked.

"Who's asking?" A short person with a halo controller around their head and haptic gloves on their hands looked at Greg and me with annoyance.

"We're with Jefferson Public Safety," Greg said. "Mr. Gibson's executive producer called us so we could check on him. We're here to make sure he's okay. Could you let us in?" I don't know what he did, but Greg could say things with just the right timbre to convey authority and trust, and people seemed to respond.

"Babe! Some guys are here to make sure you're okay!" they yelled as they let the door swing open. They hadn't asked to see our shields or the service order we had obtained from a judge. It allowed us to enter the property if we needed to, if only to verify Gibson's condition and assess if he needed medical attention.

Once we were inside, we followed the person who answered the door to a main living area. The smell hit me like a freight hauler. I pulled a handkerchief out of my pocket to cover my nose. Sometimes the living smelled worse than the dead.

A guy came out in his bathrobe. It was Franklin Gibson, based on the description we had of him. He started running around the main living space like something was chasing him. Greg and I glanced at each other, then walked toward him.

"Don't come near me!" Gibson yelled as he picked up a pillow from the floor and threw it in our direction. "You want to eat my eyeballs!" Another pillow was tossed at us. Greg blocked as I ducked.

This whole weird, one-sided yelling match played out while we stood in the middle of Gibson's massive living space. The person who answered the door continued playing the latest holo game at a completely unnecessary volume.

"So, call it in?" Greg texted me instead of yelling. I nodded after reading his message.

Greg walked toward another part of the apartment and called central communications. They sent paramedics after Greg conveyed Gibson's condition. When they showed up, Gibson lost it.

"Don't leave me!" he kept repeating. Gibson tried to grab onto us as the paramedics worked to calm him down so they could figure out what drug he was on and if they could do anything about it. By the light show in his eyes, I would guess it was Dreamweaver.

"Did you find anything in the apartment?" a paramedic asked.

Greg shook his head. "Empty inhalers. They didn't have any identifying marks."

The other paramedic had Gibson calm enough to poke him with a blood analyzer. When it lit up with a result, they turned the device in our direction. Greg read it and nodded.

"Dreamweaver," Greg said. "Most common way to take it is via an inhaler. Though this is the first time I've seen what amounts to a private label. Most of the time, they are marked with a brand identifier."

"So, someone is making a designer version?" That was new. While recreational drugs were legal, they were also regulated. If someone was skirting the system to deliver a more potent high than allowed, that was a problem.

"Maybe. I'm going to collect a few of the empties for the lab to analyze and compare to what we have on file," Greg said.

The paramedics tried to help Gibson, but nothing was working. "Nothing we have on hand is counteracting what's in his system. We should take him to the hospital. They'll have more treatment options for him."

"That sounds good. Let us know if you need anything else," I said. They finished loading Gibson onto the hovering gurney and took him to the EMS bus outside. With any luck, he might make a full recovery. At that point, if he was lucid enough, he could make his own decisions.

I walked over to the individual still playing holo games, even with everything going on around them. "Excuse me, can you pause that?" They made a hand motion that paused the game and turned toward Greg and me.

"We're taking your friend Gibson to the hospital. Could you answer a few questions?" I asked. They blinked and then turned back to their game and started playing it again. I yanked the controller off their head, which caused the game to pause.

"Hey!" they yelled.

"Do you live here with Gibson?" I asked.

They crossed their arms and squinted at us. "Yes. I live here."

"Do you know what Gibson was taking?" Greg asked.

"Dreamweaver. It's hella trippy, but hey, if that's your thing, I say go for it. Personally, I like stim. Sleep is for the mundane." They fidgeted where they stood, fingers twitching with rapid gestures, probably from the stim and repetitive gameplay.

"Can we call anyone for you?" I asked.

"No. I've been going for a record, which you are currently fucking up. Can I have my controller back?"

"Is there anything you'd like to tell us before we leave?" Greg's concern was admirable. I can't say I blame him. The gamer was shaking like a leaf in the wind.

"Franklin's not a perv or anything, if that's what you are trying to get at. I met him at a party a couple of months ago, and he's been high ever since. I've been making sure he eats something and doesn't wander outside. Bigger spaces cause bigger problems; everyone knows that." They crossed and uncrossed their arms. "Can I have my controller back?" they repeated.

I handed the controller over. They put it on their head and returned to their gameplay. Greg shook his head, and we turned toward the door. I left my information with the house monitoring system if someone wanted to know Gibson's whereabouts or needed assistance.

"Rock-paper-scissors on who ends up filing forms on this one?" Greg said, as he tried to lighten the mood a little. I nodded and promptly won.

"Two out of three?" Greg begged.

"Nope."

"How about a snack run?"

"Nah."

"The next three rounds of beers?"

"Nope, this one's all yours!"

Greg groaned as we left. It meant he was on the hook for the follow-ups at the hospital. That worked pretty nicely for me and what I had planned. He dropped me off at HQ with the empty inhalers so I could drop them off at the lab. He thought I'd be going home afterward. Instead, it gave me the perfect amount of time to get things ready.

A few weeks prior, I'd found out when Greg's birthday was at our department's blood drive. While the med techs were draining him of his vitae, we talked about how he hated making a big deal of it. Our conversation made me determined not to let the opportunity for Operation Silent Birthday to pass by. I organized folks in the detective's pool and planned a week of low-key interactions to celebrate.

Some of us pooled resources and bought him tickets to a professional basketball game with Greg's favorite team. We had various treats around the office that were Greg's favorites. I'd brought him his preferred coffee every morning, and he hadn't known that it was anything other than a more-than-usual cheerful week.

When Greg returned from the hospital late on Thursday night to find a cupcake, a digital card, and almost finished case documentation and lab requests from Gibson's health check, the look on his face was a mixture of surprise and mild suspicion.

"What's all this?" He set the vehicle keys down on his desk and stared at the cupcake and card like it might be explosive magic.

"Exactly what it looks like," I said as I finished up the forms and signed off on the logs, then sent copies for Greg to sign over to his desk.

He sat down and opened the card floating on his desktop. I had the whole detective pool digitally sign it. It included the redemption code for the basketball tickets, a couple of gift card codes, and general well wishes in audio and video that played one after the other.

We were the only ones in the detective's area as I watched Greg's astonishment change to amusement with the outpouring of support and appreciation from his coworkers. When all the media had played, he looked at me.

"I'm not sure what to say." Greg's hand covered his mouth. I inhaled and picked up joy, embarrassment, and happiness from his scent. I wondered if maybe birthdays had turned into a sore point because they ended up being about something or someone else other than him.

I smiled and shook my head. "You don't have to say anything, Lyndon." I got up, walked to his desk, and held out a cake candle. I blew a tiny flame across the candle wick. It lit with a quick pop. Greg watched as I glanced at him, and I stuck the lit candle into the cupcake.

"Happy thirty-fourth, partner." I gave him a few pats on his shoulder, then turned to leave. As I walked away, I heard him blow out the candle, which brought a grin to my face.

While Greg enjoyed his birthday, I would spend my weekend attempting to create a miracle. If my brother Denis could figure out what made the Saint George ability tick and counter it, maybe whatever he came up with could be a belated birthday present for Greg. Not only for my safety, but for Greg's peace of mind, too.

PARENTAL ADVISORY

GREGOR

Waking to the sound of the shower meant Keith was home. Things were going well, and while I wasn't big on celebrating my birthday, I was hoping to change that this weekend. Xavior helped a little in that department with his low-key birthday surprise. A warm feeling bubbled in my chest and buoyed my plans for the rest of the day.

I sprang out of bed and grabbed our overnight bag. By the time Keith walked out, I was done packing our clothes and sat on the end of the bed waiting for him. He was dripping wet and looked sexy as he walked toward me with a towel wrapped around his waist.

"Hey, you." I reached for him as he drew close and stood between my legs. He bent to give me a kiss, which I took advantage of, and wrapped my hand around the back of his neck so I could tease him with more. As he leaned into me, I reached for his towel. That's when he pulled away with one last peck to my lips before he straightened.

He glanced at the bag and back at me. "Where are you going?"

"We're going," I corrected, "to my parent's house. Didn't you remember?"

"I thought that was tomorrow."

"No, it's definitely today. I took the day off from work."

"Oh." He frowned.

I stood from the bed and wrapped my arms around him. "What's wrong?"

He pushed away a little, but stayed in my arms. "Maybe it would be better if you went on your own."

I took a step back from him. "Why? You'll make my parents think you're avoiding them."

"I am avoiding them," he said. The adamant way he said it surprised me. "Jennifer doesn't like me, and Philip barely looks at me. When I'm there, I'm a footnote to everything. Your mom doesn't even ask me to help with dinner. They don't like me, Greg. Couldn't we do something fun tonight, and then you could visit them tomorrow like you normally do?"

"I told them we'd be out for dinner tonight. Besides, this whole thing is a misunderstanding, that's all. They haven't seen us together since March. I've explained about our schedules, but they know we took days off this weekend. They're expecting us."

"Look," he said, sighing. "Don't make this weekend about me and your parents. This weekend is about you. Go home, visit your family, visit friends. Have a good, relaxing birthday," Keith insisted.

"But I want to spend it with you. You're my family, too." My plans for a special birthday were quickly falling apart. "Please. Do this for me?"

Keith sighed. "I made plans already for tonight. You'll be fine." He gave me another quick kiss, turned away, and went into our walk-in closet.

My stomach churned. When he returned dressed for the day, I tried to salvage my plans. "I'll stay then. We'll do whatever you planned. I'll have dinner with my parents next weekend." I turned toward the bed to unpack our bag.

Keith stopped me. "If you don't go, they'll really hate me. Don't make me the reason you aren't visiting your family."

"Then come with me! It'll be different, I promise." I barely kept myself from begging. If Keith came with me, I could fix things between him and my parents. My plan had to work; I knew it would.

"How do you know?" He shook his head. "I've been twice since the blowup at Yule, and they look at me like I'm. . ." He shook his head again.

In a desperate attempt to salvage my plans, I unzipped a pocket on the side of the overnight bag and pulled out a small box.

"Because I know they'll have to figure it out." As I turned back to him, I held the ring box out to him. He picked it up from my hand and opened it.

"What's this?"

As he looked at the engagement ring, I was hopeful. If we could take the next step in our relationship, it would convince my parents Keith wasn't ruining my life, and help drive any latent notion out of my head about a dragon I worked with.

"What's it look like?" He glanced at me and then back at the ring.

"I wanted to wait until we were at my parent's, but if this helps convince you, then spoiling my surprise and the speech I had planned is worth it."

"It's your birthday," Keith said, voice quiet. "You hate surprises."

"True, but I'm the one with the surprise." I smiled. "Will you marry me?" As I reached for him, he pulled away. The snap of the box lid was the punctuation on the no he didn't give voice to.

Keith grabbed my hand and pushed the box into it. "We should wait. We aren't ready for this yet."

"We don't have to be married tomorrow." I held the box like it was a magic grenade without the safety pin. "It's a promise. To show that we're serious. My parents would have to treat you differently."

"That's not how to fix things with them, Greg. I don't want to force them to see me as their future son-in-law. It would only make matters worse."

"No, it wouldn't," I pleaded.

Keith gave me an exasperated look. "I love that you're so naïve sometimes. You grew up so sheltered that you think a romantic gesture will fix things." He sighed. "Gregie, I love you, but this isn't it." He didn't know about my past, and I couldn't tell him. Not now, not ever.

Frustration threatened to turn into anger, and I refused to turn that on him. I dropped the box on the bed, went to the closet, and threw on clothes. He watched me as I came back and picked up our overnight bag. "See you in a few days." He didn't stop me as I walked past him and out of our home.

On the drive to my parent's house, my brain swam in disappointment. Our relationship seemed more tenuous than ever. The problems between us started about a year ago. Keith and I went to a party with his coven. After several years of our being together, it was the first time he had invited me. We'd just bought the house, and I'd hoped it meant things were growing more serious between us.

While I was talking with a few people at the party, Keith had disappeared. When I found him, he was being fucked by a large man I didn't know. I'd never seen him with Keith's coven group, but I hadn't met everyone either. They saw me and continued as if everything were normal. I think Keith hoped I'd join them. Instead, I left the party.

When Keith eventually made it home, instead of a fight, we had a rational discussion about boundaries and what I was willing to accept. He was upset with himself for letting things go too far with Frank. I hadn't wanted a name, but it was blazed in my memory the moment it left his lips. I wanted to respect his beliefs, so we decided he would only have sex with those in his coven, and that I didn't want to see it or hear about it, nor could he bring it to our house. It took me two weeks before I could touch him again without seeing Frank and Keith's looks of utter ecstasy and wanton need.

It wasn't Keith's fault that I didn't understand his magical practice. I'd grown to accept him and didn't blame him for what I lacked. We loved each other, and that's all that mattered. Things were alright, but not long after his slip-up, our relationship suffered another blow.

As a gesture to Keith's witch heritage, my parents put together a Yule celebration. At some point during the evening, Jennifer, my stepmom, overheard Keith on the phone with someone talking about plans for the New Year's holiday. Later, when she asked me what my plans were, and I told her I took extra shifts to help with holiday crowds, she wasn't happy about it. My parents sat me down later and asked me some very pointed questions about our relationship. A wall of ice formed between my parents and Keith, and each dinner he missed seemed to make that wall a little thicker.

It wasn't our open relationship that bothered them. Instead, they had some notion that Keith didn't care about me, and they felt I was being mistreated when he made plans without considering me. I tried to explain that Keith and I had boundaries and that I trusted him to keep to them. Jennifer never told me what she overheard that bothered her so much, but after our conversation, she never mentioned anything again.

I'd never met Keith's family. They all lived in Connecticut, and he claimed he wasn't all that close with them, but he would take a transport home to visit them occasionally over the years we dated. He never invited me. When I asked about it once, he told me it wasn't worth making me suffer his dysfunctional family.

It was mid-morning when I pulled up to my parent's house. Bag in hand, I took a deep breath, then went inside. Coming home was something I usually enjoyed. I tried to school my face and dispel my sour mood.

"Hey, I'm here," I said as I closed the front door behind me.

"In the kitchen, sweetie!" Jennifer called back. I walked to the kitchen, tossing my bag on the couch along the way, and found them working on dinner. I kissed Jennifer's cheek, then kissed my dad's. I grabbed a beer from the fridge and took a seat at the table that had vegetables piled on it, waiting for someone to dice them. They shared a glance as I worked on the pile of veggies. Likely because I was both alone and drinking before noon, but they didn't say anything.

Jennifer's dark brown hair was up in a ponytail. She'd actually been my first-grade teacher when we moved to San Francisco from Crescent, Oregon, and only retired recently. You couldn't mistake her demeanor for anything but a quiet, patient authority as her coneflower eyes watched how I cut the vegetables. She turned back to the counter, grabbing another handful of flour that was stark white against her tawny skin.

"You're here early. How was the drive?" Dad asked. Philip Lyndon worked in tech for most of his life and was recently retired. I was practically a carbon copy of him. The only difference between us, besides age, was his black hair shot through with silver, and that his tall frame had stooped a little. His intelligent gaze told me that his first question was just a warm-up.

"The usual," I said. Dad nodded and continued stirring the sauce while Jennifer kneaded dough. If I had to hazard a guess, we were making calzones. It was one of my favorites. I wondered how many of my favorites Mom planned to make this weekend.

"Are you spending the night?" Jennifer asked.

"Yeah. I brought my bag." Jennifer exchanged another look with Philip that I pretended not to see.

The next question wasn't about Keith, much to my surprise. "How're things going with the new guy at work? What's it been, three months now?" Philip turned slightly to look at me. The simmering sauce already smelled amazing.

"Brantley's good. He's smart, works hard. It's going pretty well so far." I didn't mention the few hiccups. I could be an adult and admit my partner was hot. He could be one too and not tell me what his nose picked up unless it related to a case. It was a mutual, unspoken agreement after the mildly disastrous dinner date. Nor did I mention that Xavior was a dragon. I knew they would have a lot to say about that, and I didn't want to hear it.

We talked about some of my cases along with the road trips and learning vacations they planned to take now that they were both retired. After dinner, Jennifer brought out a small carrot cake, one she had made from scratch. It didn't say anything, but the only time of year she made a cake like this was for my birthday. I smiled and cut the first piece.

"This is fantastic. Thank you," I said.

"No problem, sweetie. We're glad to have you here." We ate cake for a bit, and then Philip stood, taking his plate to the sink.

"I got some new redwood pieces in from an ent family close by. I also figured out a new technique for doing metal inlays. Would you like me to show you?"

"Sure." I gave Dad a smile. The distraction would be good. Working in the shop was always relaxing. It's something I inherited from him and Grandpa Jack.

My parents didn't bring up Keith once the whole weekend. I was thankful and annoyed, too. I didn't want to talk about why he wasn't with me, but I began to suspect Keith was right.

SIBLING RIVALRY

XAVIOR

It had been a year, maybe more, since I'd been home. I kept in touch with most of my family via holovid calls. I valued my older sister Faith's advice the most. Denis, my twin brother, was a different story. We weren't exactly fond of each other. We had been close when we were younger. As we grew older, that changed. It might be because he's a successful scientist with a successful scientist as a mate. It might be because I'd made some questionable choices in my life. Whatever the reason, we weren't close anymore. Through all the years, no matter the strife, we all had a fundamental understanding of family being important. We helped each other when we could.

I'd timed my trip to Spain the same weekend Greg took off for his birthday. Flying to Europe before modern transportation had never been easy. I'd only made the trip twice under my own power. A dragon taking a break, floating in open water, was a target for many things in the ocean. Though fishing was better before all the commercial traffic.

The maglevs on my private plane made a soft bump as they locked into place. It was a short taxi from landing to our family hangar at the private airport in Valencia, Spain.

My family's property was about an hour west of Valencia in the mountains. I could have shifted and flown to the manor, but I had important cargo that I couldn't risk. Immigration met the plane. I handed over the paperwork, and fifteen minutes later, I was in a rented vehicle on my way to my family's estate.

They built the family manor into the mountain landscape. It was ideal for dragons that liked to fly. The size and space had its advantages as well. When my sister Faith mated with Trevor Ramirez, they quickly started a family. Their oldest whelps were only a few decades younger than Denis and me. Trevor was currently pregnant with what would be their tenth whelp. With such a large brood, the manor here and their estate in northern London helped when scales bristled between the younger dragons. We weren't extremely territorial anymore. However, the trait would present itself from time to time, and it was nice to have the space to let tempers cool.

The rental pulled into the manor drive, and I quickly got out and headed toward the main entrance. As I approached the door, it opened and my mother greeted me.

"Darling, I'm so happy for your visit." Her arms went around my neck as she pulled me in for a hug.

"Hello, Mum."

Corley Cortez-Brantley was taller than me, taller than Greg, actually. She looked at me with golden eyes that gleamed red in the bright light. Her simple yellow summer dress with leather sandals accented her golden-red hair and light rose-tinted freckled skin. One trait phoenixes and fire dragons shared was the way we radiated heat. My mother might trade her sandals for more sensible shoes if there were inclement weather, otherwise, she wasn't bothered by the cold. It was another reason to live in the higher altitudes of the Spanish mountains.

"Hello, Mum." I hugged her back, though I was eager to find my brother. The package I had with me wouldn't wait much longer. My body temperature had kept it from coagulating.

"Is Denis in his lab?"

She sighed and let go of me. "Yes, of course. We don't understand why you two are being so secretive."

Denis thought it would be best to wait to tell our parents once I was here, and I agreed. If I were to mark on a calendar all the times that had happened, well, let's say you'd have a better chance of seeing Halley's Comet twice before you saw us agree on anything.

"I'll explain after I see Denis, I promise. I have something for him that won't be of much use if I delay much longer."

"Alright then, I'll let you go." She released me with a pat on the back. I hurried down the hall to the main stairway. "Lunch is at the usual time. Tell Denis. I expect both of you to be there. You can explain whatever the two of you are up to then."

"We will," I called back as I went down the stairway to the lower level, which Denis had sectioned off almost two centuries ago as his private space. The door from the outside looked the same as the rest of the nearly five-hundred-year-old manor. When I knocked, it opened of its own accord and revealed a state-of-the-art passage to another door. The inner door opened after the outer door sealed me in the passage. "When did you install an airlock, Denis?" When no answer came, I ventured further into his lab.

"Brother?" The room was stark white, neat as a pin, and hummed with machines, doing any number of things scientific, magical, or both. Denis had always been obsessed with the boundaries between science and magic.

"Xavior." Denis's brisk voice called out as he came from another room carrying a rack of test tubes. "I have the solutions ready. Did you bring the sample?"

"Of course." I removed the small case with the vial of blood I'd swiped from the office blood drive earlier in the month. When I had proposed this idea to Denis, and he asked for a sample, the blood drive had been an opportunity I couldn't pass up. I'd set up a stasis spell that kept the blood fresh until it was moved again, waiting for when I could bring it to him.

"This is a momentous occasion." Denis was practically giddy, for Denis, anyway. He'd always been rather staunch and focused, especially for a dragon. Our demeanors were opposite, but we looked the same except for the facial hair. He had a full beard, while I preferred a more trimmed-down appearance. If it weren't for that, I'd wonder if he was my brother.

"Yes, yes, a live sample of someone from the Saint George lineage. I know. I remember your study of family members resting in the crypt afflicted with the Saint George ability. Not all of them unjustly, I might add."

"As green dragons, we've had more of a long-lived family than most. There are only two other families in Europe that have existed as long as the knights. The black dragons, like Faith's mate, Trevor. And the red dragons, like the one our nephew Gavin mated with." Denis took the vial from the case and quickly went to work taking samples, making solutions, and creating slides.

"Sometimes the Knights were useful. Great Uncle Theodore practically decimated an entire village in the ninth century. It wasn't exactly his fault since he had dementia, but from the way the family talks about it, no one could talk him down, either." Green dragons were known to be capricious and rule-breakers. Our father's choice to mate with a phoenix was not a popular one, not that he could help it. There were other families of green dragons, but as he was the oldest in his family's brood, they had expected an advantageous match. Thankfully, that didn't happen much anymore. Faith's arrangement with her mate was the last time I'd heard of such a thing.

Denis looked through a scope at a slide he created. "Is that all your knight is to you? Useful?" Denis glanced up at me, and I gritted my teeth.

"No," I said with a frustrated sigh. "Greg deserves to be free of his ability, as much as you want to discover how it works." I paced around his lab as Denis busied himself with various pieces of equipment.

"It's going to take time for me to isolate his abilities and whether I can control it or reverse it. Have you thought about what you'll tell him if I'm successful?"

"I'll tell him you're bloody brilliant and that he doesn't have to worry about us taking assignments that might prove dangerous."

"He's avoided assignments?" The tone in Denis' voice indicated that he found that curious.

"Anything involving a person who might be armed. So far, we've been lucky that other detective units could respond. At some point, we won't be able to avoid a call." It weighed on my mind a lot. While our mother was a phoenix, it didn't mean any of us inherited the trait of rebirth from her. We'd all been alive for several hundred years and never presented with a phoenix cycle.

"Besides, he's a good man. I'd rather not see him suffer based on a decision I made to work with him, despite his warnings." I hadn't regretted my decision. We made a good team.

"You like him," Denis said in a flat tone.

"Of course I like him. He's a decent man, a good detective, and a good work partner." The familiarity of my words was not lost on me.

"Of course." I didn't miss the mocking tone in Denis' voice.

I glared at his back. I didn't understand why everyone automatically assumed I had ulterior motives where Greg was concerned. Was I attracted to him? Yes. Did I think his boyfriend was complete and utter trash? Yes. Was there anything I could do about any of it? Not really. Whatever Denis came up with, if he could come up with anything, was a safety precaution. Besides, Greg deserved to have a choice. There was no point in me being a casualty of his family's ability if I could help it.

"Mum wanted us both at lunch. I can go up and fend her off for a little while. But I wouldn't linger if you don't want to hear her complain."

"I'll be there." Denis said as he adjusted something with one of his instruments. "I've never been the tardy one."

"Of course," I said, mimicking his tone and voice.

Denis didn't even look up. I shrugged and left his lab.

BICYCLE, BICYCLE

GREGOR

Work was a refuge from the growing tension between Keith and me. When I returned from my parent's house, Keith was already at work, and the ring I'd tried to give him sat in its box on our dresser. We hadn't talked about it since.

Xavior and I continued to pick up cases until the central technomage group got back to us about the data request we made related to the bicycle thefts.

We walked into Detective Marcy Morales' office after she messaged to let me know she had some information. "Afternoon, Morales," Xavior said.

"Hey there, Brantley, Lyndon. I've got a treat for you today. Pull up some seats." Marcy was one of our best technomages. We'd lucked out with her catching the assignment. They would normally kick something like this to a junior in the division. By her laid-back dress style, someone might have mistaken her for a junior when she was actually one of the division leads. She wore a hoodie, T-shirt, jeans, and sneakers with vibrant colors that suited her bronze skin and braided golden-brown hair.

Both of us grabbed seats and sat on either side of Marcy's impressive desk, piled full of gear. Marcy made a hand gesture that pulled an image up on her local holo, then she used the same hand to grab the image, then used a throwing gesture to put it on a larger display behind her desk.

"These are all the missing bicycles and their last locations. The blue ones," she pointed at the image, "are privately owned bikes with tracers or trackers. Orange dots are the city-owned bikes with trackers on them."

"When we tried to trace the bikes to see if they reconnected with the local network, I found nothing." Marcy was smiling, so I knew there was something else. "But when I expanded out to other networks, I started finding connection failures. Because of how the system works, the bikes stop working once they leave the network for an allotted time. There are other networks for the city brand of bikes, but since these don't match any profiles in those systems, they're seen as errors."

She made another hand gesture that broadened the search radius to most of the western part of the country. "When I match the failure IDs in the other systems with our missing bike list, we get this."

The map lit up as she spread it out to cover most of North America. There were bikes as far away as the East Coast. I sat there in mild shock.

I looked at Xavior and watched as his eyes moved from one group of dots to another. "Can you isolate clusters of bikes? Bring up the locations from where they disappeared and where they ended up?"

"Sure. Give me a few minutes," Morales said. Her deft hands made patterns in the air that looked like a combination of typing and spell work.

"What are you thinking?" I quietly asked as I leaned toward Xavior.

"If I'm right, this is going to be a public relations problem. I don't think the bicycles were stolen. I think most of them were misplaced," Xavior said with a hint of a smile.

I was about to ask Xavior why he thought it would be a PR problem when Marcy finished her query.

"Here you are, Brantley," she said. "Oh, wow. Look at that." The clusters of dots around the city matched other collections all over the country via dotted lines.

"It's the fae," Xavior said with confidence.

I blinked at the statement. "How do you know it's them?"

"They have a network of passages they can use that don't exist in this space-time. It lets them travel long distances quickly. Jordan likes to use them to avoid fans."

Xavior grinned while I prodded for more information. "Why isn't this common knowledge?" *And who's Jordan?* The obvious conclusion, of course, was that Jordan was a fae. But what was Xavior doing with a fae besides avoiding fans?

"Only the fae can access the paths. The entrances and exits change. No one bothers to learn where they are, since most fae can find them by instinct alone. However, this seems to identify some entrances and exits. Or at least where they used to be. It appears walking through the tunnels has become passé."

"So the fae are taking the bikes through their passage system, and when the bikes stop working or the locations change, they end up abandoned?"

Xavior nodded. "Pretty much. I recognized the location of one cluster. I'm guessing about the rest of them, but I would bet one of my vintage vehicles on my hypothesis."

"Why bicycles?" I asked.

"Well, the passages aren't big enough for a vehicle, and electronic things don't survive in them. As bikes are mostly mechanical, they wouldn't break down, and are faster than walking," Xavior stated.

"How do you know so much?" His sly smile made me raise my eyebrows. Xavior laughed but didn't answer my question.

I turned back to Marcy. "Can you grab an image for us, Morales? We'll need to show the captain so he can get in touch with the right city representatives." I smiled at Xavior. He was right; the PR would be tricky, but thankfully, we wouldn't have to deal with it.

"Sure, Lyndon. I'll send it to your inbox."

We gave Marcy our thanks and went to break the news to Captain Lang. He was happy we had solved the issue, but not thrilled about the next steps. As we returned to our desks, I was curious. "I wonder how they will return all the bikes to the proper locations."

"It might be easier to suggest they update the networks to share information. That way, wherever the bikes end up, they are still registered," Xavior said. I nodded as I added the suggestion to our email to Captain Lang detailing our findings.

To celebrate, Xavior and I took a couple of city bikes out for a spin to our favorite bar. About halfway into my second beer, I asked the question that had been rattling around in my brain since he brought it up.

"So who's Jordan? Are they going to be upset you told us about the passages?"

"Jordan? No, he won't be upset. I doubt any fae would be, since only the fae can enter them. They are akin to a dragon's den. They don't exist in this reality. It takes a dragon to access a den, just like it takes a fae to access the passages. I might be able to find a fae passage, but I probably wouldn't be able to enter it."

"It seems like the fae could have a lucrative transportation business." Along with illicit activities of all kinds that I'd rather not think about.

Xavior shook his head. "Some have tried, but it doesn't go well. First of all, you have to be willing to enter the passage regardless of whether or not you're fae. Second, they built the passages with some kind of magic that requires purity of thought and intention. Splitting your focus means you can become lost and never leave the passages. So when you enter, you have to know where you are going and why."

"No one's ever accidentally found themselves in these passages?" I was still curious about Jordan, but I didn't want to pry.

"I suppose it's possible, though if someone did accidentally encounter a passage, it's because they have enough fae ancestry for the passage to recognize them as fae."

"Do you see Jordan a lot?" I shouldn't be so obsessed. Besides Vanessa, Xavior only mentioned general details about his escapades. The way Xavior talked about Jordan, he didn't sound like one of his usual hookups. With each passing day, I felt compelled to know more about the dragon sitting across from me. I couldn't help myself.

"From time to time." Xavior pulled out his phone, played with it for a minute, then turned it toward me. He showed me a picture of him standing with a tall fae with long brown hair and pink-tinged alabaster skin with chiseled features. I recognized him immediately.

"You're dating Jordan Gohansberg, the CEO of MajicMovies? Is this at a movie premiere?" It was another reminder that I could never measure up. Vanessa was a partner at a law firm, so it made sense that Xavior would date a CEO. He probably had an entire contact list of beautiful, famous, and high-profile people he had dated.

"Yeah, it was for some kind of space adventure or some such. And dating is a strong word. Jordan and I have attended events together over the years. I invested in his company when he first started it. Besides that, the fae are exceptional sex partners."

I nearly spat my mouthful of beer across the table and sputtered as I tried to regain my composure. Xavior laughed and tossed napkins at me.

"You've gotta lighten up, Lyndon."

"I wasn't expecting. . . details." I took another drink and tried to swallow the lump in my throat. Whatever fantasy I had entertained about Xavior was precisely that. I couldn't compare or measure up, which was a ridiculous thought altogether. I was with Keith, and none of that should matter.

"That was barely what I'd call details," Xavior said with a grin. I laughed as I shook my head. He was right. I needed to lighten up. Xavior took another drink, then looked at me. "You never told me how you and Keith met."

I hadn't thought about it in a while. Remembering the moment warmed me from the inside and reminded me why I was with Keith to begin with.

"You're smiling. It must be pretty good," Xavior said.

"We were working a traffic accident together. Keith was a paramedic on the bus that showed up while I was directing traffic. No one was hurt too much. Scrapes and bruises, mostly. While I was cleaning up the scene, something jagged went through my glove and cut my hand. I walked over to his bus for some skin glue and a bandage, and he proceeded to dote over me and my tiny cut for thirty minutes. His driver was snickering the whole time. When I was about to leave, he gave me his number and asked me out."

Xavior gave me his full attention. Keith and I had our moments, and I couldn't help but continue our story. Even if things weren't great right now, I knew they could be better. We only needed to find our footing with each other again, that was all.

"Our first date was the same movie as the one in your picture with Jordan. He hated it, and I was a nerd about it the entire time. We went for ice cream after and decided we wanted to go out again. Our second date was a picnic in one of the local parks. After a few years of sharing space in each other's apartments, we bought a house together."

Xavior nodded with a grin. "That's fucking adorable. Based on the movie, it's been, what, five years?"

"Yeah," I smiled.

"Are you two thinking about little Lyndon's yet?"

"We're still fixing up our house. It's a little one-story three-bed, two-bath, so I'm hopeful." Xavior nodded, and I noted the odd smile. It wasn't a direct answer. I'm sure he could smell my doubt and insecurity, but thankfully, he kept the information to himself and didn't ask anything more. "Speaking of boyfriends and home improvements, I should probably head out."

"I've got the tab this time. See you tomorrow?"

"Yep," I stood. "Night, Brantley."

"Night, Lyndon."

We heard the following week that when all the city and cultural representatives saw the data; they were shocked. None more so than the fae representative. A community notice later asked folks who used the bicycles to be aware of the difference between private and public bikes. It was also suggested that users should alert the service if they didn't intend to bring the bike back to the city of origin. The bicycle disappearances significantly slowed, which made everyone happy.

Our reputation for solving unusual cases grew. With the recognition, I knew we'd likely get more dangerous cases. My instinct to protect Xavior from my ability warred with the desire to be near him. Every day we worked together, the what-ifs circled in my head like buzzards. If I changed partners, who would keep him safe? And if I didn't, how would I keep him safe from me?

SHIFTING WINDS

XAVIOR

After six months of Greg and me working together, things were going pretty well. It was why I hesitated to mention my birthday party. I wanted to invite Greg, but the problem wasn't him; it was his partner. So while we were cleaning up the last bit of our daily logs, I gave in to my desires just a little. I wanted Greg there, but to do that, we had to talk about Keith.

"So, my birthday is in a few weeks, and I'm throwing a party at my estate. I want to invite you." I tapped my fingers on the desk as I felt the knot form in my stomach. By the look on Greg's face, I wished I'd kept my mouth shut.

"Sounds like there's a 'but' in that statement, Brantley." The annoyance in Greg's voice made the knot in my stomach solidify.

"Well, yeah, I'm a little worried. I don't want to make things awkward by only inviting you, but Keith seems like the type that would take advantage of a situation." The second the words were out of my mouth, I regretted them. I hadn't told Greg that his boyfriend was cheating on him. He knew I didn't like him all that much. The last thing I wanted to do was watch while Keith hurt Greg.

Greg stood and gave a curt nod toward an interview room. As I walked behind him, I knew I was in for an earful as I closed the door.

"Care to tell me why you think Keith is any of your concern?"

"You remember what Vanessa said?" I waved my hands around as if that illustrated anything. "My birthday parties are bigger."

"So you'd be perfectly fine inviting me because, why? I won't fuck my way through your guest list? Do you know what's best for me?"

"That's not what I meant," I stammered. The knot in my stomach swiftly lodged in my throat.

"But you certainly fucking implied it. So invite us, or don't, but stop pretending you're doing me any favors by making Keith out to be any less in control than you. Based on what I've heard, you two would probably be perfect for each other," Greg spit out.

I stood in stunned silence. I hadn't expected that comparison, or for Greg to know what Keith was up to. Maybe I missed something? Why would Greg be worried about infidelity if he knew Keith was having affairs?

He walked past me and slammed the door open. I followed him back to our desks and watched him gather his things and put on his jacket. For once in my life, I didn't have the words to fix this fuck-up, and that pained me in so many ways. I tried to think of anything I could say to make it better. My chance disappeared as the duty sergeant walked up and made a hand gesture that transferred files from her tablet to our desks.

My fingers sought the distraction and opened the case file to read the details. I assessed the included photos and smiled as I looked at the child in the pictures. Adorable and precocious were two words that came to mind.

"You two are doing a pickup and return," Sergeant Dominick said. Her hands worked at her device as she assigned us to the case. I nodded to Dominick as Greg tried to decline the assignment.

"Give it to someone else." Greg's tone was flat as he adjusted his jacket. His response surprised me. I sniffed and smelled the tang of anger and a hint of bittersweetness that I usually associated with longing and denial. The combination confused me, and while I focused on that, Dominick dashed Lyndon's hopes of escape.

"No can do, Lyndon. You're the on-call pair when the patrols are busy, and all the other day shift folks have thumbed out. You're the last detectives on the floor."

"Shit." Greg sighed. "Fine."

Dominick shrugged. Greg made a hand gesture, which grabbed the case files from his desk. As they transferred to his phone, he swiped the vehicle keys off the desk and headed for the garage. I grabbed a data copy for myself and my jacket as I pursued him.

The local shelter facility we were headed to did intakes for pretty much any sentient being, whether it was a familiar, goblin, fae, or human. As Greg drove, I knew we should talk. "Do you. . ." I started, but Greg cut me off before I could finish.

"No. I don't. I want to do this pickup, figure out where we need to go, then call it a fucking night before you say something else." I didn't push any further.

It made me wonder if something had happened recently between him and Keith. Most coworkers I've had spilled their guts within weeks. I knew pretty much everything about them: their partners, their kids. Greg was more pragmatic. The only information I had was what he deemed fit to share.

We parked in front of the shelter. As we headed inside and crossed the threshold into the welcome area, a gentle warmth drifted over me. It had to be a calming ward. There were multiple wards on the facility as a precaution for everyone who came to seek shelter or information. I watched Greg's shoulders relax and his business-like stance change to something casual and friendly. As if the last half-hour never happened.

"Evening, are you Dr. Baker?" Greg asked as the woman looked up from her desk screen.

"Yes. How can I help you this evening?" Dr. Baker was dressed in a light blue blouse and gray slacks, with her natural black hair swept back in a hair clip. Her dark brown eyes assessed Greg and me with mild concern. I had no doubt she could handle whoever walked in the door. While the contact information hadn't indicated Dr. Baker was a mage, I would bet my eyeteeth she was based on the magic I sensed from her.

"I'm Detective Lyndon, and this is Detective Brantley. We were called to pick up and return a lost pup." Greg's smile was genuine, and my anxiety about him took a back seat to the job. We showed our shields, and the doctor recorded our badge IDs.

"You can follow me." Dr. Baker came out from her spot behind the desk. We followed her down a hall as she informed us about the lost pup. "Terrance has been eating nonstop since he arrived. We found a matching snout print from a missing person's report. When I spoke with his parents, they were pretty worried and happy he was somewhere safe. They are eager to have him home." She had an efficient manner, directing other patrons who approached her with questions, as we continued our conversation about Terrance.

"In your professional opinion, do you think it's safe to take Terrance home?" I asked.

"Based on my assessment, yes. Once he shifted back, he told us he'd smelled something interesting and followed it. When he lost the scent, he realized he was lost. Another patron found him and brought him here." She turned toward us and shrugged. "It fits what his parents told us. Besides his distress at being lost, our assessment didn't uncover any past trauma or abuse." She turned down another hallway that led us to a series of playrooms. Some of them had tables and chairs with kids playing games; others with gym areas. We arrived at a room that was active, with children dashing about, some of them shifting between forms.

Dr. Baker pointed to a small boy in the middle of a whirlwind of children. "He's playing with one of our young shifter groups."

I heard a soft chuckle from Greg as he watched the kids chase each other, tag their friends, then run in the opposite direction. Dr. Baker opened the door, and we followed her inside.

"Terrance," Dr. Baker called out. "I have some visitors for you." The boy broke away from his small group and came toward us. He was slight with umber skin, soft dark brown eyes, and a stylized fade. He wore a T-shirt and jeans that were a little big on him, and his feet were bare. His files indicated he was five years old. He came over and stared up at all of us. "This is Detective Lyndon and Detective Brantley. They're going to take you home. Would you like that?"

Terrance nodded so hard I worried that his head might pop off his shoulders. I knelt down so I was at eye level with Terrance. "Have you had dinner yet?" I asked.

He shook his head, and Dr. Baker laughed. "He's had his weight in snacks already, but pups need to eat."

I dropped my voice to a whisper. "I can eat enough food for six people in one sitting." Terrance's eyes widened, and his mouth dropped open.

"Really?" Terrance said in a soft voice. "Are you a shifter too?" he asked.

"Yes, I'm a dragon." Terrance's eyes sparkled with knowledge as he touched my cheeks with his hands. He leaned in to look at my face more closely, and I rewarded his curiosity. With a blink, I'd changed my eyes from their mostly human appearance to those of my dragon form.

"NEAT!" he exclaimed. I looked up at Dr. Baker and winked. If only all kids were this easy to impress.

I offered my hand to Terrance, and he took it immediately. I looked up at Greg, and he nodded. "We'll let you know what the outcome is once we've reached his house," Greg said.

"Thanks," Dr. Baker smiled at Greg. "He's a good pup. If you feed him, make sure he goes to the bathroom afterward. Otherwise, you might have a mess on your hands." She walked to a wall of cubbyholes and grabbed a pair of shoes out of one of them. "He probably won't wear them. Most shifters don't. But just in case."

"Thank you," Greg said as he took the shoes. Dr. Baker walked us all back to the lobby. Before we left, we tried to have Terrance put on the shoes.

"I don't like them, mister dragon. My feet don't hear so well with them." Shifters had more acute senses for various reasons. Canine shifter's feet were tough but sensitive to other things.

"Okay." The vehicle wasn't too far away, but I worried he might step on something. "How about you climb on my back instead?" The grin on Terrance's face was priceless. We pretended I was flying back to the vehicle as Greg quietly followed behind us.

Terrance said he was hungry, and so was I, so we stopped at my favorite burger place and ordered a dozen burgers. Greg was quiet as we ate. Terrance and I polished off all but the one Greg had.

"The meat's weird," Terrance said, as he took another bite.

"They are a combination of soy and animal-based proteins harvested and grown, so we don't have to hunt or slaughter animals." Terrance looked a little confused at my explanation. Some shifter packs didn't eat synthetic or replicated food. I wondered if his parents belonged to a more traditional pack.

"Oh." Terrance shrugged. "It's not squirrel?"

"You've eaten squirrels?" Greg asked.

He shook his head. "Dad says to eat what we catch. I let mine go. They taste funny."

"It's not squirrel," I said. City packs had hunting rights in the forests. They stuck to small game, like squirrels and rabbits, to teach pups to hunt. Other packs had moved away from the tradition by using scenting games to fulfill the same instincts.

After encouraging Terrance to take a bathroom break, we continued our journey. His home address was over an hour away from the shelter. It surprised me that he'd made it so far on his own.

"Hey, mister, are you sad?" Terrance asked. The question sounded loud inside the quiet vehicle. Had he smelled something that prompted his question? Terrance was sitting in the rear seat of the vehicle. I swiveled my chair slightly to look at him. His eyes darted from me to Greg.

I caught Greg's attention and tilted my head toward Terrance. Greg set the autopilot and turned his seat to face the boy. I turned back to the vehicle console and took over driving while Greg talked.

"Something like that," Greg said.

"Is it because you can't shift?" Terrance asked.

I thought that was an odd way to ask if Greg was human. Terrance was old enough to know what humans smelled like. Maybe it was Greg's ability that altered his smell? To me, he only smelled like Greg. A combination of sandalwood and sage, combined with something slightly metallic. He could stand in a crowd and I'd know where he was by that alone.

"No," Greg said, as he tried to smile. "Are you sad, Terrance?"

"Yes," he said, though he didn't smell sad. He smelled as if he were planning something. Greg seemed willing to play along.

"Why are you sad?" The mild concern I heard in Greg's voice made me smile. It didn't surprise me that he was good with kids.

"We didn't have ice cream," Terrance replied.

Greg sighed and tossed his hands up with a shrug. "Well, I guess we'll have to stop for ice cream then." I almost laughed as I altered our course to add an ice cream place to our route. Greg turned back to the console to take over driving. He had a genuine smile on his face now. It was better than where the night had started, and I had Terrance to thank for that.

Terrance took less time to eat the two scoops of chocolate strawberry ice cream than we spent in the bathroom cleaning him up. Between a cleansing spell for his clothes and soap and water for his face and hands, we managed. When he let out a satisfied burp, we all laughed.

"Feel better?" Greg finished wiping Terrance's face as he gave an enthusiastic nod that belied his sleepy eyes. A few minutes after we returned to the vehicle, Terrance was fast asleep.

After another thirty minutes, we pulled up to a fabro-printed ranch-style house painted blue and white with a solar panel roof. The style was popular because the design was easy for commercial material printers to produce.

Greg stepped out of the vehicle, walked up to the front door, and knocked. When I looked back at Terrance, he had shifted into a medium bulldog, fully awake, with his face pressed to the vehicle window.

The kid smelled of happiness and a deep longing. When a person as tall as Greg answered and a slightly shorter person appeared next to them, Terrance started scratching at the door and whining. I got out, jogged around the vehicle, and opened the door for him. He bolted out of the vehicle, into the yard, and up the stairs into the arms of his parents before either adult could take a step toward the vehicle.

Greg shook hands with both of them as they thanked him, then closed the door. He walked back as he wiped at his face, though his lips were curved in a smile.

"Is everything okay?" I asked. Greg nodded as he came toward our vehicle.

"When Terrance bolted after catching a scent, they looked for him for the better part of a day, then reported him missing. They came home and didn't leave in case he showed up. They were hoping he would remember his way home. It's been a week since he took off."

I shook my head. "He's a good kid. I'm glad he's home."

"Yeah. Me too." Greg got into the vehicle, and I followed. The silence returned, but the mood was lighter.

Back at headquarters, Greg tossed me the key fob for the vehicle, then turned to walk toward his personal vehicle without a goodbye. It hurt to speak, but I had to say something. I couldn't leave the quiet between us. "We okay?"

"Yeah, Brantley, we're okay. See you tomorrow."

I didn't really believe that. But I let it go. There wasn't much I could do without making it worse.

GHOST OF A CHANCE

GREGOR

For the past two weeks, my working relationship with Xavior hadn't really improved. Each day I kept rethinking my decision as I looked at the reassignment request I had filled out. I hated second-guessing myself.

He'd told me once that Keith shouldn't dictate my career, but if Xavior didn't like Keith, how could I continue to work with him? My own chaotic emotions compounded the circumstances with Xavior as they continued to surface. I was afraid to be around him sometimes because I didn't know if I wanted to yell at him or kiss him. My ability, my curse, was more like the icing on the layer cake of crap that had become our working relationship.

My reassignment request was open on my desk once again when we were assigned a hit-and-run. I closed the file, then swiped the newly transferred case file to my phone as Xavior grabbed the vehicle fob. When we arrived at the hospital, I noticed Keith at the nurse's desk in the emergency room.

"Hey, you. You're working late." I touched Keith's back gently. We were both on duty, and I didn't want to embarrass him. I noticed Xavior give Keith a silent nod.

"We caught one more call before they pulled us off rotation for the day." Keith looked tired. "Are you the detectives they sent?"

"Yeah. We were already at headquarters this morning." Keith looked down and then back up at me and gave me a wavering smile. I chalked it up to him being tired. He launched into an explanation of the case with none of his usual energy.

"Someone called into emergency services after finding them. All the stats indicate they are a plant-based being, but they are pretty fucking pale and don't have the chlorophyll counts we'd expect. They're on CO_2, but that doesn't seem to help them much." Keith shrugged. His disappointment at his patient's predicament was apparent.

When I looked over at Xavior, his face was neutral, which was uncharacteristic. I'd never seen him shut down to the point I couldn't read him.

"Keith, do you think anyone would mind if we checked on them ourselves? We'd like to get a written report about their injuries and follow through with witnesses if we can." Xavior's tone gave me the impression he wouldn't take no for an answer. I worried for a moment but trusted that Xavior would be professional, regardless of whether or not he liked Keith.

Xavior had his arms across his chest as if he was restraining himself. It framed him in a way that caught me off guard as I took in his strength and confidence, along with his build. It was the first time I noticed he was slightly taller than Keith. That made me drop my gaze to my shoes, if only to bring myself under control. I hated that my attraction to Xavior appeared at the oddest times.

"It shouldn't be a problem. I can take you back," said Keith, before walking down the hall. I looked up to follow. When Keith turned his back to us, Xavior winked at me. Was he trying to reassure me or flirt? Either way, my face was hot with surprise. When I caught up with Xavior, he was all business again, and I wondered if I'd imagined it.

As we followed Keith into the patient's room, he moved to check various monitors. I closed the door behind me and observed Keith as he worked with the patient.

The individual on the hospital bed was a bipedal, translucent epidermis with the very faintest hint of green underneath. The air in the room seemed overly oxygenated, as if we stood in the middle of a forest. I watched the individual's whole body inflate slightly and then shrink when they exhaled, as if they breathed with every pore they possessed. The beep of the monitor noted the rhythm of their circulation organ. It was painfully slow compared to a human. Over a minute would pass before a beep sounded that alternated with a steady breath.

Xavior took a few steps toward the patient and pulled out his phone and a stylus. We had decided some time ago that if we were working on a case together, he'd take notes. My writing was illegible, according to him. I didn't argue. His scrawl was legible and showed dedicated practice. I enjoyed reading it and envied the practiced swirls. He probably had a similar style of handwriting in more than one language, though I had yet to see it.

As I watched, I caught a familiar smell that reminded me of my parent's place. "Am I the only one who smells redwoods right now?" It was so quiet that my speaking voice seemed loud.

Keith turned to me and then looked at Xavior. "I'm not smelling anything but hospital cleaning supplies and myself at the moment." He shrugged.

Xavior leaned closer to the bed. I could see him take a deep breath. He closed his eyes, hands poised with the stylus in one and his phone in the other. He set both down at the end of the bed and went closer to the patient's head.

"They're an ent, I think. But their smell is off. It's metallic, though it's very faint, right below the redwood smell you picked up, Lyndon."

"Why do you think that is?" I knew about ents and had seen pictures thanks to Grandpa Jack. The individual in front of us didn't look like one except in form. Most ents were a deep green color and had vegetation growing on them. It's possible they were a hybrid or maybe kin to a wood nymph.

"Well, for one, if they were an ent, they should be dead. The moment something separates them from having contact with the ground, they deteriorate pretty quickly. This one seems to be doing alright, but not improving."

"The dextrose drip and the carbon dioxide helped, but you're right. They've been like this since we picked them up," Keith said.

"Can I try something?" Xavior asked.

"Sure, what do you have in mind?" Keith looked at Xavior. I stayed where I was because the space was small. Whatever they tried, I didn't want to get in the way.

"It might be that what you have them on is too clean." Xavior pulled in a deep breath and held it. We watched as his face reddened and a little smoke escaped from his nostrils.

A moment later, Xavior leaned over the bed and exhaled a gray smoke into the individual's face. They responded by taking a deep breath. Xavior repeated the process, and they took another breath. The monitor beeped a little faster. The room slowly filled with enough smoke that Keith and I waved it away from our faces.

From what I could tell, Xavior used his fire breath and extinguished it internally before he exhaled. Which was smart, given the fire risk with all the oxygen in the room. I trusted Xavior but worried about what would happen if this all went wrong.

When Xavior bent over the motionless figure for the third time, they moved. Their eyes flew open, and they reached for Xavior, planting their lips on his. Xavior opened his mouth, and they opened theirs, pulling the smoke directly into themselves. Xavior braced his weight on the hospital bed railings as the ent continued to kiss him. It was oddly erotic to watch as the smoke floated around them while their vitals improved.

There was a knowing grin on Keith's face when he looked at me. I returned it as I hadn't expected what we were witnessing either. When Keith cleared his throat, whatever magic was between the two broke as they let go of Xavior.

"I apologize. I was not myself," they said. A flush of the lightest green filled their cheeks and drifted through their limbs. I realized they were blushing and looked away.

"It's alright. I'm glad I could help. Could you tell us your name?" Xavior asked. That question caught my attention and drew my gaze back to the individual in the bed.

"I am Enish." They looked at each one of us. "Am I in the city?"

Keith spoke up. "We found you unconscious on the freeway at the edge of town. Do you remember anything?"

"I. . ." they began, "I was curious."

"Do you know what happened?" I asked.

"I remember seeing lights. They drew me, and one hit me," Enish said. A large, specialized bandage was wrapped around their left arm. They reached up to touch it, then looked at Keith for answers.

"It was almost torn off. If you're able to move it like that, then you've healed fairly quickly," Keith pointed out. As we watched, the various scrapes and cuts faded from vibrant deep marks to shallow wounds. Xavior's smoke appeared to have sped up Enish's recovery process.

"You knew?" Enish asked Xavior.

Xavior shrugged. "I knew you were likely an ent, but I guessed you were a sacred one. I'm glad the smoke trick worked."

Enish nodded. "I'd like to return home now." They looked at Xavior, then Xavior looked from Enish to Keith.

"Let me see what I can do about the discharge paperwork." Keith walked past me out of the room. I followed and caught his elbow.

"Hey," I smiled at him. "Make sure you rest before you drive home, okay? I'll make it an early night and grab some takeout for us."

"I'd like that." He reached for my hand and gave it a hard squeeze. I cleared my throat as I rocked on my heels, feeling my face heat. Keith smiled and gave my hand another squeeze before letting go. Staying professional was a challenge, especially when he looked that good in his uniform. "I'll see you at home," Keith said.

I nodded and went back into the room where Enish was trying to give directions to Xavior so we could take them home. We found Enish's home in one of several forest preserves near the city. It was on a side road close to the freeway, about two kilometers from where they'd been found.

We parked on the shoulder of a gravel road, got out of the vehicle. We walked with Enish toward his forest home. They stopped several meters before we reached the treeline. "Thank you, my friends," Enish said as they turned and gave me a hug, then gave Xavior a hug that was significantly longer. I stifled my amused reaction as I watched. The ent clearly had a crush on Xavior.

"Take care, alright?" Xavior slowly separated from the ent.

"I will. Please visit. I would like to learn more about you, dragon," Enish said.

"I'll do that." The smile on Xavior's face told me he'd take the time, for curiosity's sake, and because he inadvertently gained a new friend.

As we walked back to the vehicle, I was curious how Xavior knew about ents. It was the kind of thing that made me appreciate him as a coworker and made us a good team. "So what exactly is a sacred one?"

"Locals call them ghost trees. They're albino redwoods that have little of their own chlorophyll. They obtain it by filtering toxins for the rest of their family. They are considered sacred souls among the ents because they keep forests healthy."

Given how much my granddad and dad worked and traded with different ent families, it surprised me that I didn't know about them already. "That was an impressive job today, Brantley."

"Thanks." I watched as a slight smile appeared on his face, and he looked at me. "Keith is pretty good at his job." His tone was even.

It surprised me that he'd said anything. I acknowledged his smile with one of my own. "Yeah, and he doesn't look bad in his uniform either."

Xavior chuckled. "I can see the appeal." He grinned and then sighed. "I'm sorry for what I said about him. You were right. It's none of my business."

"But you weren't wrong, either. We've had our challenges. He's a good person. Things have been difficult sometimes, but worth it."

Xavior nodded, and we left the conversation at that. I could tell he was holding something back about Keith. I didn't try to fish it out of him. The peace was too fragile between us.

After we returned to headquarters, we spent the remainder of the day filing forms. I begged off the last of it to pick up Thai food from Keith's favorite place before heading home. When I got there, an invitation to Xavior's birthday party was on the coffee table.

Seeing the opened invitation made me happy because I knew Keith would be pleased about it. I hadn't mentioned to Keith that I was thinking about asking for a reassignment. If I suggested that we shouldn't go without explaining, I knew it would lead to an argument.

The following day, I got ready for work while Keith slept. While I ate breakfast, I checked my phone for messages and noticed the reassignment forms. I deleted them before I left the house.

Xavior's Birthday Party

Gregor

It was early on a Saturday afternoon in September when Xavior sent a luxury driverless vehicle to pick us up for his birthday party. Keith was giddy, but I was shocked at the expense. I shouldn't have been, considering he owned at least one restaurant. After I put our overnight bag in the luggage compartment, we slipped into the backseat. Keith melted into the rich, replicated-leather interior.

"If this is how the weekend is starting out, I might die a happy man later," said Keith.

Xavior had invited us to stay the weekend, explaining that he had plenty of room and there would be brunch served Sunday morning. I didn't think it was smart, but I couldn't say no to Keith's enthusiasm about having a weekend together. I called my parents to let them know we'd visit the following weekend. They told us to have fun and wish Xavior well.

"Well, we know the food should be pretty good." Keith chuckled as he crawled into my lap. He kissed me as my hands landed on his hips to keep him steady while the vehicle moved.

"We have about an hour. Want to fool around in a really expensive ride?" Keith asked. I moved to wrap an arm around his back and put a hand on the back of his neck to encourage his reckless suggestion with urgent kisses.

Keith's hands went to my jeans, pulled at my shirt, undid my belt, and opened my fly. As he touched my cock, I moaned into his mouth. I glanced out the windows as Keith slid off my lap onto the floorboards. His lips wrapped around the head of my dick. I grabbed onto the seat and the door handle to keep from sliding around.

As he lavished attention on me with his talented tongue, I made small thrusts into his mouth, encouraging him to take more of me. My hand let go of the seat and caressed his head as it bobbed on my dick. His hand fisted in my shirt as he continued to tease the sensitive nerves around the tip. I split my gaze between watching Keith and the scenery through the tinted windows as it went by.

Just as I was about to spill into Keith's mouth, he moved. I groaned in frustration as he pulled my jeans and boxers down to my ankles. Once he moved to straddle my lap, I realized he'd taken off his pants, and I hadn't noticed.

Keith's hard-on bumped into mine as he adjusted his hips slightly, then rubbed himself against me. His hands went to the top of the seat on either side of my head. I spat into my hand, then reached between us. The minute I wrapped it around both our cocks, Keith groaned softly. I loved that sound. The feel of us pressed together while Keith rocked his hips had me back near that blissful edge I'd been chasing earlier.

"Fuck, I'm going to come. We can't make a mess in here," I said.

Without missing a beat, Keith waved off my worry as he continued to thrust his dick into my fist. "Relax, I've got it. Keep going."

I trusted he could handle it and let myself get lost in our pleasurable bubble.

"Yes, just like that. Fuck." Keith moved faster.

He kissed me until I was so distracted that my orgasm snuck up on me. That amped him up, and with a few more thrusts of his hips, he joined me in our mingled mess. As much as we tried, our clothes hadn't been spared. "Okay, how are we cleaning this up?" I said with a chuckle.

Keith leaned over, opened a compartment, and pulled a couple of tissues from it.

I laughed. "I think we're going to need more than that to clean this up."

"Just watch." He wadded the tissues up in his hands, said a few words, then opened his hands to reveal the same tissues, though now they had a slight purple color to them. He gently passed the improved tissues over our skin and clothing. All hints of anything we'd done disappeared. It impressed me. I had no idea he knew how to do a cleaning spell.

"The only thing it won't get rid of is the smell, but we can open a window. That should help." We cracked the windows. We were both laughing while we finished worming our way back into our clothes as the vehicle pulled up to a private gate.

When the gate opened, our transportation rolled forward. There was a parade of vehicles similar to ours going up to the house, disgorging people, then driving away. "Brantley must have rented a fleet of vehicles for the night."

As our vehicle pulled up, someone opened the door on my side, and we got out. Our bag was in someone else's hands as Keith and I looked at each other, then up at the massive building in front of us.

"Oh shit," Keith said as we looked at the sprawling limestone mansion. His sunglasses slid off his nose as he looked around. "Gregie, did you know about this?"

"No. I mean, we knew Brantley was well-off." I waved my hands around, as if that would explain the estate we were standing on or the mansion in front of us.

"Xavior has enough room for a small country," Keith said with a touch of awe in his voice.

The massive decorative doors opened, and several more people in uniform came out to greet us. I handed over our invitation and, like at the restaurant, they all seemed to shift from passive greetings to overly helpful assistance.

"Hello, Mr. Lyndon, Mr. Elliot. My name is Edward. Mr. Brant-ley has told us to make sure you receive excellent service this evening. May I show you to your room?" We nodded. Edward gave a curt nod as he took our bag from the attendant's hand. "This way, gentlemen."

Our room was a house all its own. Edward opened the double doors and explained what was available. The suite had a large, lavish bathroom, a small living room, a wet bar and kitchenette, and an enormous bedroom. Edward indicated the rooms would be available to us for the entire weekend. I was floored. Keith was in heaven.

"Holy shit, Greg," he laughed. "You're not allowed to change work partners, ever." I knew he was joking, but it didn't make me feel any better. Keith walked further into the room as Edward handed me two keys to the suite.

"Mr. Brantley said to mention that he left you welcome gifts. You'll find them in the bedroom," Edward said. "If you require anything else, any touch screen in the suite can send a message to staff who will see to your needs."

"Thank you, Edward." It was an awkward exchange that un-settled me. The last time I had to deal with butlers and house staff was when I visited my mother. This was an unpleasant reminder.

Given the local ecology, I wondered how he'd built a house this large. But then Xavior was a dragon and had access to mag-ic, material printers, modern science, and more than enough money. For all I knew, the house could be one vast pocket dimension, like the dragon dens he described.

As Edward left the suite, I went to the bedroom. I prayed by all the sacred texts that Xavior hadn't left some kinky bag of toys, or worse. I wouldn't live down my embarrassment if Keith found that first.

Instead, I found two stylish boxes, sealed with ribbon from one of the best tailors in the city. It was very exclusive and fae-owned. Each one had a tag with our full names spelled out in elegant script that I instantly recognized as Xavior's. Keith came to stand next to me as I stared down at the boxes.

"No. Fucking. Way." Keith plucked the lid off his box. Inside was a suit I would guess was tailored to his body with precision and worth a few months of mortgage payments on our house. It was a deep blue with a peacock mosaic tie and vest to match, including a creamy white shirt that set off the suit's blue and the deep greens and reds of the patterns on his vest and tie. The box also contained a matching changing robe, cufflinks, black slacks, and dress shoes with a coordinating belt.

When I opened mine, I noticed the slacks and jacket were dark green, paired with a pale green shirt and a creamy white tie and vest.

Keith and I smiled at each other. Xavior could be eccentric, but the fact that he went out of his way to make sure we had clothes nice enough that we'd feel like we fit in was appreciated. We grabbed a shower and helped each other get dressed.

Keith adjusted my tie as we looked each other over. "Fuck, babe, you look spectacular," he said, smiling.

"You clean up pretty well yourself, sweetheart." I brushed his shoulders.

"We should save these," he said. He turned toward the mirror to smooth his tie again.

"Oh?" I breathed. I dared not hope and waited for what he could say next.

"Mmm hmm. Maybe someday we'll have a reason to use them, you know."

I chuckled. "For what, exactly?"

He turned around. "Maybe," he kissed me softly, "a ceremony involving that ring you showed me." He shrugged. "Just a thought."

I felt my heart skip a beat, then slam hard in my chest as it started up again. That Keith even brought up anything close to marriage made my throat dry.

"Familiar catch your tongue, Gregie?" he teased.

"Uh," I breathed, not sure what to say.

Keith gave me a smirk. "Come on, babe. If these clothes are any sign, we have a fucking fabulous party to attend." He offered me his hand, and I took it while thoughts of spending the rest of my life with this man danced in my head.

"Shit, wait. I almost forgot." I let go of his hand and went to our bag and fished out the small present I'd made for Xavior. Keith said it was a cute gift. I only hoped Xavior thought so after giving us the clothes we were wearing.

Once I was back at Keith's side, I slipped my hand into his as we left the suite to join the party downstairs.

THE SHEPHERD'S HOOK

XAVIOR

Guests began to arrive in a steady stream. Everyone I'd known in the last fifty to a hundred years that could make it wandered around my property meeting each other. That is, everyone but my family.

Birthdays with my family were mostly a quarter-century affair. For someone's twenty-fifth anniversary, we'd come together at the manor property in Spain and celebrate. But, as I was only turning three hundred seventy-four this year, it spared me the intimate yet boring family celebration that would usher in an aging cycle.

With dragon aging cycles came the biological drive to find a mate, so I wasn't looking forward to next year. I'd avoided having to deal with my aging cycles by not being around or involved with anyone for extended periods. As I've done a similar dance for the last three hundred years or so, I assumed I'd reach my half-millennium mark without becoming attached to anyone. I liked my independence, and while I cared about people, I hadn't found anyone I was in love with enough to want to be mated to them.

My personal suite was set above and back from the entry to the main house. It featured a landing with a winding staircase on either side. Directly below my suite was the main foyer and a passage through several sets of French glass doors to the main garden, which led to the main sauna, hot tub, and pool area with a patio. Or guests could take the left and right passages, which led to wings of the house that featured conference rooms, sitting rooms, the kitchens, dance halls, and an art gallery. All the rooms on the lower floor, except the library, would be open to guests. The second and third floors of the wings had guest rooms of various sizes and luxuries. Those were reserved for guests who stayed overnight. The estate could easily host two hundred individuals, especially since we were fully staffed for this weekend.

I adjusted my tie and walked down the staircase to the foyer, and was instantly immersed in the crowd of guests making their way into the party. Staff members carried trays of drinks and hors d'oeuvres, offering them in welcome and giving directions to areas of the estate.

Most of my events had an initial party, one where the dignitaries, CEOs, lobbyists, politicians, and philanthropists would gather to discuss any number of subjects. Then the afterparty would start when polite society disappeared back to their homes and hotels or stayed to indulge in more clothing-optional activities. With safety wards in place and my staff monitoring the event, I didn't worry much about things getting out of hand. It's why my parties had an excellent reputation. Everyone went home happy, regardless of when they left.

A tray of cocktails floated past me, and I grabbed one while I mingled with people, shook hands, and tried being the gracious host and birthday guy. There were always those who thought they needed to bring something. My staff would collect those items at the door and store them later for sorting. I rarely kept anything, and most of the time, I auctioned the items off and donated the proceeds. Others who knew me better were smart enough to contribute to one of my preferred charities.

As I moved through the crowd, greeting people, I made my way to the art gallery in the left wing of the estate. I picked up the soft tones of the string quartet that played as people admired the art. It didn't surprise me to see Jordan there. Fae were always attracted to things they found beautiful.

Jordan admired a newer contemporary piece that took up half of one wall when I walked up to him and whispered, "You're looking rather ravishing tonight."

He gasped, then spun on his heel. His arms came around me and pulled me into a tight hug. "Fuck you, gorgeous. How have you been?" Jordan's ice-blue eyes looked me over as I took him in. He was impeccably dressed in a white cloak over a soft yellow shirt and a pinstripe vest with pants to match. His shoes were the same color as the cloak. His soft brown hair was plaited down his back, and a derby hat the same color as his shirt covered his slightly pointed ears.

"I've been fairly good. I transferred headquarters, so I've been busy."

"You're still working as a public safety officer?" Jordan's voice conveyed his astonishment.

"Well, I'm not doing it for the money, you know that. It was the easiest way to handle my nature." I shrugged and took a sip of my drink.

"Ah, the mystery. Are you finding plenty of mysteries, then?"

"You have no idea." He laughed as I'd hoped, but it was the truth as well. Learning a new department wasn't hard, but Greg was a mystery, and that was before you added his Saint George ability.

As I thought of him, I realized he should be here by now. I had mixed feelings about inviting Keith, but I had buried those, hoping to give Greg and Keith a night of luxury they could enjoy. Whatever their relationship was, Greg was right; it was none of my business. As his coworker, I was determined to be more supportive.

I gave Jordan another hug and left him to admire the art with a promise that I would find him later if he was staying for the afterparty. He indicated he wouldn't miss it for anything. Jordan wasn't with anyone tonight, and I could definitely get behind—or in front of—spending a few hours with him in my bed later.

As I finished my drink and handed the glass to a staff member. I made my way back through the left wing, venturing from one space to the next until I reached the dance hall where a live band played. That's when I spotted them. To my minor shock, Keith and Greg were holding their own on the dance floor to some kind of upbeat music. Greg executed a couple of twirls, and Keith smiled and laughed as they continued to circle the crowded dance floor. I held my place and watched.

Keith noticed me first and left the dance floor, bringing Greg with him. I hadn't expected that. The other thing I hadn't expected was Greg to look so fucking breathtaking in the suit I'd picked out for him. I knew Keith would look pretty good. His build was like mine, although I was a little taller.

"Xavior!" Keith yelled over the music as he came toward me. Greg held Keith's hand, but his eyes were on me. As he got closer, I got a dose of his scent with attraction and desire woven into it. It hit me like I'd had five shots of something expensive and smooth. Keith said something, but I wasn't paying attention. Instead, my eyes were on Greg. Greg grinned, then winked, which caught me by surprise. I hadn't expected him to flirt like that.

"What did you say?" I returned my attention to Keith, who rambled on about something. I pretended the music was too loud for me to hear him properly.

"The party is spectacular! We've met a dozen stars already, and the band is totally killer. And the clothes, holy shit, thank you so much, Xavior. I can't. . . we can't thank you enough for inviting us." Keith looked at Greg and kissed him on the cheek. Greg pulled Keith close and smiled.

"No problem. What's the point of having a party if you can't invite your friends?" I gave them a friendly smile, for Greg's sake, more than anyone else.

"Will Vanessa be here tonight?" Keith asked.

"Yes, I imagine so. I invited her." Keith nodded. Greg took that moment to pull something out of his pocket.

"We got something for you, or rather, I made it. Nothing expensive or anything, but thought you'd like something practical," Greg said as he handed over a slender pouch about twelve centimeters long.

"Thank you. That's thoughtful." I meant it. Regardless of how I felt about anyone else bringing me a present, the fact that Greg had made me something had my stomach doing little flips. I opened the little pouch, and a piece of redwood slipped into my hand, weighted by metal at both ends.

It looked like a mini shepherd's hook. However, the hook was a small, stylized flame carved and plated with the same silver as the bottom. I held it for a moment to figure out what it was precisely, and then I looked up with a smile. "It's a bookmark."

"He got it on the first try. You said he wouldn't," Keith said.

"I was wrong," Greg said, looking at me. That statement was so heavy, I wasn't sure what to say exactly, so I forged ahead, admiring Greg's artistry.

"It's excellent work." I turned over the bookmark in my hand. It was clear Greg had spent time with it. The silver and wood piece was polished to a bright shine, giving the wood a rich color.

"I do some woodworking in my off-time. Small pieces, nothing fancy," Greg said. I watched as Keith grabbed two drinks off a tray. The server stopped next to me and offered me one, but I waved them off.

"It's beautiful. Thank you. Both of you." They both smiled and gave a brief nod as I noticed they were holding hands again. I buried the odd spike of jealousy with a smile to match theirs.

"Happy Birthday, Xavior!" Keith held up his glass, and I nodded again. Greg echoed Keith's sentiment.

"I'm going to put this in my library and catch up with you two later, okay?" They both agreed to catch up later, then set their drinks down before they went back to the dance floor. I wandered away, practically on autopilot, saying hello and receiving well wishes until I reached my library. Inside, it was quiet and dark. There was a lit lamp next to my favorite reading chair. I sat down and admired the bookmark again.

Emotions threatened to leave me in tears. No one, save my family, had ever given me something so significant and sentimental. I knew exactly what it meant. Greg remembered the story I'd told him about the shepherd and his wife.

I got the subtle hint. Greg wasn't scared of me. It hadn't clicked with me how much I wondered if his fear of hurting me came from a place of fear in general. I wiped my eyes and laughed. It seemed Greg and I were destined to one-up each other. I was satisfied with that prospect. At least I knew things would always be interesting as long as Greg was around. I placed the bookmark back in the pouch and put it on the table next to my chair. I headed back out to the party with a lighter step and a smile on my face.

TRIGGER WORDS

GREGOR

I hadn't expected Xavior to respond to the present like that. Part of me was happy he liked it; another part felt bad for invoking something deeply personal to him. Personal enough that he ditched his own party for a while, according to some guests. If I saw him again, I'd have to apologize for catching him off guard.

While my concern about Xavior bubbled in the back of my head, Keith and I spent another hour enjoying the dance floor. The swing classes we'd taken had come in handy, and when people started asking us to trade-off dance partners, we both enjoyed the attention. Keith was much better than me and made it look like everyone he danced with was graceful, while I managed well enough.

After the whirligig of people, I stepped off the dance floor for a break. Keith was still going strong when Vanessa showed up beside me.

"Who knew you two could dance? If I'd known, I would have made Xavior take us all dancing. Though he would probably have been a wallflower most of the time. He's never liked dancing in public."

I was taking another swig of water from a bottle one of the staff had brought me. "Nice to see you again, Vanessa."

"I don't have Xavior's nose, but I think we both know you're not that happy to see me," she said.

I sighed. "You caught me off guard, that's all. The entire night did. I did it for Keith. Xavior doesn't talk about any of this at work, and he certainly doesn't flaunt any of it." I took a deep breath. "A little warning might have been nice," I grumbled.

"About me or his money?" she purred, all too happy to keep interrogating me.

"Both?" I huffed out a smirk.

"Listen, Greg." She set down her empty glass on a tray as a staff person passed by. "I've never seen Xavior take to someone like he's taken to you. He wants to make you happy. For me and others, it's kindness, but for you, there's something there."

I looked at her, then looked down at my shoes. Everything I wore, which Xavior had purchased, fit as if I'd stood in the boutique shop they had come from while tailors measured everything by hand. It was the exclamation point on her words. "Why are you telling me this?"

"Maybe because I'm jealous." She smiled and picked up a fresh drink from another tray as it went by. "Or maybe it's because Xavior's a friend, and I'm protective of my friends."

"Vanessa, we're coworkers. That's it." My explanation fell flat, and her smile thinned.

"I can't tell if you really believe that or if that's what you want to believe, because if you give up that little lie, your whole, carefully constructed world changes. Life's too short, Greg. I hope you figure it out."

She took a long drink while she watched me, put down the glass, then wandered onto the dance floor. I stood there, holding my water bottle, a little dazed. I took another drink as I watched the dancers revolve around the room again. Vanessa found Keith talking with another group. They hugged and began a lively conversation before returning to the dance floor. I barely kept from shaking my head. I wondered for a moment if she would say anything, but the look on Keith's face made me believe otherwise.

I wasn't exactly worried that Keith would do something with Vanessa. He had clear preferences, but she was someone Keith could be attracted to or have interesting experiences with, if given the opportunity.

After a couple of revolutions on the floor, they stopped next to me, and I could tell Keith was excited. "Hey Gregie, Vanessa is going to take me around to meet a few more people. Wanna come with us?"

I saw Vanessa raise an eyebrow. After our brief discussion, the last thing I wanted to do was spend more time with her. "I think I'll sit this one out, babe. Wanna meet up later for a swim?" While Xavior had neglected to warn me about the opulent house, he'd made a point to warn me about the afterparty. I saw Vanessa smile as Keith gave me a quick kiss.

"See you soon," Keith said, with a dreamy look plastered on his face. He turned and took Vanessa's hand, and I watched as they wandered off together. I moved back toward the main hall, grabbing snacks along the way. People were already leaving, and it looked like the staff was handing out some kind of party favor.

When I got back to our room, I noticed someone had organized our things. Our clothes were neatly folded and placed on the dresser, and they had stored our overnight bag on a luggage rack. There were two more small boxes on the bed near the pillows. Inside the boxes were chocolates. I took one and popped it into my mouth. It surprised me how good it tasted. I wasn't a big fan of chocolate, but I had to admit, these were rather notable. It shouldn't surprise me that this place worked like a hotel.

I noticed trays on the table in the kitchenette area as I took off my coat. Upon investigation, I discovered one tray had a pastrami sandwich and fries. It was still hot, and my stomach made noises like it contained a monster ready to devour everything in sight. I quickly stripped to my boxers, then returned to dig in. About five minutes into my total grease fest, Keith walked in, followed by Vanessa.

"Greg, you here?" he said. He went toward the bedroom first while Vanessa stood with a hand covering her mouth, staring at me.

I was likewise frozen, with half a sandwich filling my cheeks and the other half in my hand. When Keith saw me, his eyes went wide, then he burst into laughter.

It took forever, but I finally chewed my mouthful and swallowed. I answered Keith and Vanessa, as they laughed. "I didn't want to ruin the suit, and I was hungry."

"I guess I should be glad you're wearing underwear," Vanessa said.

"We came up to change for the pool. Vanessa is staying down the hall," Keith said, as he wiped tears from his eyes. "I didn't know you'd be elbow-deep in carnage when we came by."

I growled and took another bite. Vanessa laughed and turned to leave. "Catch you two later." As she left, Keith came over and opened the lid on the other tray. It was a version of the spicy basil Thai dish he liked. I recognized it from ordering it so often from his favorite Thai food place. Xavior had done his homework.

"Okay, I'm sorry for laughing. Fuck, that smells good. I'll be right back." Keith retreated to the bedroom, then returned wearing only his underwear and sat down. I chuckled as I ate some fries.

When we were done, we both wandered back to the bedroom. I hung our suits in the armoire while Keith grabbed our swimming suits. The night was going pretty well, and I was looking forward to a dip in the pool.

"Greg, did you eat one of the chocolates?"

"Yeah. It was pretty good. I wonder where Xavior got them."

Keith chuckled. "Babe, did you read the note in the box?"

"No. Why?"

"Because they are magic-laced chocolates," Keith said. I heard the serious tone in his voice and turned to see him looking at the note in his hand. He held his box and sat down on the bed.

"Really? I don't feel any different." I walked over and sat next to him.

"It's because all the chocolates have different trigger words. How long ago did you eat one?" Keith looked at me with a distinct amount of concern on his face.

"Um, before I had dinner. So, maybe thirty minutes ago?"

"Okay, well, the spell only has potency for an hour." Keith continued to read. "It says that after an hour, without the trigger or the dispel word, it fades. If triggered, it can last for an hour or more, depending on the spell." He turned to me and spoke a list of nouns. "Relaxation, euphoria, amativeness, and exuberance."

I felt a sudden shift in my mood. Desires and needs I kept under tight control burst to life. Sticky wetness from my erection quickly accompanied the tightness in my balls and lightheadedness.

"Let me guess, the trigger word was the name of the chocolate?" I asked as I tried to control myself, breathing in through my nose and out through my mouth.

Keith watched as I lay back on the bed. "Oh, that one," he chuckled and put the small boxes on the nightstand.

"I have about five seconds of control left before I tackle you to this bed or spend the next hour jacking off in the shower." I was thirty seconds away from an orgasm, so I hoped Keith took me seriously.

"Oh, I'm not passing this up. Want me to dose myself too?"

"Oh, fuck no, one of us should be sober for whatever I've gotten myself into," I said.

"Only if you promise to return the favor later."

"Absolutely, sweetheart. Please, please help." My light-hearted laugh turned into a small whimper as he moved my boxers. A groan followed it as my dick throbbed when he wrapped his hand around it.

"It's alright, babe. I have you." Keith's words caressed my skin as he wrapped his lips around me. I closed my eyes and lost myself in the sensations.

It wasn't Keith's face I saw in my mind's eye. When familiar emerald orbs stared back at me, I fell into them like they were pools of water. The sensation of bliss crawled up my spine and bowed it as I came in several drowning waves of intense desire. A choking noise caught my attention. My gaze found Keith covered from face to chest in\ spunk. The sight was so shocking and satisfying. In the back of my mind, something dark stirred and rumbled its pleasure at marking its territory. If I'd been sober, the thought would have scared the shit out of me.

"Fucking hell, Greg. That shit must be potent," Keith said as he stood.

"You have no idea," I said with a low growl in my voice as I grabbed Keith and pulled him onto the bed. The mess didn't matter. In fact, it turned me on even more. I was hard again, and Keith's body responded to mine.

"Holy shit." He laughed as my lips fell on his. "Greg," he whispered breathlessly, as I reached between us while my other hand searched for one of his.

"It's alright. I'm going to take care of you."

FAE-TASTIC

XAVIOR

I wandered a bit and noticed Vanessa showing Keith around. It made me wonder what Greg was doing without them. I turned to find him when someone came up behind me and dropped a blindfold over my eyes. A quick sniff told me it was Jordan, much to my delight.

"Darling, I have a surprise for you. Will you come with me?" Jordan whispered.

"Have I ever told you no?"

"There's always a first time," Jordan said. His voice was non-chalant. Frankly, I was happy with the distraction. I shouldn't be thinking about Greg at all. But my thoughts kept returning to him repeatedly, like a recording on a loop.

I let Jordan guide me back to my suite. I knew it was mine by the smell, then caught a few more scents besides. Most of them were lust-related; some smelled like massage oil. Jordan was still behind me, but I knew the scene awaiting me was erotic and comprised multiple people.

Jordan opened my bedroom door, then closed it behind us. When he took off the blindfold, in the dim light, I could make out at least ten naked bodies on the floor, all arrayed in the center of my bedroom. They were pouring massage oil and hot wax on each other.

"Happy birthday, Xavior." Jordan removed my suit jacket before I could formulate a response. I noticed a protective mat covered the floor, which meant Jordan had enlisted Edward's help.

"They're magnificent. Who are they?" I glanced at Jordan as he took off his coat and hung it next to mine. Sounds drew my eyes back to the scene playing out in front of us.

"Well, they are a small erotic fae dance troupe that does nude performances." I saw a few sets of wings flutter as Jordan whispered in my ear.

"Oh? What does that entail, exactly?" I asked.

Jordan wrapped his arms around me and rested his chin on my shoulder. His touch made my breath hitch a little. The sight on my bedroom floor was unbelievably erotic.

He pressed in a little closer. The feel of his body lined up with mine sped up my heart rate. "We have options. We could watch them, participate, or do our own things while they make a beautiful soundtrack. So what do you feel up for tonight, my friend?"

"All of it." Jordan's laugh in my ear was seductive as he started picking each button open on my shirt.

We watched as the scene evolved. Hands and tongues disappeared between legs and into mouths. The group was various hues of bright pink or red. The moans and soft sighs that echoed from the vaulted ceiling were enough to make me hard. Once Jordan and I finished undressing each other, we joined the orgy. We were immediately covered in oil, kisses, hands, and other body parts as we became part of the group, collectively seeking sexual bliss.

I didn't keep track of how many times I came before I pulled Jordan away to my bed. I grabbed a few more things from the half-empty baskets filled with various kinds of protection and lube. The troupe continued as we pressed our oil-slicked bodies together.

"You give excellent birthday presents," I said, after I'd ardently kissed him.

"Only because we enjoy similar things," he said. "Are you ready for your next present?"

"There's more?" Jordan smiled, and I distracted him for a moment as I pressed my groin to his and teased him.

"Stop, you wicked dragon, or I won't give it to you." His voice alone was enough to make me groan with need.

"Okay, I'll stop," I said with a sheepish grin, and teased him instead with small kisses on his chest. He reached for something on the nightstand. Before he could reveal what he had, his nipple was in my mouth while I caressed the other. He moaned in response as his skin flushed a darker red. We continued with my distraction until Jordan gave me a gentle push and we sat up.

"Here," Jordan said as he held up a small bag.

It was tiny, and the aroma had an interesting spice to it, like pepper or ginseng. Smells I often associate with earth magic. Jordan's magic was focused on illusions and architecture. He was a builder of dreams. Someone else made the elemental magic in the tiny pouch. "What is it?"

"It's supposed to let you connect on a deeper level when you're having sex with someone." He handed me the bag.

"Like the chocolates?"

"Not quite, more like a metaphysical connection."

"Interesting. Shall we try it?" I asked.

Jordan grinned, and I opened the bag. I dumped two small pieces of something that looked like bark into my hand. I took one, and Jordan took the other. It only took a few minutes to take effect.

Colors blossomed between us. A shared body language sprung up, and I traced kisses down Jordan's body until I reached his hard length and slid it into my mouth. One moment I felt Jordan's hand in my hair, then he pulled it. But Jordan would never do that. When I looked up, I was between Greg's legs, and he looked directly at me.

I continued to watch, mesmerized. What the hell had Jordan given me? When Greg came, the connection shifted back to

Jordan, and it disoriented me for a moment. When the link reasserted itself between Jordan and me, Jordan's desire hit me full force, and I swam into it, seeking the safe harbor of the familiar.

Jordan spoke in a language I didn't recognize. I knew some Altus, a fae language Jordan had taught me, but this wasn't the same. I wasn't entirely sure he was even talking to me. His eyes were focused somewhere above me.

He pulled me up for a kiss and rolled me under him. I went willingly and allowed myself to drown in the sounds, colors, and feelings, if only to chase away the images from a few moments earlier. I felt light and disconnected until Jordan pressed himself into me. That's when my perception shifted again.

Greg was panting above me, holding me down, determined in a way I'd never seen him. I was stunned and disturbed at the same time. I couldn't look away, and the sight of Greg made me reflexively tighten around the solid length in my ass while my cock became painfully hard.

It all seemed like a fever dream. I knew I was with Jordan, but all I could see was Greg. I couldn't focus on either man, but seemed connected to both simultaneously. Greg rocked into me, determination on his face. His lips moved, but I had no idea what he said. When he shoved into me hard, I could tell he came, and that's when I let go, coming with a roar that vibrated in my bones.

Greg faded from my vision, but Jordan was still above me, thrusting into me as I felt another orgasm building. It washed over me so quickly; I gasped for breath as my own cries of pleasure stuck in my throat. Jordan came moments later, calling out in the strange language I'd heard earlier. We lay together, heedless of the oil-slick, cum-covered mess we'd become. The cacophony of sounds from my floor hadn't stopped. It continued to be punctuated with cries, grunts, and screams as various individuals came.

"How long?" I panted out. Whatever this magic was, it was potent. I wanted it out of my system before we did anything else.

"Not much longer," Jordan said.

Jordan gave me a gentle kiss. As we looked at each other, I had a distinct impression that Jordan's plan had not turned out the way he wanted. We lay together, touched each other gently, and smiled until the effects of the bark wore off.

"Jordan, what was that exactly?"

He pursed his lips. "It's supposed to connect you spiritually to the person you are with. Strengthen your orgasms, or some shit." He laughed. "The second part worked fairly well, I think."

"Yeah. I'd say that," I chuckled. Jordan kissed me again. I gave him a contented sigh in return and reached over to brush a few strands of hair out of his face.

He returned my sigh with a heavy one and laid a hand on the center of my chest. "I need to go," he said. Under all the lust and desire still floating between us, I barely caught the sadness and regret. I realized he was using his glamour, as his skin showed a pale pink, with no hint of the passion we'd experienced before or the tinge of sadness I smelled.

"You don't have to, Jordan." I reached up, tucked a lock of hair behind his ear, and used my thumb to trace it. I wanted to convey that I understood, that it wasn't his fault the magic hadn't worked like he wanted.

He cleared his throat and put his hand to my cheek, then kissed me again. When he pulled back, he sighed softly. "Work, sweetums, that's all. Let's get cleaned up so you can walk me out." It was almost the truth, and I didn't say otherwise. I think we were both a little confused by our experience.

We went to my bathroom. I started the massive shower, then invited anyone else who wanted to clean up. The rest of the troupe slowly joined Jordan and me. Showering took another thirty minutes and a few more orgasms we happily shared with the troupe.

GREEN-EYED DREAMS

GREGOR

Whether I was possessed or mentally broken, I wasn't sure which. The drive to wrap the man under me in everything I had didn't stop with the blow job I'd received only minutes before.

Keith quickly lost his boxers as I pinned him under me with his wrists captured in one hand above his head while my other hand worked at our erections. He whimpered as I pressed for more. I gave both our dicks a solid squeeze before I moved my cum-covered hand to the back of his neck to control his movements while I drove my tongue into his mouth, fiercely claiming it and tasting myself on his lips and tongue. With each grind of our hips, and drag along our dicks, I felt him lose control and give in to me.

Somewhere in the back of my head, two voices warred. One told me I was completely out of control, and the other told me I was claiming my mate. I'd never had sex like this. The magic running through my system must have knocked down some mental barrier. Keith had specific needs and desires, and I let him have what he wanted because I loved him. It never occurred to me I could or should ask for more than a blow job or the occasional jerkoff. I'd taken what he had offered, and I was happy with it, until now.

Keith's gasp made me press a grin into his lips as he panted and his cum mingled with mine. I pulled back but kept his wrists pinned, then took my hand from his neck to swipe at the mess covering our abdomens. I smeared it into his crack and pushed my middle finger into his tight hole. Keith grunted as I buried my finger inside him and resumed my possessive kisses. The exploration of his mouth consumed me while I made slow thrusts with my finger.

His grunts and moans vibrated along my skin, enticing me to see what other noises he could make as I added a second finger, opening him wider, massaging his prostate with each thrust. When his moans turned into a mantra, my unrelenting fingers stopped as the word "lube" finally reached me. I growled at the distraction, and let go of Keith's hands long enough to wrench open the bedside drawer to find precisely what I expected.

There was a complete kit of toys, condoms, and lube, all neatly arranged. The lube was even the closest to the bed in the drawer. I snatched the bottle, not bothering to close the drawer. The cap clicked open with a flick of my thumb, and I poured the cool liquid onto my fingers. I quickly worked them back in while I poured lube on my dick to slick it up. I was determined. Any new distractions be damned.

Once I worked Keith open with a third finger, his moans had shifted to a soft begging. "Greg, fuck me. Please. Please…"

The feral satisfaction I got from his cries of pleasure as I replaced my fingers with my cock and worked into him was like nothing I'd ever experienced before. At first, my thrusts were measured. Then I saw his wanton gaze and lost some restraint, snapping my hips, thrusting faster. As I drove into him as he grabbed the headboard to steady himself. I wanted him to scream, cry out, say my name in a fit of passion. I needed him in an all-consuming way I'd never felt before. When his tight heat contracted around me, I lost any sense of control. I thrust in and out of him with wild abandon, gripping his hips tight, slamming into him with a piercing need coiled deep in my groin.

"Greg!" he cried, as he lay under me, his hard dick flopping between us. He shot his load all over my chest as he came yet again. His sticky mess was more fuel for whatever flame would not be extinguished. Determined to hear my name on his lips again, I grasped his shoulders and pulled him up to sit on my lap. My cock slid deeper into him, his hole still clasping tightly from his orgasm. He groaned and whimpered as I thrust up into him, with my arms around his waist, my lips sucking hickies into his chest and neck. I wanted to merge with him, be one person, one soul. When I finally came, I unloaded enough liquid that it leaked out onto my lap and down my balls.

I buried my nose in his neck and held him as I shook with pleasure. After I caught my breath, my lips wandered from Keith's chest to his shoulders, tasting his sweat and delighting in his languid strength as he panted. With his body still connected to mine, I inexplicably responded, growing hard once again. As I thrust into him, Keith's hand snaked into my hair and pulled my head back. Our eyes met, but I didn't see his face; I saw another. He yelled, and I flinched.

"Stillness, Greg. Shit! Gregor, stillness!" Keith said. It was like he doused me with a bucket of ice water as the magic dissipated.

I sucked in a deep breath. "What was that. . . what happened?" I shivered from the effect and held onto Keith even as he tried to pull away.

"I used the dispel word to break the magic."

"Are you telling me you could have stopped it from the beginning?"

"Yes," Keith admitted.

"Why didn't you?" The betrayal I felt was nearly the same as the shame that coursed through me from how I had utterly used him.

"I mentioned there was a dispel word, remember? Plus, I've never seen you high on anything. You're always so controlled. I had no idea you were holding all of that back," Keith said as his hand carded through my hair and pushed it out of my face. His gaze locked with mine when he asked, "Where did you go?

It was like you were here, but you didn't see me. You seemed lost in your head."

"I was, I think. There was so much desire and need." I shook with the realization that it hadn't been for him.

"That was pretty apparent. You were so aggressive. Have you ever been that way with anyone else?"

I shook my head. Losing control scared me. I remembered everything I'd done. I remembered having Keith under me. Then I saw someone else, someone I shouldn't be with until Keith dispelled the magic. "I can't stop shaking." I shivered as if I'd been outside in winter weather without clothes.

"Magical side effects. If you're not used to it, coming down can be fairly harsh. Come on, babe, let's get you into the shower. We can go to the sauna after we clean up, okay?"

I nodded and followed Keith into the bathroom. I caught the time on the nightstand. Inexplicably, all of that had taken less than an hour.

"Do you think we used up the magic?"

"It's a onetime use thing. Once you call it off, it's done. You're okay unless you eat another chocolate."

"Fuck, I might be off chocolate for a while after that."

Keith laughed a little as he turned on the shower, then walked us under the spray of warm water.

As we cleaned up.

I saw flashes of the other person. Memories of his face as I thrust into him. It seemed real. I could only hope Xavior was occupied the rest of the night. I wasn't ready to see him, not after what the magic had unleashed in my mind.

DECAYING ORBITS

GREGOR

After we cleaned up and changed into swimsuits, we went downstairs, back to the main entry, then out the garden doors to the walkway on the right that took us on a trek to the pool and spa area. The outdoor pool and hot tub area were rather large, and next to it was a building with a sauna, changing rooms, and showers. Several dozen people had already exchanged their formal attire for swimsuits or bare skin. While the party had shrunk in size, the general bawdiness had grown tenfold.

Once we reached the sauna, we stripped down, hung up our things, and wrapped towels around our waists. I followed Keith to the back of the room and sat next to him. My insides perked up as we enjoyed the fresh steam that blew out of the vents, scented with something like citrus or lemongrass. The smell calmed me as Keith caressed my back, and the last bit of anxiety faded along with the post-magic tremors. That'll be the last time I put something in my mouth without reading the wrapper.

It didn't take long for others to drift into the sauna. They took benches across from us and closer to the door. Keith and I stayed in our little bubble of solitude until someone from one of the other groups called his name. He looked up as they waved at him.

"Who's that?"

"Someone Vanessa introduced me to earlier. Let me go find out what they want." He left a peck on my cheek as he left my side.

I closed my eyes, feeling the temperature change as his body heat disappeared. When he hadn't returned after a few minutes, I looked around and noticed Keith's group was in an animated discussion. I sighed and went to find out what was keeping him. When I gently put a hand on his shoulder and kissed his temple to gain his attention. He turned slightly and gave me a relaxed smile as he put his arm around my waist.

"We were talking about going for a swim. Wanna come?"

I have him a quick kiss and shook my head. "I think I'll head back to our room instead."

"Yeah? Okay, babe." He gave me a quick kiss as I slipped out of his embrace.

"See you later," I waved, then went to gather my things. I didn't bother dressing since it was warm outside. With a guest towel around my waist, I ventured back through the garden and enjoyed the soft breeze on my skin after the heat of the sauna.

Even though our room was on the second floor of the left wing, the fastest way was the stairs near the main foyer leading to the front entrance. When I reached the foyer, I saw the one person I was hoping to avoid.

It mesmerized me as Xavior, dressed in only a robe, kissed freaking Jordan Gohansberg, who looked like he'd been thoroughly fucked. My fascination with watching the private moment kept me rooted where I stood. All I had to do was turn down the hall to reach the stairs. Instead, I listened as their conversation echoed in the whisper chamber the foyer had become now that it was empty of partygoers.

"You could stay, Jordan," Xavior quietly pleaded with the fae.

"I know, Lo dragone. But work waits for no one, and I have a flight to Hong Kong in two hours, which gives me enough time to put myself back together. I'll snooze on the plane," said Jordan, his face pressed close to Xavior's.

They kissed again, and I must have made a noise because they parted and looked directly at me. Jordan gave me a subtle smile, and Xavior's emerald-green gaze locked with mine. The moment stretched for an eternity, and I wondered if the drug-induced images were more than my imagination. Xavior had more willpower than me, returning his gaze to Jordan as he opened the door for him. The fae glided out into the night with a quiet goodbye.

While my brain told me to escape to the stairs, my feet carried me further into the foyer. Xavior met me halfway. This meeting was oddly like our first one at headquarters. I was only wearing a towel, and I'd bet almost anything that he wasn't wearing anything under. . .

Nope, don't think about it, not after what happened earlier.

"Having a good time?" Xavior asked as he crossed his arms, his hands coming to rest on his elbows, framing his chest in a way that drew my eyes. I fought to bring my gaze back to his face.

"Um, yeah." I cleared my throat. "It's all been a bit over-whelming, but enjoyable. However, I have learned my lesson about eating anything in your house that comes in a box with directions."

Xavior's soft laugh filled the space and slid down my spine. It made me shiver in ways that echoed fantasies from earlier. "Oh? Which one did you try?"

I crossed my arms and stared as Xavior burst into a full laugh. "Oh, shit, Lyndon, I'm sorry. I really am. People are used to getting those at my parties. I'm sorry I didn't warn you."

"Keith was smart enough to read the box first," I said, adding my chuckle to his. "At least it turned out alright, but coming down was a little rough."

"That happens if you don't use magic a lot. You'll want to make sure you eat and drink some water before you sleep. That should stave off any magical hangovers, hopefully." He smiled, and my whole body responded as if he had said a magic word. Thankfully, I hadn't tented my towel, but the physical manifestation didn't matter when Xavior inhaled, exhaled, and then inhaled again. I had a pretty good idea of how I smelled. When he took a step forward, it all but confirmed it.

It wasn't on purpose, but I took a step back. I knew better than to do that in any situation with a dragon. If I hadn't felt so relaxed by the sex and the sauna, I would have planted my feet. Instead, my backpedaling didn't stop until I'd hit the corner of the wall between the foyer and the passage to the left wing. We were centimeters away from each other, with nowhere for me to go.

"Xavior," I said, my voice pleading, though whether it was to leave me be or kiss me until I passed out, I wasn't sure. We didn't touch, and the tension stretched between us. Someone clearing their throat turned my head, and I saw Keith as he approached us. Xavior took several steps back, and I exhaled.

"Are you still heading back to our room?" Keith asked as he came up to me.

"Yeah." I didn't try to explain. My guilt and shame felt like a living thing. Keith's response dripped with caustic nonchalance.

"Good. Can you take my robe and trunks back with you?" He handed them to me without waiting for a reply. Xavior went still, and I grasped the clothing as if it would shield me from what might happen next. Keith kissed my cheek, caressed it, then walked off, wearing only a towel.

Xavior glanced at Keith, then looked at me and shook his head. He didn't have to say anything. His previous warnings about Keith rang in my ears. "Night, Greg," Xavior said, walking away from me as well.

I stood frozen, holding a pile of clothes in front of my inexplicable hard-on as I watched both men walk away. Frustrated with how I'd handled myself, I returned to our room. I found Keith's room key as I put our clothes away.

The feeling of betrayal rose to meet my guilt and shame in a dance of pure emotional turmoil as I fell into bed. I didn't heed Xavior's warning about water and food before I closed my eyes, hoping I wouldn't dream of emerald pools and citrus smoke.

In the Library with a Conscience

Xavior

I felt agitated. With Jordan leaving the way he did and Keith blatantly leaving Greg there with his clothes, the best place for me was somewhere without guests. So I returned to my library.

With a book in hand, I tried to relax while I lost myself in the story. I'd been relatively successful for a few hours, with both occupations, until the library door opened and closed with a great deal of laughing.

"Can I help you?" I called out.

"Oh, shit. We didn't know anyone was in here," said a voice unfamiliar to me.

I stood and adjusted my robe. "It was my mistake in leaving the door unlocked. This is a private area. Guests are not permitted."

"Well, seeing how it's private, would you be interested in having a private party? It's just me and what's your name again, babe?"

"Keith," the familiar voice said with a chuckle. "Though somehow I don't think he'd be interested in us, would you, Xavior?"

"Wait, Xavior Brantley, the guy that owns the estate?" asked the slightly younger man, who was just as naked as Keith. I didn't know who he was, but if he found himself on my guest list, it probably was because someone had wanted to meet him, fuck him, or both.

"Yeah, Ashton. We should go," Keith said as he tried to guide the man back toward the door.

"But his parties literally made my career." He came toward me, his arousal evident and his judgment clouded. I could smell magic and more conventional drugs in his odor. His desire, which was previously focused on Keith, had switched to me. If Keith and I hadn't played this particular scenario out earlier, I'd find it comical that Keith lost someone he was interested in to me yet again.

"Mr. Xavior, I mean, Mr. Brantley, thank you so much for inviting me. A few years ago, I was on the wait staff for one of your parties and was scouted for holo movies. I landed my first role, and I've been working ever since. Thank you so much," Ashton said.

"Ashton, I'd be inclined to take your thanks a little more sincerely if you weren't standing in my library, naked, with someone else's partner."

Keith shot me an evil look, and I gave him a shrug.

"Is he serious?" Ashton asked Keith.

"Don't worry about it. Let's go, Ashton."

"I think maybe it's time for me to turn in," Ashton said. He gave Keith his own dour look, and I tried my hardest not to laugh. I gave a serious but congenial face when Ashton turned toward me. "Thank you again, Mr. Brantley. Have a good night."

Ashton walked past Keith and out of my library. I sat back down and gave Keith a pointed look while I waited for him to leave.

"You're such a fucking hypocrite, you know that?" Keith yelled.

I smiled at him and, in the calmest voice I could muster, said, "Am I?"

"You've fucked more than a dozen people tonight alone, so I heard." Keith took a step toward me. It was brave, whether he knew I was a dragon or not. But as much as it would satisfy something primal in me to scare the shit out of him, I wouldn't. If only because of the man we were both interested in. "There's a connection between you and Greg. I saw it in your auras. And don't think I didn't notice the color of his clothes. You'd probably be fucking him right now if I hadn't interrupted you earlier."

"Gregor keeps his commitments. While you, on the other hand, go out of your way to break them." I got up from my chair, which got Keith's attention. "He's one of the best men I've ever known. No matter how much you hurt him, he won't leave you."

"And you would be so much better? Please. He clearly has a type, or he wouldn't be so infatuated with you."

"Maybe he does, but I'm not the asshole taking advantage of it."

Keith responded with a scoff and left. I paced until I found another book on a low table and threw it across the room. It hit the wall with a satisfying thud, causing several loose pages to flutter to the ground after it.

As I tried to calm myself, I returned to my chair and reached for the book I had been reading. It held the clever bookmark Greg had given me.

My argument with Keith cut too close to the truth. I wasn't good for Greg either. While I hadn't pushed our attraction into something more, I continued to take advantage of our connection at work. I looked forward to being near him each day, and I wasn't ashamed to admit that it made me happy. I could tell that Greg had been struggling with our mutual attraction and tried to stick to a professional relationship. Tonight's episode in the foyer confirmed it.

To take my mind off things, I cracked open the book and put the bookmark on the side table. The story was about a wolf shifter trying to understand their position in a pack they hadn't grown up in.

Sometime later, I blinked my eyes as light streamed through the high windows around the library. I looked up to notice Edward standing next to my chair, still as a statue. He was the only individual I knew who could sneak up on me.

"Morning, sir."

"What time is it, Edward?" He was still dressed in his clothes from the night before. I couldn't imagine he'd actually slept yet. Not a centimeter of his immaculately groomed white hair or beard was out of place, and his tawny face held no hint that the previous night had taxed him in the least.

"It's half-past seven." He handed me a cup of tea, and I took a long drink.

"Can you tell me if Greg Lyndon has left yet?"

"He hasn't. Mr. Lyndon is in the accommodations you designated for him. His partner found other accommodations with a different guest," said Edward, in a careful voice.

While I was in the habit of throwing things at walls occasionally, I'd never turn on individuals who worked for me. Or be upset when they told me something I didn't like. I drank the rest of my tea and handed the empty cup and saucer back to Edward.

"Could you manage a tray for Mr. Lyndon? I'll meet you at his room in fifteen minutes if that's alright?"

"Of course."

"Thank you, Edward. And please make sure you take the next couple of days off after this. Everything went very well last night. Your expertise and organization were invaluable, as always."

"You're welcome, Mr. Brantley."

I stood and patted Edward's shoulder. He was a good man, though to be honest, I wasn't sure if he was a man. He'd looked the same for quite some time and might have been an immortal, but I'd never asked. It was none of my business.

Edward met me at Lyndon's door with a breakfast tray after I went to my room to change first. I scanned my personal key to open the suite door and took the tray from Edward. Greg was sprawled under the covers with an arm over his face.

"Keith, is that you? Do you have any idea if we packed any pain relievers?"

I froze. "Sorry, not Keith, but I have breakfast, caffeine, and fairly decent pain relievers for you," I said, as I took another few steps toward him.

He lifted his head slightly and looked at me from under one elbow, then flopped back on the bed. "Fuck."

Indeed.

CONSEQUENCES OF THE MORNING

GREGOR

I was trying to decide if the throbbing pain in my head caused the hallucination of Xavior or if he was actually here, standing in my bedroom, or his bedroom. Even trying to figure it out made my head hurt.

"Greg," Xavior spoke softly. "You should eat something. Did you eat before you went to sleep?"

I groaned. Fuck, no, I hadn't done that. I should have, but I'd fallen into bed, unwilling to think of anything after what happened in the main hall. Xavior came closer, and I pushed myself up. I had never been more thankful that I had a habit of sleeping under covers, or at minimum a sheet. The duvet was enough to hide the very physical reaction to how early it was, as well as Xavior's presence.

He put the tray across my lap, and I immediately grabbed the pills and the orange juice. I tossed the first into my mouth and swallowed them with a few mouthfuls of juice.

"So, do you normally deliver breakfast to your guests?" I asked as I grabbed a piece of bacon off the plate. It was perfect.

Crispy and greasy, it settled my stomach instantly. It figured that Xavior could afford the best replicated meats on the market.

He laughed. Fuck me, that laugh was going to make me come or kill me, at least until the pain relievers kicked in.

"Not usually. You're a special case. I can't go back to Captain Lang on Monday and explain that you're not at work because you took magic chocolates at my party. He'd have a dozen stern words and a reprimand ready for my file."

"Ah, so this is you saving your own ass. Good to know," I joked, as I took another bite of bacon.

I watched as his lips twitched. It wasn't like him to hold his opinion, which made me note what else was off. Keith was nowhere to be found. My throat thickened with emotions I didn't want to voice. I finished chewing and choked down the pieces in my mouth.

"Where is he, Xavior?"

"A few doors down with another guest."

I nodded. "Um, I'd like to get dressed now," I mumbled. My stomach churned. "Thank you for breakfast and the pain pills."

"No problem. If you need anything, tap a panel, and someone can bring it to you."

"Thanks," I said with as much sincerity as I could muster.

When Xavior closed the door behind him, I moved the tray off my lap and ran for the bathroom. Everything came up in an emotional torrent. I was mad at Keith, mad at Xavior for being right, and mad at myself for believing everything would be okay. I wiped at my mouth and eyes to dash away silent tears.

It wasn't our house; I told myself. It likely wasn't with a coven member, which was the other half of our agreement. But in my emotional turmoil, I held onto anything that made sense. I told myself those words over and over as I took a shower, then got dressed. Keith came in sometime later, though I wasn't sure how without his key, and went about his morning as if nothing had happened.

It wasn't in our house. The rules we had weren't broken. It wasn't in our home. Everything would be fine.

It was nearly noon on Sunday when we walked down the stairs and got into the luxury automated vehicle. There was no sense of excitement or desire between us this time.

"What's wrong with you, babe?" Keith asked as he relaxed into the seat.

"Hangover." The one-word reply was enough to silence him for the rest of the trip.

When we returned home, Keith napped the rest of the day, then left for his usual night shift. I ate the relaxation chocolate and slept for several hours. When I woke up from that one, I ate Keith's and slept until he fell into bed next to me around six o'clock Monday morning.

I moved by rote. Showered. Put clothes on, then drove to work. The whole time, a litany floated in my mind: *It wasn't in our house. Everything will be fine.*

I hoped it was true.

MONDAY BLUES

XAVIOR

Another year, another celebration, and another day at work. I wasn't sure how Greg was doing. I was worried for all sorts of reasons, but most of all, I was concerned about our friendship. When Greg finally showed up for work, it was apparent I was worried about the wrong things.

As Greg walked in, I noticed two things about him that were different. First, he wore his sunglasses inside the building and had yet to take them off. The second was the large coffee he brought. I wondered if he was still hungover from the stuff he'd taken at my birthday party. Given our line of work, it would be strange if he were that sensitive to magic.

Greg was quiet as he thumbed into his desk. I watched as he took another drink of his coffee and then took off his sunglasses. The dark circles under his eyes were noticeable.

He went through the case files I'd already organized for the day. I didn't stop him, giving him time to figure himself out. There were a couple of follow-ups from the night shift. Another cease-and-desist, or what we called a C&D, that needed to be delivered for the landlord that was still fighting his tenants about bringing the building up to code for magic, and a pattern of home break-ins that involved a magical bypass of the security features.

Greg moved the C&D to his phone with a hand wave. When he stood and put on his sunglasses, I got up to go with him.

"I've got this," he said as he picked up his coffee.

"Not in the condition you're in. You've barely got anything right now." I knew Greg could be stubborn, but I wasn't about to let him push me out of our working relationship without a fight.

"Brantley."

"Lyndon, I'm going with you. That's final." I snatched the keys off the desk, and when he noticed, he made a low growl of frustration. Any other time I might have teased him about it, but I had the better sense at the moment to rein in my flirtatious joking.

While we were having our silent standoff, Captain Lang walked up and cleared his throat. "Good morning, detectives. Is everything good here?"

"Fine," Greg said.

"Yes, sir," I replied.

"Good. There is a special unit being organized for a case that's come to our attention. I'm putting you both on it. Follow me, please," Lang said.

As we walked into the main conference room, it appeared the Federal Crimes Investigation Bureau had set up shop. You could always tell federal folks from locals because they dressed in business suits regardless of the climate. Case in point: we followed Lang to an individual dressed in a lovely light gray business suit. "Detectives, this is Special Agent Naomi Ives. Agent Ives, Detectives Gregor Lyndon, and Xavior Brantley."

There was a round of handshakes. We followed Agent Ives over to a holo with images of several art pieces, most thought stolen or lost to history. She pressed a button, and the photos enlarged and displayed details one by one.

Ives turned toward us and pointed at the wall behind her. "We have reason to believe that an underground art auction is happening somewhere in the area. Some of these pieces have been missing for years, and we think they might be at the auction." Her dark brown gaze met mine. I held it for a few moments, but had to look away. I'd rarely met anyone who looked like they could size you up with one look and know they were right. Ives had a gift, and I wasn't even sure it was magical.

"How can we help you, Agent Ives?" I asked. I had an idea where this was going, but wouldn't volunteer myself like that if I didn't have to, and she knew it.

"We need a local operation. Considering your connections, Brantley, and the impact the two of you have made so quickly, the captain and I considered you both as our first choices for this case," she said. I couldn't help but notice her flawless bronze skin, with a perfectly pink blush to it. I wasn't conceited enough to assume I'd given her that blush, but I liked to think I had.

"We'd like to gather faces of buyers, and even the auctioneers would be helpful, but unnecessary. The primary goal is to verify where these pieces are, verify if they are the real things, and quietly retrieve them at a later date." Ives pointed at the pictures, then looked directly at me. "Our first objective will be to obtain an invitation to the auction. Do you think you can manage that, Brantley?" I took a step toward the board to look at the images she had displayed. She glanced at me again, and I noticed the shine to her onyx hair and the dark makeup that accentuated her eyes. She blinked and looked away. I tried not to smirk as I answered.

"Sure, but that makes this a one-shot deal. If anyone offers me an invitation, find out I used it for surveillance; that's it. Not that many outside of a few individuals know I work as a public safety officer, but it's a risk. We might need to come up with a cover story as to why I'm there."

"Isn't being a dragon enough?" Ives asked.

"Maybe. It depends on who runs the auction. It might be the last thing to help me." I shrugged. Greg interrupted the banter.

"I take it I'm backup and running comms?" Greg asked.

Greg's sunglasses hung off his shirt. Even in his somewhat wrecked state, he had a calm seriousness about him that was alluringly handsome. I'm glad he didn't protest the assignment.

My stubbornness wouldn't let me give up on our working relationship, even if I knew I might have to resign myself to the reality that it wasn't repairable.

"Yes. My team will piggyback off your setup. We want to keep the presence on the ground minimal to maintain the idea that the local public service is the only one that has this information," Ives said.

Lang looked at Greg and me. "This has priority over your other cases. If anything is urgent, let the staff sergeant know and we'll reassign them to other detectives," Lang said. "I want progress reports as we move forward. Other than that, I'll leave them in your capable hands, Agent Ives."

"Thank you, Captain Lang." Ives nodded to the captain, then looked at us. I wasn't sure what the sly smile on her face was for, but I was willing to find out.

Greg, coffee in hand, found a seat at the operations desk. He thumbed into the desk, which instantly recognized him as part of the special unit. He pulled up the operation files and reviewed them. I sighed and did the same. The distance between us felt like a canyon, even though we sat next to each other.

I didn't like Greg's silence, but I would accept it for now. It made me wonder what Keith might have said to him. If I knew Greg at all, he was likely angry at both Keith and me. On the one hand, I knew I should let him stay mad at me if it made things easier with Keith. On the other, I couldn't bear it.

FRIDAY NIGHTS

GREGOR

Several weeks went by while we worked with Special Agent Ives, during which Xavior and I didn't talk to each other unless it dealt with casework. He was too busy schmoozing his connections. I was busy making sure our equipment was ready for whenever he obtained this rare and elusive invitation. They deferred the rest of our caseload to other detectives while we were on the special unit.

When we reached a second Friday with no new leads on the art auction, I decided our current working arrangement was for the best. After this case, I'd ask Captain Lang to be reassigned.

I needed to work on my relationship with Keith, and Xavior was worse than a distraction. Keith and I weren't talking very much, either. Our relationship was more tenuous than ever, and our six-year anniversary was next week. While I had enjoyed working with Xavior these last eight months, I couldn't help thinking that my life would be different without him. If what Vanessa said at his birthday party was anything to go by, so would Xavior's.

"Hey Lyndon," Ives said. "Brantley and I are going for a bite to eat. Want to join us?" Xavior was nearby, gathering his coat. Naomi bent over with one hand braced on my desk, which gave me a relatively unobstructed view of everything her blouse wasn't covering. Did she have any idea she was pointing those at the wrong person? Her forwardness reminded me of Vanessa, putting a smirk on my face. Xavior had a type, after all. "Something funny, Lyndon?" she asked.

"Um, no, ma'am. Thanks for the invite, but I need to head home. My partner and I are starting a painting project this weekend, and I need to stop off for dinner."

"Okay, maybe next time." She straightened up and shrugged.

"Sure. Have a good night."

"Catch you next week, Lyndon," Xavior said.

"Later." I gave him a half-assed wave and packed up for the night.

When I got home an hour later with Thai food, most of the furniture was covered and Keith had started painting. I gave him a kiss on the cheek, then went to the kitchen to drop off dinner.

"How was your day?" Keith asked as he worked on the section of wall. I came up behind him and looked at the color.

They built some houses with color tech that would let you change the pigment on a whim. A program would run an electric current through the layer of paint to cause molecular realignment to available color ranges. The alternative to the tech option was magical pigment spells. Keith had tried to learn, but it failed horribly. The color was never right, and half the spell materials were still stuck to the walls. That had taken a bit to clean, even with Keith's magic. After he gave up, we picked out a light gray and painted by hand. It was dark enough to make the room cozy, but bright enough to keep it feeling light and open.

"That looks great, babe." I put a hand on Keith's shoulder and rubbed it, avoiding his question about work. "You wanna take a break for dinner? I can change and help after."

"Yeah, that sounds good."

He put the roller in the paint tray, followed me back into the kitchen, and helped unpack dinner. "You didn't tell me how your day went. Everything okay at work?" he asked. Trust Keith to focus in on the one thing I'd rather not discuss.

I sighed. "We're working on this big case, and we haven't had a break in it yet." I dished out some noodles and then traded containers with Keith to add veggies and tofu. It was on the tip of my tongue to tell him about my decision to be reassigned after the case. Instead, I passed the spring rolls and left the emotional grenade alone for the carefree moment we were having.

"I'm sure you'll figure it out."

The smile on his face was genuine. It felt like I hadn't seen it in some time, and I wanted more. "I know we're working for our anniversary, but I thought maybe we could take a real vacation as soon as this case wraps up. Rent a house, go to the beach, just get out of here for a while. The last time we took a vacation together was before we bought the house. We should do something fun."

The smile grew into a grin, and he nodded. "Yeah, I think that would be great. Spend some time together and work on our tans." I took a breath and relaxed as we ate and talked about what home improvement project to tackle next.

We stopped painting around midnight and took a shower together. If there was a way forward for us, for our life, I wanted it.

If only I could ignore the emerald-green eyes filled with desire that haunted my dreams.

JURISDICTION

Xavior

Naomi and I were under no illusions about how dinner that first night would end. She knew I was a dragon, and while that was enticing enough for her, we couldn't help the volatile chemistry we had. The first night in her hotel room, we used a gag because she couldn't stop screaming every time I made her come. After that, I couldn't leave her alone.

The two of us fucking around was a questionable career move, at best. We knew it was temporary. It had to be. There wasn't a relationship here, only work and sex. We were okay with that. We both had frustrations we couldn't really talk about, which made us good at taking them out on each other.

Each quick fuck, each long working dinner that turned into a long fucking night, worked the day's tension out of us. After a week of going to her hotel, or having a quick interlude in her rental vehicle, I took her back to my place. If anything, it would be a chance to hear all the noises she could make without trying to be quiet.

The minute we were inside, our mouths connected, intent on starting with each other's lips and wandering from there.

We made it up the stairs in record time. Once we hit the second-floor landing, I wrapped my arms around Naomi's waist and carried her down the hall to my bedroom. As we kissed, she dropped her overnight bag to the floor, which was promptly followed by our clothing.

She smelled like everything I wanted, but something was missing. It was like having someone present your favorite meal, but it wasn't quite right. It didn't have all the ingredients you remembered. But it was still pretty good, so you ate it anyway.

I laid her back on my bed, then put her legs over my shoulders. When I picked her up, my mouth found her wet and needy. Her hips pressed into my face as her feet kicked at my back while I suspended her in my arms. I could pick up five times her weight and not blink, so this was nothing but instant gratification for both of us.

When she came, I laid her back down on the bed and teased my hands over her heated flesh. Each time I saw that blush of rose on her bronze skin, I knew the reason. My lips lit on her wonderfully sensitive breasts. With each lick and suck, she was moaning again before I snaked a hand into her hair and slid my condom-covered cock inside her. My hips moved of their own accord. Never one to be passive, she reached up and grabbed a handful of my hair and pulled my lips to hers, biting and sucking as I thrust into her.

"That's it. Let it out. All that pent-up need." She grunted as I pulled her head back and exposed her neck. I sucked and bit at her skin until she pulled me away by my hair, and I moaned my frustration. "Do you need me to fuck you tonight?" she purred. I nodded, not trusting my voice, barely in control. The sound of my hips meeting her ass echoed in my bedroom, and her exquisite pussy already had me on the edge.

"Thought so. Fuck me until I come again, and I'll return the favor." I did as she asked, and she was screaming within minutes. I gave her another just to hear her curse me out after she moaned my name. The moment I let up, I was on my back. I barely registered the change in position when her lips fell on mine. If I thought she would let me finish, I was wrong. She shoved herself off me, reached for my hand, and wrapped it around my dick.

"You keep that nice and hard until I'm ready for you."

Taking off the condom, I closed my eyes and fisted my hard-on. A familiar image surfaced of brown eyes with a playful grin. I squeezed myself to stop that particular influence from making me spill like it had so many other nights since my birthday. I don't know how long I stayed in that limbo. When I heard Naomi's voice, I nearly whimpered at the anticipation of relief.

"Good, X. You waited for me."

She pressed her strap-on into my inner thigh before I saw it. The obscenely orange phallus had lube on it, and I groaned with need from the size of it. We hadn't played with this toy before. Naomi leaned into me, trapping my hand and cock between us, letting the dildo slide along my dick and balls.

"You think you'll be able to hold out until I'm inside you?" Her low voice whispered in my ear as she slid the toy between my legs, warming it with our body heat. I nodded in response. In truth, I wasn't sure, but I absolutely wanted to try.

She slipped a slightly cold, lubed finger into me first. I almost came then, so overstimulated and on the verge. Pre-cum leaked all over my hand. It's not as if this was new for me, but something about Naomi made it different, more intense. She quickly worked in another finger. Before I understood the rapid litany of "please" coming from my mouth, she had already replaced her fingers with the head of the dildo. She was still standing next to the bed when she grabbed my legs and pushed them to my chest, then put me on my right side, with my dick still in my hand.

The position gave Naomi more leverage, and my toes were curling within moments as she took up a steady rhythm. My hole stretching for her. My gland was stimulated with every press and pull. I clung to the edge of my orgasm out of sheer will. When she leaned over me, pressed all the way in, and said, "Come." I honestly wasn't sure what had happened until she caressed my cheek and kissed the side of my face while ropes of cum were plastered all over my stomach.

Partners had usually wanted me to take the lead, and this was a singular moment in my life when a partner knew what I was and took control without hesitation. I hadn't even known I'd wanted it, and the realization made me lightheaded.

At Naomi's direction, I followed her to the bathroom to clean up. Afterward, wrapped in towels, we returned to my bed. She moved behind me, wrapped her arms around me, then kissed my ear. After the intense sex and a hot shower, my circling thoughts were quiet for once.

"Feeling more relaxed?" Her hand caressed my chest in a way that was calming.

"Light and heavy at the same time," I said in a sleepy voice. "I know we talked about you pegging me, but for whatever reason, I didn't take you seriously."

"It wasn't only being pegged. You liked that you weren't leading or controlling. Have you done that before?"

I shook my head a little. "Most of my partners want me to lead or initiate. I have to be careful with them. They rarely realize that the same doesn't apply to me. This was the first time someone took advantage of that."

She kissed my shoulder. "Hopefully, whoever you end up with will come to know that about you." She petted my hair for a moment and kissed my neck. "Sleep, X." The authority in her voice was enough to make me close my eyes and let me drift into a dreamless space without another word.

When I woke the next morning, she was already gone. I found her note on my bedside table. I recognized my expensive stationery, which she must have found somewhere in the house. It had a lipstick imprint. I grinned when I read it.

X,

Any time you want me to fuck your pussy, you let me know.
— N

"Fuck, that woman is something else." I flopped back on the bed and thought about what she had said the night before. An image of Greg taking me like that, holding me down, and thrusting into me came to mind. I shook it off. Everything I'd seen from him with Keith made it seem like it was the other way around, but at work, he was in control, confident, and capable.

That it was likely Greg's relationship with Keith that made him question all those things about himself had me gritting my teeth. I caught my mood shifting. I'd been floating peacefully on a fucked-out brain moments before. It figured that thinking about Greg would fuck it up.

Why the hell was I obsessed with him? It was clear that we would never happen. He and I were practically oil and water. It complicated our working relationship enough, not to mention his Saint George ability.

All I knew was, after this case was over, I needed to keep myself distracted. Start dating more. Besides Vanessa and Naomi, I hadn't been on a date with anyone in months. I hadn't called Jordan to see when he might be back in town. I needed to get myself together. If I didn't solve this obsession once and for all, I'd lose Greg as a work partner and a friend.

The thought of losing him, even as a friend, hurt. My chest ached and my skin itched, which frustrated me. Impermanence was a fact of life, and Greg's life was relatively short compared to mine. I knew this, so why couldn't I leave well enough alone?

A Lead

Gregor

Something was going on between Xavior and Naomi. I was sure of it. Over the last several weeks, while they were trying to be discreet about it, their furtive looks and subtle touches said otherwise. It was as if they shared an inside joke. I was happy and jealous at the same time. It made no sense whatsoever, but helped solidify my plans.

So when Xavior showed up one morning for a run, it was unexpected. We started on the usual route and exchanged little but pleasantries. When we were about a mile in, I commented on the current state of things.

"I'm surprised you're here this morning. I figured you would be with Ives."

Xavior smiled. "She took a transport last night back to head-quarters in DC. She should be back in town by the weekend."

"Do the two of you have plans?" I asked. Some sadistic part of me wanted to know. Technically, we were all colleagues, but only for this case. If I didn't want him prying into my life with Keith, I certainly shouldn't question him about his personal life. Things weren't tense between us anymore, but we weren't talking like we used to, which stung. I blamed myself for that more than Xavior.

"Not really," Xavior said as he easily kept up with me. "How about you? Still working on the house?" I noticed how he avoided asking about Keith. We were tiptoeing around each other, but I would take that over the silence.

"Yeah. The living room is a pleasant shade of light gray now. Brightened it up from the dark blue we had before." At least the house was safe territory. I was excited about it. I had ideas about what it meant for Keith and me, but I didn't voice those to Xavior. "We have a kitchen remodel coming up. We hired contractors for the plumbing, the electrical, and the cabinets, but we figured we'd do the paint and tile work ourselves."

"Considering how this case is dragging on, at least you have something you can look forward to when you get home."

I hadn't expected him to sound lonely. That was odd. Or maybe I was reading too much into it. "Maybe you could find a cat roommate."

Xavior laughed. "A cat? I wouldn't have any idea how to live with a cat. Though, come to think of it, most cats like me. Horses are always a little skittish. Dogs and wolves just pee on everything."

"Really? Why's that?" It made me wonder whether he had horses on his estate or not. Probably not if they were skittish around him. Come to think of it, I hadn't seen animals on his estate.

"Something about being an apex predator, probably. They tend to be that way around wolves, too, whether or not they are shifters."

"Interesting." While I usually curbed Xavior's trivia knowledge, it felt like a tiny sliver of how we had started, and I missed it.

Xavior regaled me with other interesting facts, and I prompted him with questions. It stayed that way for the rest of the run. The small glimmer of how we'd started as coworkers made me doubt my decision again. Like the renovations on the house, if Keith and I were going to take our relationship to the next step, I needed to make changes. I couldn't have doubts about that, so I shoved it away.

Once we were back at headquarters, we cleaned up and headed to our desks. On the way, Xavior got a call and stepped into an interview room to take it. I sat down, thumbed in for the day, and went to work arranging things from the night shift. When Xavior came back, he was excited.

Xavior tapped my shoulder playfully. "We have an invitation."

I turned to look up. "Shit, really? Will you be able to keep quiet about who you got it from?"

"I hope so, because I certainly don't want to piss this person off, and if they find out what I'm using it for, then I'm going to get an earful."

Xavior leaned on my desk, and I could smell his soap. I tried to keep my cool and whisper my question, but I was excited about too many things. "Is it a certain CEO we know?"

"No, it's a little closer to home than that." Xavior seemed worried, but continued. "The auction is next week. They've been moving pieces for the last few weeks for the show." He leaned a little closer, and I tried to check any errant thoughts about how much closer I wanted him to be.

"The problem is, if they use too much magic to ship things, then it's flagged by customs. It's normal for some magic to be present, depending on the spells used to preserve items. This means that the auction house has to be creative about how they smuggle their pieces. They hide some inside other things or use glamour to make it look like something else. I've even heard of magic that would physically morph items into other things and then reverse it back into their original form when it's in the right place."

"That information wasn't in the case file." The special unit had access to other related cases. None of those contained the information Xavior was divulging.

"Well, I wasn't always a public safety officer," he quipped.

I looked at him for a long moment. "Shit, Brantley. Sometimes I forget how old you are." A laugh tumbled out of my mouth before I could stop it.

He smiled and moved to his desk. I watched as he thumbed in. I felt buoyed by the good mood and risked a small collaboration.

"We should do a test run with the equipment and make sure it works," I said. I was looking forward to playing with the earwigs and the crystal imaging button. I was hoping Xavior felt the same.

"That's a good idea. I'd rather not figure out that our equipment is useless inside whatever security the auction set up for this. It could be a combination of things, and we'll need to test the earwigs to make sure they still work even under wards." Earwigs were bio-mechanical worms that crawled into your ear, out of sight. They were paired with a receiver. Supposedly, they created an unbreakable, unique comms signature. They had to be grown in labs and were highly regulated. Most local headquarters didn't have access to this kind of biotech, and ours were international military grade.

"Ives was confident everything would work even with wards, but if you can set up a few, we can test it."

"Let's clean up the night shift paperwork, and then after lunch, we can run some tests in the parking garage," Xavior suggested.

"That sounds like a plan. Should we order lunch in so we have more time to test things?"

Xavior nodded. "Yeah, let's do that. Pizza?"

"Yep. That works." I had to admit, it felt nice to get back to something that resembled our old work habits. We were a good team as long as we ignored everything else going on around us. My thoughts strayed to my reassignment request. After I deleted the last one from my desk, I kept the current one on my phone. Sure, I could work with someone else, but would I still be as effective at my job if I did? After all these months, my doubt was like a twisted tentacle creature living in my chest.

Xavior drew me out of my odd contemplation to let me know he'd divided up the night shift work, and the files were on my desk. I opened the first report. It was another complaint about a woman who had paper constructs attacking her neighbors as they passed on the sidewalk. I shook my head. I wondered why there were so many reports on one person. What could happen? A paper cut? No one had reported any injuries, only that the paper constructs were harassing them. I filed it with a request to have a mobile unit follow up.

The rest of the morning went quickly, and the equipment tests went exceptionally well after lunch. When we called it a day, both of us were in a good mood and happy to be moving forward with the case. It carried me through my evening. I spent it pulling tile off the kitchen walls while Keith was at work.

UNDERGROUND FANCIES

XAVIOR

"Brantley, any progress?" Greg's voice was calm, but I felt a small thrill every time I heard it.

It was an interesting way to start a Saturday evening. Once the auction started, you couldn't leave until it was over. Everyone was required to wear a personal magic-dampening device that could only be removed once you left the venue. Thankfully, that didn't interfere with the magic devices I had on.

Turns out, when you have money, you can send a representative to bid for you. Several of them had comms units similar to mine, which means they had friends in high places, or they had access to the earwig tech somehow. If anyone was using crystal imagers, I couldn't tell.

There were contingency plans for guests if someone crashed the auction. As far as we knew, no other agency knew about the auction other than our special unit and the FCIB.

"If this place wasn't illegal, it would be like walking into a Christie's or Sotheby's. Just in time to buy something pricey for the winter holidays." I said, amused. I stopped in front of each piece I saw to record what was there. So far, I'd seen a Salvador Dali work which was listed as missing for at least a decade. A Picasso, several antiquities, and even a Banksy. Though no one was sure if it was real or not. This auction was amazing in its variety and audacity.

Greg's voice held some amusement and a bit of sarcasm as he replied, "Of course you would know what one of those auctions would be like." I could picture his face as he spoke, and it made me smile.

I'd been picturing Greg a lot lately. My attempts to supplant the memory of him with memories of other people and places over the last few weeks had not worked. My mind kept spinning fantasies about what it would be like to be in a relationship with Gregor Lyndon.

Morning exercise with Greg gave me the chance to have a conversation with him, but his smell was almost too much. It was a test of my self-control not to corner him and bury my nose... somewhere. He wouldn't appreciate it in reality, but his smell always said otherwise. It was frustrating as fuck, as every interaction became more of a calculated risk.

Like sending me into the auction instead of sending a proxy from my staff. It was another calculated risk. I didn't want to risk someone I cared about. Especially if something went wrong. I hadn't been approached by anyone or their representatives so far. It was slightly disappointing that the evening was going so smoothly. I could have used a distraction from the voice in my ear.

Bouncing between frustration and distraction wasn't healthy, but I was managing. Sex with Naomi seemed to take the edge off my frustration when we could find the time. At least her scent matched her intentions. She could compartmentalize like no one I'd ever met. All business one minute, desire and lust the next. It made me wonder if she regularly worked with shifters. As the case kicked into high gear and the auction surveillance became the priority, we'd been too busy to see each other. Maybe after tonight, we could catch up before she went back to DC.

As I threaded my way in and around individuals packed into the small, makeshift auction house, I found an unexpected guest. While it was on the list of missing items, finding it here was a slight shock.

The painting was simply called "The Dictator." His real name wasn't said in some circles because some thought he was a demon or cursed. However, Joseph Florentine was a necromancer. He raised armies of the dead and compelled vampires to keep out various peacekeeping units from Eastern Europe. He started the war to protest the Magical Species Pact, or at least that was the excuse that was used. A lot of other horrific things happened under his rule. The stories were gruesome, and some of my family members who had been in the war refused to talk about what they had seen.

The Vampire Accords of 1878 resulted from his unprecedented ability along with his bloody-minded ways. It became illegal for necromancers to control vampires or raise the dead unless it was under certain conditions. There were minor violations from time to time, but nothing before or since that rivaled Florentine's.

I was in Aotearoa, what some call New Zealand, during the war. Several of my family members participated in the dragon corps that used their fire breath to slow down the undead armies, while others carried magical ordnance to drop into enemy territory.

The painting depicted Florentine with his undead hordes languishing in rows and columns behind him. Sometimes I wonder if I did the right thing staying out of the war. My parents thought so. Denis, my twin, had been part of the science corps, but well away from the front lines.

"Earth to Brantley, hello? Did the auction start?" Greg asked.

Even annoyed, Greg was endearing and frustrating. I don't know how many times he'd asked for a status report before I heard. My lack of focus was becoming problematic.

"Don't get your boxers in a bunch. It's started." I took a seat in the main hall as the things I had viewed were quickly shown and bid on. My bidding was to appear as if I was participating, picking things so others would outbid me.

"I'm only checking in. You keep spacing out on me. I was worried. You okay?" Greg cared. It was in his voice. I'm sure the rest of the team back at headquarters heard it too, but I didn't care.

I took a breath. Greg was right. I kept spacing. I was here to do a job, get an inventory, case the participants, and leave. "Thank you," I said to the staff person as I picked up my sixth champagne glass of the evening. I needed to get my head back in the present and stop daydreaming about my coworker.

"No problem. I'm here if you need me." Greg said.

Another person came by with a tray of hors d'oeuvres. It gave me a reason to reply to Greg. "I'm good, thanks."

"Copy that," Greg said.

We had a designated meeting point after the auction wrapped up. Five hours later I sat in the comms van with Greg; his smell in contained in such a tight space, soothed me and made me fidget. I distracted myself by packing up the devices and sealing them with evidence tags. I'd deal with them when I went back into the office on Monday. The last thing for the evening was a debrief with the FCIB.

"Good work, detectives. Any issues, Brantley?" Naomi asked. She dominated the view, but I could see her agents packing up behind her on the holo.

"None that I know of. I have the evidence sealed, and I'll pull images from the crystals in the scrying lab on Monday. I've given Lyndon a rundown of what I saw. About half the catalog of items you have were there, including 'The Dictator.'" That small tidbit of info was like a silence spell.

"Well, it figures he would show up where he was least expected. Good work, both of you," Naomi said. A text from Naomi came through just as we were wrapping up. She wanted to meet. The relief and excitement I felt made me fidget more.

"Thank you," Greg said. I nodded. Greg ended the call. He and I said goodnight to each other and split up. I couldn't get out of the van fast enough.

"Where are you going? Don't you want a ride home?" Greg asked.

"No, I'm going to fly. Too worked up right now."

He nodded. "See you Monday, then."

"See you Monday." I grabbed my backpack and left the van. I watched Greg drive off, then found a secluded spot to take off my clothes and shift. The flight home wasn't long, thankfully. I took a quick shower and threw on a robe, and waited for Naomi.

As soon as she was inside my house, her clothes came off and my mouth was on hers. I could feel my frustration and desire like a physical thing. It was a live wire that somehow kept missing its intended target, only briefly connecting in these frenzied moments.

Naomi wasn't gentle. She threw me against a wall at the top of the stairs. It knocked the air out of me, and I growled. She smiled. "That's it," she said. "Let me take that fight out of you." We knew this would be our last night together.

She dropped to her knees, and her mouth found my solid cock. I panted as she worked me over with her hand and mouth in a rough, fast motion. I didn't have time to think before I came down her throat. When she stood, our eyes met, and for a moment, her gaze reminded me of someone else before she kissed me, breaking the spell.

I switched our positions and lifted her, guiding her leg over my shoulder as I pressed my face into her soft flesh. My hands cradled her with every intention of devouring her pussy until she came. It didn't take long. She shivered and kicked while my tongue teased each wave out of her until she pushed my mouth from her heated flesh, then took her from the hallway to my bedroom.

When her back landed on the bed, we struggled for control. Frantically kissing and touching each other, in a test to see who would submit next. I kept pulling away until we slowed things down. She sat up as I got a condom from the bedside table and put it on.

She came to me, eager to take my cock, as I returned to the bed. She put herself on my lap and thrust down onto it, taking me easily. I supported her as she chased after another orgasm. As she panted, I spilled her onto her back and pressed into her with slow, methodical thrusts. I kissed her again, teased, and pulled back the moment she tried to take control or demanded more with her mouth. She tried to turn us so she could be on top, and I wouldn't let her.

She growled, and I replied with a rumble more akin to my dragon form than my bipedal one. "Oh, I see. You're trying to be fierce, hmm?" She moved her hips, and I tried to press her into the bed further. She raked her nails up my back; I grunted with the slight pain. The scratches would fade quickly, but I still felt them. When her hand snaked its way between us so she could rub herself, I sat up and brought her with me.

"Let me have your hands," I demanded. Naomi gave me a curious look as she offered them. I took them, placed them behind her back, and held them there with one hand while my other sought her hips and encouraged her to move. My orgasm was not that far off, and when I closed my eyes, Greg was there. My frustration bubbled up, and I tipped Naomi onto her back again and fucked her for all I was worth.

"You see something you want, X? Are you gonna fuck your way into it? Let it swallow you? Is that what you want? What's in your head? What do you see right now?" I didn't argue or respond. I kept going. "It's where all your frustration is coming from, isn't it?" I whined, her voice breaking the illusion in my mind's eye. "All that pent-up need and desire, and you can't get enough because you can't have it. Answer me," Naomi demanded.

"Yes!" I hissed. This wasn't fair to her. I knew that. Guilt almost made me stop.

"I didn't tell you to stop; you keep fucking me." I let out a strangled cry. All I could see now was Greg under me, me inside him. It's all I wanted. I pulled out, unable to articulate my pain, still hard as fuck.

"Talk to me, X. What do you need?" I showed her with my finger. I pressed it in, and she gasped a little.

"Let me have your ass." I was so far gone in my head that if she let me keep going, I'd take whatever she gave me. That, I realized, was what was special about Naomi. We understood what we needed. For me, it was distractions and a way to work through my frustrations. For her, it was power over someone that intentionally gave it to her.

"Take it." Her voice was full of need and anger. This wasn't really about her anymore, and I was beyond fighting for control. I could feel her heated gaze as I grabbed the lube and used it to work myself into her. She moaned as my cock sank into her ass, inch by inch. "Does that feel better? That tight heat wrapped around you?"

I moaned an affirmative, stripped bare of any sort of higher cognitive function. Once I bottomed out, I tried to gulp down some air and think about what I was doing. I felt her hand slap my side.

"Fuck me, asshole. Do it. Finish what you started. I want to feel you come so hard in me you don't know which way is up. Do you hear me?" She wrapped her legs around my waist, feet settling on my ass.

"Yes, ma'am." I went at her like I was in a steep dive and wasn't sure I'd pull up in time. I needed to breathe. Everything constricted. All the feelings and emotions I'd bottled up for months were surfacing, and I couldn't deal with them.

Naomi reached up and pulled my head down next to hers as I continued to pound away. She whispered in my ear. "Do you see them, the person you want, the one you need so bad you can't think?"

I nodded.

"Say it."

"Yes, yes, I see him." I kept going. I was so close, and her voice wasn't the one I wanted, but it was lulling me into a place that I wanted so badly I couldn't help but follow.

"That's it, baby, keep going. You're almost there; I can feel it. Tell me his name."

I moaned from everything that was wrapped up in the orgasm I was about to have and then let go of a sob at the truth being pulled out of me as if by magic. Still, I didn't stop.

"Xavior, say his name."

"Gregor," I whispered. The dam began to break. I whimpered.

"That's it, baby, a little more." She moaned and thrust herself back onto me. I sobbed into her shoulder. "Say his name and come for me, Xavior." And, fuck if I didn't do just that.

I collapsed on top of her and cried. It reminded me of the first time my mother burst into flames from her phoenix cycle. I was a child then, and I wailed as if I were the one on fire. But I didn't burst into flames; I imploded.

"Shhh, it's okay. You're okay. I have you." Naomi moved us to lie next to each other, then pulled me to her shoulder, wrapping her arms around me while I sorted through my mess of emotions. She kissed my forehead, petted my hair, and prompted me to take deep breaths between sobs. Eventually, I calmed down enough for her to help me clean up.

"Are you going to leave me?" I hated the desperation and need in my voice. The rawness and sheer vulnerability made me feel like someone had sliced me open and pulled my guts out. I was ready to beg her to stay.

She sighed softly, but there was a smile on her face. "No. I'll stay. My transport isn't until tonight." I nodded and felt relieved.

"But you're going to have to figure this out at some point, X. Other people can't be your substitute forever. They won't be as understanding as me." Her words were a comfort, yet they wounded me. She laughed softly as I whimpered. She had to understand it wasn't so simple. I told her everything.

"Wow." She kissed my forehead. "That's a tough spot."

"Yeah."

"Does he know how much you're in love with him already?"

I shook my head. "Of course not. I wasn't all that sure myself until you forced it out of me."

"Yeah, that was kind of a dick move. I'm sorry for that."

"Fair is fair. I was using you, and you knew it."

"I know. But at least I know who and why. Lyndon is a good man, X. If you can wait for him, it will be worth it."

"I know."

We slept for a few hours. When we woke, we ate, had a few more orgasms, cleaned up and went to grab her things from her hotel room before I took her to the transport station.

"Stay in touch, Xavior, okay?" I nodded. We walked to her transport and kissed one final time before she boarded.

Naomi waved at me from her transport. I waved and felt calmer than I'd been in months. I knew the moment I saw Greg again that calm would slowly disappear. The smart thing to do would be to walk away. But for the life of me, I couldn't bring myself to do it.

SWEET DREAMS

GREGOR

I could feel the rain pounding on my skin through my clothes. It didn't hurt, but it beat a kind of rhythm that kept pace with my racing heart. I wasn't exactly sure what I was running toward. The street was unfamiliar, the lighting poor, and the cold was seeping into my bones.

A roar stopped me in my tracks. It was a sound I'd never heard in my life, but I knew exactly what made it. From the recordings and images I'd seen in my childhood to the hundreds of hours of training they had forced on me, you couldn't mistake that roar for anything other than a dragon.

The dragon landed about twenty meters in front of me. Their wings flapped and slowed their descent. When they saw me, they roared again. The sound washed over me as fear and bile crawled up the back of my throat. The fear pheromones were a trigger that would make a dragons attack, but this one didn't.

The mythic beauty quieted and came closer. Each step was carefully exaggerated, as if they were afraid of spooking me. I walked closer, heedless of the danger their claws or teeth could do. This one was the size of an elephant. Smaller than most dragons I'd seen in pictures. Some could be as large as whales.

We had a calming effect on each other. The dragon settled and relaxed as I approached. My fear bled away to awe with each step. A low warning growl rippled through the air. I paused less than a meter from them as my fear returned. Had they changed their mind? Their gaze moved to the object in my hand.

I looked down at the long sword in my left hand. The weight of it was excruciating, which was odd. I'd practiced with one most of my life. It was the first time the weight of it seemed unbearable. I opened my hand, and the sword fell to the ground with a loud clatter.

Each step I took toward the dragon brought a clarity of purpose. I would dare to touch that which I was meant to kill. I wanted to with all my heart. The emerald eyes were patient and waiting. They knew they were dealing with a frightened beast of a man. And I was frightened. I shouldn't want this.

When I was young, they taught me I was one of the few who created balance, chosen to keep dragons from destroying humanity. Instead, that fear had turned into a need, and it drove me closer until my hand came into contact with their snout.

My whole being lit with joy at that momentary touch. Their scales were smooth under my fingers, and the sound they made was an ethereal white noise with layers of harmonics that conveyed a kind of peace and contentment. In the dim light, their primary color was green, but I caught flashes of other colors in their scales too complex to describe. It filled me with wonder and happiness that was only ever described in a fairytale.

In a flash of lightning, the dragon became a bipedal being. One I knew well, with eyes the color of emeralds. The rain changed from a torrential downpour to a spring mist. He smiled, and that smile was everything. I couldn't help but kiss him, taste his lips, and feel his body pressed to mine.

We were wet, but no longer standing in the street. We were in bed naked, his lips inviting me into deeper kisses and his tongue teasing me with each plunge into my mouth. His hardness was pressed against mine, and we thrust against each other as we panted and kissed, unable and unwilling to separate for even one moment.

The electric tension that built between us was palpable. I clung to my dragon, unwilling to let go, as my hands braced across his back and his buttocks. I whispered, "I love you." He whispered something I did not understand. I tensed and pressed myself up against his heated skin as I came. He growled his release into my neck as it splashed across our skin.

I swallowed and looked up into those emerald eyes and smiled. He returned my smile and kissed me again. In my soul, I felt complete.

"Gregie, are you awake? Greg?"

That wasn't Xavior's voice. As the dream slipped away, fear and panic returned. I barely kept from shoving Keith off me. Our sticky mess commingled on my body. I opened my eyes, and Keith looked down at me with a furrowed, steely gaze. My stomach churned with the reality of what had happened.

"Let me up, please." My calm voice sounded strange. Keith moved without me having to repeat myself. As he did, he grabbed part of the sheet to cover his nudity. It was uncharacteristic of him to be embarrassed about being naked.

"I came home and crawled into bed. You reached out for me, and I thought you were awake, Greg." Keith's voice sounded small and scared, as if he'd done something wrong. "You seemed like you were awake," he repeated. I pressed a hand to his cheek.

"Hey, hey, it's okay. I don't know what happened either." It was a lie, but Keith didn't call me on it. His eyes widened slightly and watered, but he didn't cry. He knew something was up, but we both seemed to decide the lie was easier to live with for now. I reached for his hand and led him to the bathroom to clean up.

I tucked him back into bed with a kiss as I got ready for work. There was paperwork left to do for the art auction. The transfer request on my phone became a talisman in my mind. I needed to use it if I was going to save my relationship, and maybe even my career.

IMAGES

XAVIOR

When I returned to headquarters on Monday, I went to the lab to develop the images for the special unit case. I didn't know if Greg was in yet, but I left a message detailing my whereabouts. I had mixed feelings about being near him. With each interaction, I felt desperate for more time with him, yet I was too raw after the weekend with Naomi to figure out what to do next with my feelings.

I checked out the crystal image button from the evidence manifest system in the lab and opened the storage container. After I verified it was still in a good state, I set up the scrying projector, popped the crystal in, and pressed the button to start the spell work. Some spelled devices take time to warm up, but this one didn't. It quickly displayed the images from the crystal.

"Shit." Thankfully, I was the only one in the lab.

Every third or fifth image was of Greg instead of art or a buyer at the auction. I'd picked up some faces and a picture of the person who bought the Florentine painting, but I'd lost half the art images to my memories of Greg. I kept going through the crystal structure, hoping I'd find more from the auction.

The strongest images by far were of Greg, all from previous memories. I fought down my frustration and saved what I could for the case, swiped copies of the images of Greg to my phone, deleted the digital versions, then wiped the crystal so we could reuse it.

It was early afternoon when I returned to my desk and checked to see if it had transferred the images from the lab. After I thumbed into my desk, I wrote a message to Naomi with the pictures attached. I was upset and ready to be done for the day. It was better to leave before I ran into Greg.

As I put on my jacket, I saw Greg come out of Captain Lang's office. When he saw me, Greg paused for a moment, then continued walking toward me. When he reached our desks, he gave me a half-hearted smile.

"Hi." Greg's greeting had a tinge of regret to it. I tried really hard to take shallow breaths. The last thing I needed was to smell some confused emotional mixture from him.

"Hey," I replied. "I finished those images from the case and sent them to Ives. If you've finished the paperwork, I think we're officially clear."

"I finished it this morning." He paused. "I asked Lang for two weeks off. Been a while since I took a vacation."

"Oh. That makes sense. When are you going on leave?" I didn't want to think about him leaving. An odd sensation crawled up my spine that told my brain not to let him go, which contradicted my logical need to avoid him.

"Soon as I'm out the door today," he said with a smile. Then his face changed to concern. I half wondered if it was because usually he would have mentioned something like that to me before he went to Lang. Instead, I'd be working for two weeks without him. It was one more thing to add to the list of how much had changed between us. "You alright?"

I must have made a face if he was concerned enough to ask. "Just tired. I'll see you when you get back." The last I saw of Greg was him standing next to his desk while I scooped up my phone and practically jogged to the front door, then down the street, toward my place.

Once I was home, I tossed the images of Greg I had inadvertently captured on my holo. After Naomi pushed me to see what was right in front of me, I tried to process it. To understand my need to be near him, and the fear that drove me away.

Was I in love with Greg? Probably. Did that explain my mental state? I wasn't so sure. So I did something I was sure I'd get shit for later. I poured myself a glass of wine, pushed the images aside with a hand gesture, then called my sister, Faith.

The video connected after a few rings, and her smiling face was the bright spot I needed. The significant huffing and groaning in the background came from a dragon in late-stage pregnancy.

"Hey sis, how are you feeling? How's Trevor?"

"Not bad, but we're stuck in his den until he can pass our egg. It shouldn't be much longer now," Faith said. Then eyes the same color as mine seemed to drill into me, even through the holo. "But I think I should ask you that question. You look like shit, baby bro. What's up?" She always knew when Denis and I weren't doing well. It was weird because Denis and I didn't share that kind of bond at all.

"Love your way with words." I deflected like usual. I didn't want to talk about what I felt, and I was afraid I already knew the answer.

"Yeah, yeah, spill it. What's going on?" She sat on the ground next to her groaning mate. She leaned against him, and I could see how they both relaxed at the contact. Jet-black scales smoothed as Faith ran her hand along Trevor's side and patted him reassuringly.

I gave Faith a rundown of how I met Greg and everything with Keith. Getting through what had happened between us and the most recent situation had me draining my wineglass, and then the bottle.

"Xavior." Faith's voice was somewhere between sad, happy, and sympathetic. I didn't like her tone in the least, and wouldn't like what she said next. "You're early."

"What does that mean?" I knew what she meant, though I didn't want to acknowledge it. Fuck, I was good at not accepting things, but I knew Faith wouldn't let it stay that way, which is probably why I called her to begin with.

"You're coming up on an aging cycle, brother. You've been avoiding them most of your life. I'm shocked you managed to for this long." I heard the rhythmic breathing that accentuated Faith's words, which indicated that Trevor had fallen asleep.

"You know I didn't. Not really. And that wasn't my fault." My family took two tactics about what they privately called The Incident: either tip-toed around it or shoved it in my face.

"I wasn't going to bring it up."

"And I appreciate you for that, but Bianca was, well, if she wasn't a vampire, it might have turned out differently. Or maybe the same. I gave up playing what-if about that a long time ago."

Mercifully, she didn't give me crap about it. Denis would always bring it up when my parents became concerned about my solitary status.

"But since then, you've avoided it. I'm surprised you're as functional as you are, little bro. We're not meant to be loners. Our biology literally forces us not to be, yet you've managed it longer than anyone I know."

"The trick is not to settle on any one person for too long. Instead, keep moving, never spend enough time with anyone, so your biology doesn't get the better of you."

"How's that working for you now?"

"Well, until this point, it worked fine."

"How much time do you spend with your Gregor?" I could hear her leading me to a conclusion she'd already made, and I wasn't ready for it.

"He's not my Gregor."

She chuckled at the way I said his name. Even I had to admit it sounded wistful. "How much time, Xavior?"

"A lot."

"More than the last person you were seeing?"

"Yes."

"And you both like each other." Her tone was flat as she stared at me from the holo. It practically asked if I was this obtuse on purpose.

"Faith. Are you going to get to a point sometime this century?"

She held up her hand and counted off each point as she made it. "You spend a lot of time with him, you think you might be in love with him, and I would bet you're marking him, too. Whether or not you're aware of it." She shrugged. "It all points to an early aging cycle, Xavior."

I sighed. I could remember a half dozen times or more where I'd touch Greg on the shoulder or arm without realizing it. It definitely might have been biology at work. I had thought nothing of it until Faith put it together.

"Tell me I'm wrong," Faith said in a soft, understanding voice.

"You're not. I know you're not. But none of that helps." I wiped at my face in the odd hope that maybe my reality would shift and my hormones would stop fucking with me.

"No, but at least you're aware of it." The dragon behind her continued to sleep, and I wondered if I could ever have a relationship like she had with Trevor. Well, not exactly like she and Trevor had. It had its own complications. "You always had a thing for complicated people."

I groaned at that. Faith wasn't wrong. Greg, being a Saint George Knight, was the least of my worries, let alone all the other non-magical problems we'd have to overcome before anything happened. "Greg doesn't want to be with me, and it's taking every bit of my self-control to give him space."

"You can only manage your biological needs by being near him."

"Well, that doesn't help me now. He's on vacation for two weeks."

"Xavior." Her voice was sharp. "You need to figure something out. You need to be near him. Or something that smells like him at least, or your mental faculties will deteriorate." She caressed her husband's side as he groaned in his sleep. "If you can manage that, maybe you'll come out of your cycle with no lasting effects."

I gave her a smile. No lasting effects could mean something as simple as not mating to not developing dementia, crippling disorientation, oh, and dying. It wasn't as simple as staying away or staying near Greg for a couple of weeks. Aging cycles were as short as a month if a dragon was already mated. Finding a potential mate but being unable to complete the mating process could make a cycle last for years.

"Thanks for the conversation, sis. Can you keep this between us for now?"

"I will. For now. Call me if you need help. Okay?"

"I will."

"Promise?"

"Promise."

I waved my hand to end the call and sighed. The images stared at me from the holo. The thought of Greg on vacation with Keith, doing what couples do on holidays, infuriated me. I had no right to be jealous of him and his life, and yet I was, and I hated it. Was it my biology, or was it me? If it was both, then the question became, how do I survive someone that doesn't want to be with me?

REST &
RELAXATION

GREGOR

Keith and I rented a lovely beach house in the Baja, took walks, and enjoyed simply being with each other. We didn't fight about anything, which was a surprise, but a gift, too. Our two weeks together were absolutely perfect. Well, it wasn't quite two weeks, but it was close enough that I felt like things were on the upswing.

It was the shield I needed from the weirdness going on between Xavior and me. Finally, Keith and I were on solid footing again, talking about what we would fix next in the house since the kitchen was done. I was hopeful for the first time in a while.

After our vacation, I felt lighter and ready to get back to work. I took a seat at my desk and thumbed in. I brought up the list of cases and noticed we had nothing on our assignment board. That couldn't be right. I looked across to Xavior's desk and saw he wasn't in yet. That was strange, too. I pulled my phone out of my pocket and went through my contacts until I found Xavior.

I started a voice call, but got the message prompt. It worried me until I heard Xavior from the front of the building saying hi to everyone as he came in. He had two coffees in one hand and a paper bag in the other. He wore a T-shirt, jeans, sneakers, sunglasses, and a suit jacket with rolled-up sleeves.

As he got closer, I recognized it was the suit jacket I had left on the back of my chair so that if I had to meet with lawyers, caseworkers, or judges, I could just throw it on.

I stood and leaned against my desk as he walked in. "Hey, Brantley."

"Lyndon! Hey! Welcome back, partner. Here's your coffee. And I grabbed the pastries you like from the spot around the corner." He handed me the pastry bag and coffee.

"Thanks." I was suspicious. He hadn't been all that happy before I went on vacation, but maybe a break was what we needed to reset everything. Perhaps I was the problem. That realization struck pretty hard, but it made sense.

"No problem. Glad to have you back," Xavior said in a cheerful tone as he sat and thumbed into his desk.

"Glad to be back." I sat back down and watched as he opened his communication folder.

"We don't have any assignments?" I was still curious about that.

"Nope, I've been picking up stuff from everyone else while you've been out. We'll probably catch a case now that you're back."

"Is. . ." I almost didn't want to ask. "Is that my jacket?"

"Oh." There was a moment where he looked embarrassed, then recovered quickly. "Yeah, I had to meet with a couple of social services folks this morning. It's kinda sweaty. I'll have it cleaned and get it back to you. Is that cool?"

"I guess. Not like I want to wear your sweat." I did not say it looked good on him, even though it did. If I didn't get it back, I wouldn't mind, if only so I could imagine him wearing it. I shook my head at my own thoughts, chastising myself, then giving up and at least letting myself admire him. That was safe enough, I hoped. It had to be.

We spent the day running down cases for other teams. Overall, it wasn't a bad day. The drive home was peaceful, and when I walked in the door, I was looking forward to cooking dinner with Keith.

When I went into the kitchen, I found our favorite instant meal waiting in the synth-bowl. It could make nearly anything, and often we had our favorites programmed for nights we'd be together if I wasn't getting takeout. There was a note propped next to it. I smiled as I recognized Keith's handwriting. If I'd known what was in the letter, I wouldn't have opened it.

Dear Gregor,

These last few years have been amazing and challenging in turns. I knew we were growing apart. We knew that. The house was our last-ditch effort to find our balance again. I know you had a lot of hopes.

I think you hoped the vacation would help set us right. For me, our vacation was a swan song, love. It was beautiful, and it reminded me of all the things I loved about us and all the things that I am not for you. I desperately wished I were those things. I wanted to be. You might not believe that, but it's true.

As for the house, we can figure things out in a few weeks. My half of the house payment is in the envelope. I'll keep up my half until we figure out what to do next.

Promise me you'll stop ignoring what's right in front of you, love. He needs you as much as you need him. It was my duty to let you go.

I loved you, Gregie. In some ways, I always will.
Keith

I sat on the kitchen floor and reread the letter until it was smeared with tears. There was a sharp pain in my chest, and then I took a deep breath. I felt lighter. All the fighting and heartache were over, and while I was sad, I was relieved. In some ways—in a lot of ways—Keith knew me better than I knew myself.

I wouldn't have stopped trying as long as he stayed. I stayed because I thought it was the braver thing to do. The right thing. The self-sacrificing thing. It's what I was taught to do. I laughed and wiped my face. The irony was not lost on me that the very thing I had learned to do in my adolescence caused Keith and me so much suffering.

Maybe this was a break instead of a breakup. I scrambled to check our bedroom. Keith's things, clothes, toiletries from the bathroom, and the few pictures of his family he kept on his nightstand were all gone. As his absence sank in, a painful flutter spread in my chest. I couldn't be here right now.

I grabbed my overnight bag and packed quickly, pausing long enough to shove the thoughtful dinner into the cooling unit on my way out the door. I didn't remember getting into my vehicle or driving down the highway toward my parent's house. My relationship with Keith was built on my desperate desire to stay together. I wanted what my mom and dad had. I wanted it bad enough to hold on to someone who said he loved me, even when everyone around me knew we didn't fit together.

Would things have been different between Keith and me if I'd told him about my past? I'd pretended to not have an ability for so long I believed it until Xavior showed up. What if he knew? If he had, would he have seen my attraction to Xavior for what it was: an infatuation?

When I thought about it like that, I cringed. It was bullshit. Was Keith right? I hated the confused feeling that sat in my chest.

Tears fell from my eyes as I barreled down the highway. Green and white rollers lit up behind me, and I winced. A public safety mobile unit signaled for me to pull over, and I complied.

"Shit." I pulled my registration and license chit from the dashboard storage, my badge from my belt, and opened my window. "Evening, officer," I said, as I took another swipe at my face.

"License and registration, please." A light floated over her, illuminating her face and uniform. I handed over the info chit and showed my badge.

"Detective Lyndon. I clocked you at thirty kilometers over the posted limit. Do you want to explain why you were driving so fast?" the officer asked.

I broke up with my boyfriend. My coworker might have feelings for me, and since he's a dragon, I could kill him with a spork because I'm cursed with a fucking ability I hate. She got the mundane answer instead. "I realized it when I saw your lights. I apologize. It's been a rough night."

"Give me a minute," she said as she scanned the documents. She waited for the readout to verify my information and handed everything back to me. "If you promise to slow down, I'll let you off with a warning." She smiled, and I tried to smile back.

"I appreciate that, Officer. . ."

"Fairbanks."

"Officer Fairbanks. Thank you. I'll slow down." She nodded and walked back to her vehicle. The floating light followed. After taking a moment to collect my thoughts, I called my parents to let them know I was on my way.

As I pulled up to the house, Dad and Mom came out onto the front porch. I got out of my car and walked up the steps. They both hugged me when I reached them.

"The spare bedroom is ready. You can stay as long as you need to," Dad said.

"Have you eaten anything, Greg?" Mom asked. I shook my head. "We have some leftovers. I'll go heat them up." She patted my back and left me with my father.

He gave me another hug. "Truth be told, I always thought you were too good for him," he said in my ear. I laughed and felt tears well up as I hugged him tighter. "Come on, let's go inside." He took my hand and led me into the house. My parents wrapped me in the love and comfort I always found when I came home.

That night I tried to sleep, but tossed and turned. I was watching Xavior fly over me. I heard him roar and swoop down toward the street. A man was running, but he wasn't going to make it. Xavior was going to eat him. I watched in horror as Xavior dove toward Keith. I heard Xavior's roar again and saw him open a mouth full of teeth, then his jaws snapped shut.

I woke up with a start, gasping for air, and glanced around. The floating, angry red numbers above the nightstand said 4:15 AM. I groaned and flopped back on the bed.

When I got to the office the next day, Xavior was sitting at his desk, picking his teeth with a fancy toothpick, and still wearing my jacket.

"Morning, Lyndon. Coffee?" he asked as he held out a cup.

I took the caffeine offering. "What's with the toothpick?"

"Oh, you know, villagers' clothes. Always getting stuck in my teeth," he said as he worked the toothpick with that damn tongue of his.

I stared at him for too long.

"I'm kidding! The seeds from an everything bagel are a pain. Lighten up, Lyndon."

"Right." I wasn't sure if I wanted to believe him or offer him a human-sized snack. I smiled internally at the idea. Okay, so maybe I wasn't wholly magnanimous about the breakup. I watched Xavior for a minute.

"What?" He gave me a curious look.

"Nothing." I waved away his concern. "Should we figure out what we are doing today?" I thumbed in. I still felt drained, but the day was looking up.

ROCK, PAPER, FIRE

GREGOR

A few weeks went by. Things seemed to settle a bit. I managed the commute to headquarters from my parent's place, but missed the time I'd usually take for my morning exercise. Xavior didn't ask me about it, and I didn't offer any information. I wanted to sort through my feelings before I told him anything. The least of which was the guilt that manifested any time I spoke with Keith.

I moved my things out of the house into storage, and Keith picked up the rest of his things. He moved in with a friend and transferred to another district for work. That kind of transfer takes time, which meant he'd planned this long before our vacation, maybe even before our anniversary. The house needed a few more repairs and paint, but I could manage that alone. Once I was done, we planned to sell the house.

Xavior's behavior at work became more erratic. He showed up late, left early, and sometimes I had to call to find out if he'd be at work at all. He'd taken several sick days and wouldn't talk about it. The captain hadn't asked me anything yet, but it was only a matter of time. We only talked about work now, and neither one of us volunteered personal information. Even though Keith and I were no longer together, I wondered if putting in a transfer would be the smart thing to do. To save both our careers.

One morning I called Xavior because he was nearly an hour late. He eventually answered, audio only. I had barely said his name before he hung up, and I called back.

"Hello?" Xavior answered. He sounded weird, maybe half asleep, but I couldn't be sure.

"Brantley?"

"Oh, Lyndon, hi. Terribly sorry I hung up on you. I'm in the middle of something at the moment." I heard muffled voices and what might have been a moan.

"In the middle of what, exactly? You were supposed to be at work an hour ago."

"Oh, shit, right. I'll be there in thirty." He hung up. I looked at my phone and shook my head.

I reviewed case files from the night shift and noticed a case I had referred to mobile units about animated paper attacks was in our queue, and it seemed to have escalated. The officers who stopped by indicated Ms. Sawyer had resolved the issue. Since nothing happened while they were there, the officers closed the reports. Recently, the reports of incidents had tripled.

When Xavior finally showed up, he had two coffees and an apologetic look on his face. "Hey, I'm sorry. I spaced on what day it was." He put a cup of coffee in front of me, then shrugged.

"Did you space the lipstick on your cheek, too?" I was amused, and it was even better when Xavior's face showed a moment of shock for a split second, then smug satisfaction as he wiped the bright red lipstick off.

"You're buying lunch." I kept my tone light, hoping the minor penalty I'd imposed for his tardiness might encourage him to talk later. I picked up my coffee, grabbed the vehicle fob, and handed him my phone so he could review the case file. "Read up on this while I drive. It should be interesting." He pivoted to follow as I headed to the garage.

By the time we'd reached the vehicle, he'd transferred the file to his phone and handed me mine. Through the drive to our destination, the only sound in the vehicle was voices on the main channel from central communications calling out where patrol vehicles were headed and for what reason.

When we pulled up to Georgia Sawyer's house, it seemed unassuming and quiet. We watched for a few moments until a cat strolled by on the sidewalk. As soon as they crossed some invisible border in front of the house, the quiet front yard erupted as paper animals leapt at the tabby. The cat shredded two of its paper foes before it dashed off.

"You're right, this is interesting." He said as he looked away from the chaotic yard and glanced at the report on his phone. "People have complained, but no one's been hurt. When the officers came by, it was quiet. I wonder if the constructs will recognize us as public safety officers," Xavior said.

"We'll see, I guess. If the constructs swarm, you distract them, and I'll try to reach the front door." Xavior nodded as we got out of the vehicle.

The second we crossed the threshold from the sidewalk to the walkway of the front door, they leapt out from everywhere—hundreds of them. It was a maelstrom of small, snarling paper beasts. When the sound of rushing flames and a burst of maniacal laughter reached me, I didn't know if I should be concerned for Xavior or not. All the constructs swarming toward him mesmerized me for a moment. It was as if they knew who the greater threat was.

"That's right, you didn't expect fire, did you? Want some more? Come on, I'm right here!" Xavior blew out a stream of fire, and the paper constructs retaliated as they tried to dive-bomb him. He grew claws and breathed at them again. "Lyndon, the door."

"Right." I sprinted to the front of the house and kept an eye on Xavior as I knocked. "Ms. Sawyer, we're detectives from Jefferson Public Safety. We'd like to talk. Can you call off your creations?" An older woman opened the door, still dressed in a housecoat and hair bonnet, ushered me inside and slammed it.

"I'm trapped! I think something happened to my magic. One minute I thought they were gone, the next, they were like rabid pixies hiding in my yard." Her dark brown eyes were wide with panic as she went from the front door to the living room window. I followed, and we watched as Xavior fought off the paper swarms.

"The report said you told officers you dispelled the constructs," I mentioned, glancing at her.

"I thought I had dispelled them! When the officers showed up last time, everything was fine. The clever things saved themselves by making more copies with my replicator and slipped into the attic. Can you help me? Please, I can't stop them! My magic isn't working," Ms. Sawyer begged.

"We'll let Detective Brantley finish while I call medical assistance to get someone here with an inhibitor for your magic until they can find out why it's gone haywire." I pulled out my phone and called it in.

Xavior was still hunting rogue paper beasts by the time the medics arrived. Once they gave Ms. Sawyer the inhibitor, the last few paper terrors lost power and floated to the ground, lifeless. She told us how grateful she was while we helped secure her house and gather a few things so she could stay for observation at the hospital.

Xavior and I stood on the sidewalk and watched as the EMS bus rolled away with their patient. "Did you have fun?" I couldn't help but smile.

"Oh, that was spectacular. It reminds me of this one time with Jordan and a troupe of acrobats. . ."

I cut him off by holding up a hand. "For the hundredth time, whatever you were going to mention, I'm good with not knowing the details."

"Such a prude, Lyndon." Xavior grinned. It seemed his fire-breathing adventure had put him in a better mood. I hoped it lasted for a little while, at least. Moody dragons were never a good thing.

I shook my head and walked back to the car. "You're still buying lunch."

"Fine. If that's the case, we're going to the deli I like, and you're going to sit and wait instead of being antsy." He gave me a pointed look. That particular deli was upscale as fuck and they treated Xavior like he owned the place. Now that I thought about it, he actually might own it.

"Your call, fire breath." I smirked as I tossed him the keys on our way back to our vehicle. Whatever was up with him, I figured I could wait him out. Besides, I wasn't ready to talk either.

At A Loss

Xavior

Our caseload had lightened. They finally settled the landlord dispute in favor of the tenants. The landlord promptly turned around and put the property up for sale, stating he lacked funds to do the sufficient upgrades. The new owner would need to invest in the requirements. If not, the city might become involved and condemn the building for not being up to code. If that happened, it would displace those who had fought hard to have their homes repaired.

Greg held out hope that the right thing would happen. I made a few calls and had the right investor pick up the property and schedule the needed repairs. It was a gray area where I was concerned, since I owned the investment company. Still, I couldn't sit by and watch an entire building of people suffer through another landlord dispute over requests that should never have been an issue.

Later that week, Greg took a half-day to see to some repairs at his house. I was curious but didn't ask, so I took the afternoon off to visit Jael at their art gallery downtown. When I showed up, they gave me one look and escorted me back to their office. Jael had a deep voice, a tight body, and wore anything and everything. Today, they were dressed as a Victorian nanny, complete with heels, hair, and a dress that covered every centimeter of skin below their neck, petticoats included. Though it turned out they had skipped the bloomers, but not the corset.

"Aren't you hot in all these layers?" I reached for them and worked on their dress.

"It's the layers that give the mystique, darling. You know that," Jael purred. When the outer layer came away, I bent them over their desk and spread their legs.

I tossed the layers of petticoats over their back, and they helpfully gathered them out of the way, exposing their ass for me. "This brings back so many memories."

"Oh darling, you and I both. Now, do me a favor and put that work of art in your pants to good use."

We made enough noise that Jael's assistant closed up and left for lunch. When we were done, I helped Jael back into their dress as they worked on resetting their hair to pre-nooner status.

"I missed you at my birthday party," I said, as I put myself back into my jeans.

"Oh, Xavior. I'm getting too old for one of your parties. It's best left to your younger friends."

"You're a deity. A work of art that age has only improved. An irresistible jewel." I kissed the back of their neck. I also knew they didn't get along with Jordan much, which might have been another reason they declined my invitation.

"Flattery?" Jael made an amused noise and picked up some paperwork that had fallen off their desk. "You're after something. Is it the new Fredrickson piece? You can't have it. Besides, I did that favor for you a while back, remember?" Jael tried to be playful. "Did you find anything you liked at that naughty auction?" The salacious look they gave me should have made me laugh, but it didn't. That auction had put what I was avoiding front and center, but of course, they had no idea.

"I saw a lot of things, but nothing I really wanted." What I wanted hadn't been at the auction. It was in a comms vehicle down the street.

Jael sat me in their office chair as they perched on their desk. "Okay, out with it."

"I'm at a loss." I really was, too. How was I supposed to keep working with Greg? His relationship was okay, and it seemed their vacation turned things around, but how long was that going to last? At the same time, how long was I going to survive if what Faith said was true? It all added up to something I was barely handling.

"That's new. Fifty years we've been friends, and not once have you ever seemed lost." Jael reached over to straighten my jacket. Greg's jacket. The one I said I would clean. He knew I was still wearing it, but didn't ask for it back.

"It's my coworker. He's in a situation that isn't sustainable, and I'm not sure how to help." Was I talking about Greg or myself?

"Why are you so worried about him?" Jael narrowed their eyes. "Did you do something?"

"Let's say, hypothetically, the thing I've been putting off for a long time caught up with me, and apparently, the one person I'm now biologically geared toward is in a committed relationship. Even though it has problems, if I do anything to mess that up for him, he won't take kindly to it."

Oh, and he's a Saint George Knight, with an ability that could kill me with no more effort than Jael might take to inspect their illustrated fingernails. But they didn't need to know that part.

Jael blinked at me in surprise and pointed one of their artfully done fingernails at me. "So you, the dragon who has practically everything and literally fucks everyone, can't have the one thing you actually need. That's ironic." They shrugged and rolled their eyes. I'm not sure they believed me.

"Thanks," I said, with a pointed look and all the sarcasm I could muster.

They leaned toward me and caressed my face. "Oh, sweetie, you know I'm here for you when you need me. Though if you manage to snag this piece of love toast and hang onto him, I'll be impressed. You're usually not the stick with'em kind. Of course, you'll need to bring him by so I can meet him. And you still have to purchase the Fredrickson from me." They smiled as one eyebrow raised slightly.

I would absolutely not bring Greg to see Jael. They would eat him for lunch. "Wait, I thought you didn't want me to have the new Fredrickson."

"It's called negotiating, Xavior. Over three hundred years old and you still need lessons," Jael playfully scoffed, and I laughed as I looked up at them.

As long as I could be near Greg, I could manage my biological instincts. When he'd first left on vacation, I threw myself into work. I stole his jacket and the clothes from his locker. When Greg returned, he'd stopped coming early in the morning to work out and hadn't noticed they were gone. Whether it was because he was avoiding me or spending more time with Keith, I couldn't tell.

At the very thought of Keith, I felt a simmering rage take hold. The sound of twisting metal and plastic caught my attention, and Jael gave me a sour look. "I'm billing you for that too," they said.

I looked at the left arm of their chair. It was completely bent and hung in disjointed pieces.

"Sorry, Jael." I frowned. Maybe I wasn't handling this as well as I thought.

"Dragon." Jael's voice had a warning tone that meant they weren't messing around. "You need to get your shit under control. It's one thing to come here and have a little playtime, but this isn't playing around for you, is it? You're avoiding things. That boy is all up in your head, and you're fighting it. You need to tell him."

"I can't, Jael. It'll make things. . . complicated."

"Complicated is your middle name. Figure it out, hmm?" They gave me a couple of pats on the cheek and proceeded to write me an invoice for the Fredrickson painting and the chair.

Jael was right. Maybe it was time to tell Greg and figure shit out. If I needed to find another job, transfer, or quit altogether, then I'd do it. I couldn't fuck up Greg's life over my own feelings, and certainly not for a biological instinct I had little control over.

SCALES & BULLETS

GREGOR

Xavior and I had been lucky to have a lot of cases with nothing too hazardous in the months we'd worked together. Our luck in that department ran out on our latest on-call shift. A domestic disturbance was never easy to de-escalate. This one had reports of shots fired, which immediately meant we had to handle it as a hostage situation.

As we arrived, I got out of the vehicle and went to grab protective gear from the storage space. Xavior stood there and watched me.

"Are you going to gear up?" I asked.

"Why?" he shrugged. "My scales act as armor. Nothing as simple as a bullet or knife could make a scratch."

His flippant response put me on edge. "First off, you have no idea what kind of bullets are involved. Second," I stepped closer, "I'm going to be in the room with you, and I don't know what range my ability has." I gave him a very pointed look and saw a flicker of fear in his eyes. It reassured me and scared me, too. If Xavior was this cavalier with his life, and it only took my ability to scare him, could we actually have a relationship?

I put on my vest, then checked the pouches for stop-goo and my deployable shield spell. While some thought it necessary for public safety officers to carry firearms, especially in situations like this, others decided long ago that it was better to look for alternative ways to protect people, even from themselves. Magic and technology didn't solve everything, but they went a long way toward providing a different solution.

Xavior finally put on his protective gear and followed me inside. Other officers were evacuating the building in case of stray bullets. We used the emergency access via our badges and went up to the tenth floor in the elevator.

Xavior danced from foot to foot and scrunched his shoulders several times. The body armor wasn't comfortable, but I didn't think it was that bad.

"You alright?"

"Yeah, just. . ."

"Just what?" I asked, striving for a calm I didn't feel.

"Smells. Tight spaces." He glanced at me, then faced forward again.

I didn't ask. Maybe I should have. I trusted Xavior to say something if it was important. There were a lot of factors going into this situation, and I was worried. I had kept us off de-escalation duty by claiming we were too new a team to put in the field. After our de-escalation field training, Lang insisted we go on rotation to provide more coverage, so here we were.

"Follow my lead. I'll distract while you extract, just like we practiced." I put my helmet on and secured the strap under my chin. As Xavior did the same, I glanced at him and tried to take a calming breath.

"Yeah. Yeah. Okay." He nodded. I hadn't seen him this focused in a while. I worked on taking even breaths and centered myself. It helped that I had my other training to fall back on from time to time, even though I hated what it represented.

When we arrived on the tenth floor of the apartment building, I noticed a couple of officers had set up a shield generator near the apartment where the disturbance was located. We walked up, and the officer maintaining the generator gave us a status report.

"There are two individuals present. One unarmed, sitting in a chair across from the individual holding a weapon. The individual with the weapon is impaired. We have the apartment bubbled, and the evacuation of the building is nearly complete."

The shield worked to manage possible projectiles that could be produced in a dangerous situation. It wouldn't protect people in the bubble, but it would protect everything outside of it in a three-hundred-sixty-degree radius. The evacuation was an extra precaution if the shield failed, but I couldn't remember a time when that had happened.

"Either of them have magic abilities?" I asked.

"Auras read as non-magical humans," the officer closest to us said.

"Do you have a pair of goggles?"

The officer handed me a pair of goggles that allowed me to see the situation through the wall. Use them too much or too long, and they'd give you migraines. Or at least that was the case for humans, including ones with magical abilities. Sometimes even the most helpful tech and magic had significant drawbacks.

I confirmed what the officers had said. I handed the goggles back to the shield team officer and took out my hand shield.

It was shaped like a gauntlet, with a trigger handle for my palm and polycarbonate braces on both sides of my forearm. While the shield was activated, those braces acted as stabilizers. I pressed the trigger, and the shield flared to life in an oval shape that covered me from chin to shins. They modeled it after an ancient Roman scutum shield in shape and size. I liked it because it was still maneuverable while providing adequate protection.

I glanced at Xavior. He gave me a nod to indicate he was ready.

"Open it."

The officer manning the generator opened a small portal through the bubble to let Xavior and me through. Once the shield closed again, I tested the door and found that it was locked. Kicking it open would definitely unsettle the situation inside. Xavior was unnaturally quiet.

"Brantley." I extracted a lock helper from another pouch and held it out for Xavior. It was a onetime use device for security reasons. "You unlock. I'll maintain the shield." He took the device and crouched into position.

The lock opened a moment later, and Xavior gently pushed the door open. I had the shield in place while Xavior backed up. We moved into the room together, like we had practiced.

The front door swung inward. It concealed Xavior while I stepped out from behind it with my shield. The person in the chair across from the person on the couch glanced in our direction quickly. She could see Xavior while the man on the couch couldn't yet. His weapon swung toward me as soon as I cleared the door.

"Evening. You realize you are breaking and entering, right?" the man said.

"We apologize, but we were called to this apartment with a report of individuals in distress." I tried to keep his attention on me while Xavior moved behind me, closer to the woman.

"My wife and I were having a conversation. She was being unreasonable and started yelling." He glanced at her, and I took a step forward. He was a little too calm. Either the man didn't care who he hurt, or he had already decided what he wanted to do. That wasn't good for everyone else in the room.

"Would it be possible to try this discussion again without the weapon? Your neighbors might appreciate it," I said.

"Fuck the neighbors. Noisy fuckers anyway," he said quietly. The weapon wavered, swung to his wife, then back to me. I took a few more steps forward to put myself between the gunman and the woman. Xavior took the opportunity to move closer to the chair. I tried not to feel nervous about that. Another few steps myself and I'd effectively block the weapon, but that was only if I could keep him talking.

"I understand that. These apartments are old and not up to sound codes. I'm surprised you're able to sleep at night." Empathy worked sometimes. I lived in a similar apartment when I was in college. You could always hear more than you wanted to, regardless of the soundproofing.

"Kids running, people snoring and farting. It's so fucking loud, I can't get any peace. Then she goes and wakes me up for some kind of dinner with her parents. I've been at work all day. I don't want to deal with her parents," he said.

"What do you do for work?" I asked, as Xavior made it to just behind the woman's chair. She was utterly still and hadn't made a sound. If I hadn't seen her chest move when we walked in, I might have thought she was dead already.

"Factory stuff. Tech. I work in a quiet room all day. It's cold, too. Testing circuits. Just me and the buzz of electricity with a tingle of magic. It's peaceful, in a way."

"It sounds like it." I was nearly in front of the woman's chair, then took another step forward. The coffee table was between my shield and the guy holding the gun. I couldn't get any closer without doing something drastic.

"But I have a solution," the man with the gun said as he waved it a little. "It will fix everything." He said it with a calmness that didn't match the shaking hand holding the weapon. His words sounded final.

"Can you tell me your name?"

"Parker."

"Parker." I tried to make eye contact, but his gaze kept shifting between Xavior and me. "Parker," I said again. "Can we talk about your solution? I'd like to talk about it."

"Nah. You'll find out soon enough." He swung the weapon toward his wife and pulled the trigger. I kicked over the coffee table to reach Parker and tried to block the first shot, but the whoosh of heat that zipped past me meant I missed. The shield absorbed the second shot as I threw a stop-goo pack. Parker froze, and so did the gun, just as he was about to pull the trigger for the third time.

I shut off my shield and checked Parker to make sure he was secure before I turned to check on Xavior and the woman, but I was the only one in the room. I went to the hallway and asked for help with Parker's detainment.

"Where's Brantley?"

One officer stopped on his way into the apartment. "He took the other individual downstairs."

Satisfied that Xavior and Parker's wife were okay, I went back into the apartment to read Parker his rights. Afterward, I left to find Xavior while the officers disarmed the weapon and removed Parker from the goo.

When I found them, they were chatting inside one of the EMS buses where Parker's wife was receiving treatment.

"Everyone okay?" I asked, as I took my shield off and stowed it.

"Yeah. A couple of bruises and scrapes, but alright," Xavior said. His smile was light, but I could see his concern. "Detective Lyndon, meet Emilia." She was wrapped in a blanket as she sipped something warm. She was calm, considering what had happened.

"Hello, Emilia." She gave a small wave, and I nodded. My gaze moved to Xavior, "We should probably report back to the captain." Xavior nodded and came with me as I got out of the bus.

He turned back toward Emilia. "I'll come back to check in with you. We'll figure out arrangements for tonight and next steps, okay?" Emilia nodded, and something caught my eye.

"Brantley, stop." I noticed a hole in his shirt on his upper left arm where the vest didn't cover him. "Your shirt."

"What?" Xavior reached for it and fished around for a minute. His fingers came back with a bullet. "Huh, guess I got hit. Didn't even feel it." He looked at me with a stupid grin on his face.

I stood there as my brain spun worst-case scenarios that hadn't happened. His scales had stopped bullets, and my ability hadn't made him vulnerable. But what if it had? It was all I could think of as Xavior pocketed the bullet.

Anger boiled under my skin. The risk was too much. How could he be so blithe about it?

Officers brought Parker out of the building. I hadn't realized I'd taken a step in that direction until Xavior caught my arm.

"Hey," Xavior said quietly. "I'm alright, Lyndon."

My focus on Parker didn't stop as he made eye contact with me. His zombie-like eyes barely held any recognition of his surroundings. Our eye contact broke when the officers put him into a mobile unit. Xavier led me away from the response teams once my focus shifted. We ended up in a quiet spot under a tree before I took a full breath and calmed down.

"I'm alright, Greg." The concern on his face registered. "I'm safe."

I nodded, but I was an emotional mess. I wanted to hold him, make promises I had no right to make, and tell him all the things I felt for him. My gaze met his as I tried to contain my shaking hands by stuffing them into my armpits. Xavior rubbed my arm, speaking quietly.

"He shot at you, too. I knew you had the guy secured, and I had to get Emilia out of there like we'd practiced. It took every ounce of willpower I had to leave. If I had smelled one drop of blood. . ." He squeezed my arm.

I tried to swallow past the lump in my throat. "You're right. We did it like we practiced. The outcome was good."

It was rare for guns to be involved in a violent altercation. It was usually magic, with more brutal consequences. I wasn't sure which I liked less.

My brain screamed to tell him exactly what I was feeling, but I bottled it up. If Xavior could act professionally in our first proper test in a highly volatile situation, I could too.

When I dropped my hands to my sides, his hand slid down my arm. He took my hand in his for a moment, squeezed it, then let go. "Let's report to Lang and make sure Emilia is settled. Then we can find some dinner and a beer. How does that sound?"

There was a slight tingle in my hand after he let go. It was similar to a sensation I'd had around magical items sometimes. A few moments later, the fog of anger lifted, and I played back Xavior's words in my head. "That sounds good."

Xavior tilted his head toward the direction of the command tent, and I fell into step beside him. Later, we found a quiet pub with greasy food and excellent beer, then stayed up most of the night. We talked about sports, the trouble we used to get into as kids, what it was like for me being a somewhat-only child.

When we finally left the pub, I went back to my house instead of my parents' to stay the night. The house was empty except for the bed and a few other things I had kept there while I finished the work it needed so Keith and I could sell it.

I crawled into bed without taking off my clothes. Emotions I'd held in check the entire night manifested as I cried myself to sleep. The next day, Lang left a message reminding me that I could take the day. I turned off my phone and went back to bed.

MISSED OPPORTUNITIES

XAVIOR

A week after our first de-escalation call, something was still off between Greg and me. I'd catch Greg looking at me sometimes, and afterward, I'd pick up an array of scents. The more time we spent together, the more pronounced the unique underlying smell was, and it hit me. It was proof that I had marked him.

My nose finally confirmed what my sister had suspected, and I couldn't ignore it any longer. Unfortunately, I wasn't brave enough to tell Greg what was happening to me, let alone explain to him why I was marking him with my pheromones. I was only slightly thankful that Keith was a witch and not a shifter. They had enough problems with their relationship without my biology involved. Though I had to admit, some dark part of me liked the idea of picking a fight over Greg. It scared the more rational part of my brain to death.

As we left for the day, I expected it to go like every other day, where we said our pleasantries and avoided each other until the next day. Today, something changed. "You wanna go to Jackie's for beers?" Greg asked.

Of course, he would ask me after I finally contacted Jordan and planned a date.

"Maybe next time." I tried to sound disappointed, but really I was fucking scared of anything Greg might want to say to upset our weird stand-off. "I have a date." He frowned. I couldn't sniff how he felt because he was downwind and far enough away. Greg's frown could mean he was disappointed, or something else I couldn't sense right now.

"Oh?" he said.

A motorcycle came into the garage and stopped. We both turned our heads in time to see Jordan flip up his visor and wave. I looked back at Greg to see him swallow, and then he looked at me.

"With Jordan?" I nodded. He shrugged in return. "Okay then. Next time. Have a good night, Brantley."

"You too!" I said, a little too enthusiastically, and tried not to think about what a good night Greg might have with Keith. I didn't want to be in a foul mood.

I walked over to Jordan. As he tossed me a helmet from the side of his bike, I put it on and got on the back. When he took off like they had cleared him for flight, I saw Greg following our trajectory from where he stood next to his vehicle. That image burned into my brain, and I almost told Jordan to stop and let me off. I didn't, though. I needed to be saved from myself and from wrecking Greg's life.

Jordan tapped the table to get my attention. "You're distracted tonight." We were at one of our favorite restaurants, enjoying a bottle of wine and two of the best entrees on the menu.

"Just work. Sorry. I'll try to be better company."

"Any new acquisitions you'd like to regale me about?"

"Acquisitions" was a code between us. It could mean anything from some trinket to bedding someone interesting to buying out a company. Jordan was a mirror in some ways. Physically, we were different, but the similarities we shared around relationships, friendships, and proclivities kept us in contact and a bit more. Fae and dragons have had a tenuous history. The fact that we continued to be friends delighted and surprised me at times. If he couldn't help me get my mind off Greg, nothing would.

"Nothing new recently." I gave him what I thought was my most charming smile. Luring Jordan to bed was never hard work, but one was always required to exert some effort. "A few of the fae from the troupe we spent time with on my birthday stopped by, but other than that, it's been quiet."

"That was a remarkable group." Jordan sighed. "I regretted leaving your party early. However, I would be up for a nightcap to make it up to you if you were so inclined."

Oh, I was definitely up for a nightcap.

Jordan's place was a modern two-story back in the San Francisco hills. Heated kisses started before we got from the garage to the house. We lost clothes along the way. When Jordan laid his pale pink-gray flesh out on a bed made for orgies, I joined him and curled myself around his lithe body.

He seemed pleasantly surprised when I took the lead. I watched as Jordan's eyes danced and brightened with lust, and his skin went from pale pink to a blushing rose with his long brown hair splayed out on the bed. When he came, the bluish-white fluid splattered up his chest and made a wonderfully debauched picture. That image alone was enough for me to join him. When I caught my breath a bit, I got out of bed and went to the ensuite to clean up. Jordan's voice followed me.

"What are you thinking about? You seem distracted."

"Distracted?" I asked playfully, as I tried to avoid giving any kind of meaningful answer to his question.

"Somewhat, yes. I know you well enough to see when your mind is somewhere else."

I walked back out to find him rolled on his side, watching me. He wore a devious smile, and I couldn't quite meet his eyes as I wiped him down with a warm washcloth. He made some rather delightful noises, and my dick perked back up at the prospect of round two.

"That's lovely, darling. I feel much better," Jordan said. While I was interested in more sexual gratification, Jordan wasn't. "Are you unable to answer me, or are you avoiding something?" I tried to use my hands and lips to encourage him away from his question, but he wouldn't leave it alone. "Xavior." Jordan touched my face, which brought my gaze to his. "While this is very pleasant, I want you to answer me."

I tried to kiss him again, but he pushed me away. I sighed. "We're having an enjoyable time. Let's not talk about my problems, Jordan. They'll spoil the mood." I laid on my back next to him, annoyed that yet another of my friends seemed to be too perceptive.

"I've known you for a long time. Something is different. Tell me," Jordan all but pleaded.

"I must be losing my appeal if you want to talk about my problems more than you want to fuck me."

"No. You're perfectly fuckable. The problem is that you want a distraction, not a lover. So, out with it. What's wrong?" I must have made a face because he gave me a lopsided grin and pulled me into his arms. I put my head on his chest and tried to find some measure of comfort. "Let me guess. Is it the tall lad I saw all forlorn and pining when I picked you up?"

"Shit, Jordan. I don't know." I did, but I didn't want to. It was complicated, and I didn't like complicated. So why was Gregor Lyndon so stuck in my brain? Fucking biology. And why was everyone else noticing it? Was I really that fucking obvious?

Jordan glanced at me. "By the beard of the great one, you're in love." The astonishment in Jordan's voice made me flinch.

I did what you should never do with the fae: I lied. "It's an infatuation."

I knew it wasn't. I knew it was more. Naomi had pulled that much out of me. I couldn't confront Greg and force him to choose between his relationship and me. As much as I wanted him, I couldn't do that to him, even if I suffered for it.

"Did you lie to me just now?" Jordan pushed me out of his arms. His skin quickly changed from a lovely blushing pink to a stormy dark blue-gray. He was pissed. "Xavior Brantley! You lied to me." He pointed at me as if I were a wayward child. "You're either trying to piss me off so we have angry sex or you're really fucked up about this guy."

"Is it working?" I was game for angry sex. I'd do anything rather than talk about what I was willfully ignoring. Besides, angry sex with Jordan was pretty fun.

"No, dragon-brain." I watched as he sat up. I followed, then he reached for my face. His warm hands bracketed my gaze. His eyes showed a mixture of intensity and determination. "Tell me the truth. Do you love him?" I nodded. "Does he know?" I shook my head.

Jordan shook his head. "What a lucky fucking asshole." He let go of my face and lay back down.

That sounded like. . . could Jordan Gohansberg be jealous? "Lucky? Jordan." I moved and lay down next to him again. I wrapped my arm around his waist. "Are you trying to tell me something?"

He shifted toward me. "Maybe." He sighed. "In all the time I've known you, after all the things we've done together, I'd give my eyeteeth to have you feel about me the way you feel about him."

"You've never said anything!" I felt Jordan tense in my arms. Talk about fucked-up timing. When I opened my mouth again, I whispered, "Why didn't you say something?" I caressed his side and tried to soothe the anger I'd ignited in him.

"We're having fun. I didn't want to ruin a good thing with one-sided emotions." He sighed, then leaned into me. "Besides, I'm patient. I take it he's human?" That last question had an oddly hopeful tone to it. That worried me if Jordan really was jealous, but I answered him anyway.

"Yeah."

"Oh, that's rough. I've been there. It was before I met you. Let me give you a word of caution, my friend. Those relationships are fierce and fleeting, as far as we are concerned. Enjoy it with everything you have. Have children and families. Don't look back and regret nothing."

This was going in a direction I had not expected. Jordan had a human lover? It only reinforced how alike we were in a lot of ways. "Who were they?" I needed to know. Was he happy? Did they have a good life? Did they have children? In response to my question, Jordan's smile was sad, but his scent had something in it I rarely ever smelled. I might describe it as reverence or love. It was hard to tell. Maybe it was both.

"She was the absolute very best of me in every way. Anitha was a witch. She had ample hips and massive breasts. She was short with beautiful long black hair that went to her waist, and she could bake unlike anyone I've ever met. Our children were plentiful, and making love to her was like watching a sunrise or seeing a full moon. I couldn't get enough of her. She would sometimes joke that I looked so frail she worried she'd break me."

The emotion in Jordan's voice hurt. I'd been his friend and lover for hundreds of years, and he'd never told me this story before.

"She never broke me, not physically. The day she died, I thought I would die with her. Our youngest was ten. She made me promise that I wouldn't leave him. Once he was settled, I wandered, and that's how I met you. I figured at the time it was a small blessing that fate put you in my path. I still consider it an absolute honor to be your friend, and more."

Jordan wiped at his face, and I sniffled, holding back tears. I wanted to comfort him, but didn't know how. He smelled of deep grief and longing. If that was what waited for me, if Greg and I became a reality somehow, I don't know that I'd want it. Though maybe dragons were lucky in that regard. We rarely outlived a true mating. Maybe it's the grief and longing that kills us. Then again, avoiding a true mating killed dragons, too.

Sorting my emotions from my dragon biology was nearly impossible. Somehow I'd fallen in love with Greg, and my biology was re-enforcing it. I was playing a dangerous game by ignoring it, as several had pointed out to me lately.

Plus, here was one of my dearest, oldest friends pouring his heart out. His long hair splayed across the bed in disarray, eyes brimming with tears. Skin dotted with pink blushes with a kaleidoscopic effect of blue, yellow, and black in various shades and swaths across his body.

Jordan hadn't used glamour to hide what he was feeling tonight. It was one of those rare times when what I smelled matched what was on his skin. His honesty was beautiful, and yet it made me feel horrible for not being able to return that level of trust and honesty to him. I had a great deal of affection for Jordan, plus adoration, attraction, and lust. But it wasn't love. Not the kind that he wanted from me. Not the kind he had with Anitha.

As if he sensed my thoughts or read my aura, Jordan attempted to lighten the mood. "You'll invite me to the wedding, won't you?"

The tease in his voice was there, but also the sorrow. I hit him with a pillow. "Ass," I said, amused but worried. "Greg's in a long-term relationship, monogamous, gay, and frankly, kind of a buzzkill. Biologically, I can't seem to get enough of him, but I'm pretty sure we'd be miserable together. It's fucking laughable to even entertain the notion."

"It's ill-advised to ignore your heart." Jordan placed his hand on my chest where the aforementioned organ was located. "If you care about him, you'll figure it out. And hopefully, so will he."

That sounded like it was all too real for him, and I suddenly felt guilty for not knowing how Jordan felt about me all this time. I pressed a kiss to his lips and held him tighter. "I. . ." Jordan stopped me from saying anything more by pressing a finger to my mouth.

"Don't apologize. Never apologize to me, for us, or him. Xavior, I'll miss you. I know as well as anyone that monogamy is a bitch, but worth it for the right person." We both laughed because he was right.

We spent the rest of the night together, enjoying each other's company. It was a goodbye of sorts, but I knew Jordan was right. Whatever happened, I needed to see this through. I hoped that somewhere along the winding road of time, maybe Jordan and I would have time to explore the things left between us. I hoped for his sake that he would also find someone that he could be with again who loved him as much as Anitha had.

A High Note

Gregor

After I watched Xavior drive off with Jordan, I went home, had dinner with my parents, and tried not to feel like a total loser. I resolved that when Xavior came into the office tomorrow, we'd have a conversation. If what I suspected was true, and he was avoiding me because of it, then I needed to make sure he could live his life. I didn't want to torture him. He wanted his life to be uncomplicated and carefree. We were opposites in many ways, and he deserved to be with someone like Jordan who understood him.

Based on all the training I had concerning dragons, Xavior was likely in an aging cycle. He was fixated on me because we worked closely together. And if I was right, he'd be better off dealing with his aging cycle without my interference. It was for the best, or so I tried to convince myself. Sleep eluded me while my head fought with my heart.

Xavior showed up at work the next day with two coffees and a smile on his face. I felt the weight of what I had to tell him like a millstone around my neck. When he handed me my coffee, I thanked him, and at the same time, we said, "We need to talk."

He nodded, and I tried to be casual about it. "Let's go for a walk."

Xavior followed, and we walked a block or two, drinking our coffees, before I spoke up. "I'm going to request a transfer."

"Really? Why?" I thought I heard a note of concern in his voice, which wasn't surprising, but he must have known this was coming.

"We're doing alright as a team, but we keep avoiding each other. It's not like when we first started. Things have shifted between us. I'd like us to go out on a high note. They offered me a promotion. It might be time to take the captain up on that. I could transfer to another department, and we can move on with our lives."

"No."

I stopped walking. "What?"

"You heard me. I said no." He had his arms crossed over his chest, coffee cup tucked under one shoulder, with frustration and worry etched into every inch of his body.

"You don't have a choice, and I think it would be easier on you, considering your situation."

"What the fuck do you mean by that?" Xavior asked, as his voice rose in volume.

"You've been erratic and somewhat emotional." I could hear the frustration in my voice. Why did he have to be so stubborn about this? "Does any of that sound familiar?"

"Maybe," he said, and looked away.

The flippant answer pissed me off. "Don't maybe me, asshole. You either are or are not in an aging cycle. Which is it?"

"You know about aging cycles?" He looked at me with wide eyes and seemed to be on the verge of a panic attack.

I nodded. "It was part of my training. Right now, you are at your most vulnerable, regardless of my ability." Especially if he was in the process of mating, which might be why he was with Jordan last night.

Xavior rocked on his feet as he stood next to me and looked at the ground. "Maybe I am, but that has nothing to do with us working together."

If you could catch a dragon in their cycle, then you had leverage. I hated to think that way, but you don't forget things when they were drilled into your brain throughout your childhood.

I took a sip of my coffee. "It's dangerous, Xavior." He didn't respond to that. "You're taking an unnecessary risk by working with me. It's for the best." When he stayed quiet, I decided I had said enough. I started to walk back toward headquarters. He didn't deny he was in an aging cycle. I wanted to ask if he and Jordan were mates now, but I couldn't bring myself to do it.

I was half a block away when Xavior yelled, "Best for whom?"

I turned around and shook my head. "Xavior, go home. I'll square things with the captain and tell him you took a couple of days off. When you come in on Monday, you can start over with a new partner and not worry about me."

He caught up with me and grabbed my arm. "Like fuck you'll square it with anyone."

He pulled me a few steps into an alleyway. I assumed he wanted more privacy since we were practically yelling at each other. Instead, Xavior pushed me up against the brick wall and kissed me. Xavior's lips. Fuck, it was all I wanted for months, and now that it was happening, I'd frozen up. I was afraid of the contact, yet I wanted it more than anything else in the world.

Xavior pulled back, and I read a hint of fear in his eyes. I knew I had to chase his worries away. I turned us and pressed him against the wall instead and kissed him with everything I had, determined to let him know he had done nothing wrong. He moaned, and I could feel it vibrate through my body.

When we finally stopped, we were holding each other between two recycling units, our coffees painting the pavement beneath us.

"Okay, new plan," I offered as I pressed my forehead to his. Xavior chuckled. I was still trying to think of one when Xavior spoke up.

"You're right, by the way. I am in an aging cycle. It caught me by surprise."

I brushed my fingers along his face, and he leaned into them. "Why is it early?"

"Because I've mostly avoided it. I thought if my biological instincts weren't triggered already, then it wouldn't happen."

I looked at him, kissed him again, and then took a few steps back. "Let's find someplace to talk that, preferably, isn't an alley.

And maybe more coffee. I'll call central comms and let them know we are taking a training day."

We had to figure this out before we went back to work. My first idea still wasn't a bad one. If we were involved, working together was even more dangerous, especially in our unique circumstances.

"There's a hotel around the corner, if that works," Xavior said.

I nodded and followed him.

CROSSED WIRES

XAVIOR

I often wondered if individuals didn't realize how much information they transmitted in their scent. Greg's smell and his body language betrayed his calm demeanor. From his hand in his pockets, to the way he glanced at me, to the intoxicating mixture of all the distinct scents that I wanted to bury my nose in so that it would block out anything else. My brain was on fire with the information and the possibility of unraveling the mystery around the man who had captured my heart.

Logically, I knew Greg had feelings for me that came across sometimes when he least expected. What happened in the alley, though, was reality meeting the underlying fact. We acknowledged, finally, that we had something between us, and I was giddy with it. Like I'd taken the best drug in the world, and nothing else existed.

I had so many questions and so many things I wanted to do. Talking seemed like a good, logical idea. But biologically speaking, I needed more. My brain was on fire with the instinct to find my mate and complete the pheromone connection.

We entered the hotel lobby, and I quickly rented a room as Greg acquired more coffee. His smell hadn't changed, but his demeanor was off, like all he needed was coffee and somehow it would magically help settle what we started in the alley.

This was important for us. Greg looked surprised when we went to the penthouse suite. I wanted to make this as meaningful a moment for him as it was for me. We deserved this.

Once we were inside the room, I took his coffee and set it on the entryway table. I pulled his badge from his belt, took mine from around my neck, then tossed them on the couch. I kissed him as I undid his tie. He kissed me back, but I underestimated how much Greg wanted to talk.

He pulled away for a moment. "Xavior. Aren't you afraid?"

"Afraid of you? No." I emphasized my words with another kiss as my fingers worked on divesting Greg of clothing.

Greg put his hands on mine and gently pulled them away. His silent protests were not lost on me, but his smell was too intoxicating. If it were up to me, I'd let my biological drive take control, to the elements with the consequences.

"Xavior. I'm a Saint George Knight. You're a dragon. This makes zero sense," Greg pleaded, as he kissed me again.

"Why?" I absently said as our kisses grew urgent. I took off his tie and unbuttoned his shirt. My heart thudded as my hands touched his skin. Something like tumblers in a lock fell into place in my brain and matched the beat of Greg's heart.

I pressed a kiss to his neck. Greg responded with a soft moan. I already had a cockstand, and Greg's hard-on brushed against my abdomen through his slacks. He tried to talk again, but I pressed another kiss into his flushed skin. When I reached for his belt, he grabbed my hands and pushed them away. The smell of his frustration and annoyance hit me like a punch to the face.

"Damn it! Because of my ability. Not to mention, we work together, you're in an aging cycle, and I don't do casual relationships." His voice became more intense with each point he made. It came at me like boxing combinations to my guts that knocked the wind out of me.

We were both breathing hard as he put his hands on my chest and gently pushed me away, further into the bedroom. He looked like something I wanted to eat, framed in the bedroom doorway with his open shirt and the strip of flesh I'd touched moments before laid bare, taunting me.

Something finally penetrated my pheromone-soaked brain: the one reason Greg didn't list. "Wait. You didn't mention Keith."

"Keith and I aren't together anymore."

"Then what's the problem?" Everything else was simply things to work out, or so I thought. Greg didn't seem to see it that way as he crossed his arms over his chest and stared me down.

"You're not monogamous. So it doesn't matter how attracted we are to each other. I can't be in a relationship where your needs are met, and mine take a backseat, not again," Greg said. "And what about Jordan?"

"Jordan and I are friends, that's all. He's not the individual I have a biological connection with." Greg's eyes went wide with that information. Fuck, this was complicated. I really wanted to find Keith and punch him for causing so much damage to Greg's confidence that he had so many doubts about himself and us, and what we could be to each other. I couldn't let his concerns stop us from being together, not if I could address them. But I couldn't do that with him half-dressed and this close to me.

I took a moment to breathe so I could get control of myself. "Greg, don't take this the wrong way, but I need you to leave."

"What?" He stood up straight, and I caught a whiff of fear in his scent. It threatened to derail my decision.

"I get it. You want to have a rational conversation, and I want to give you one, but I can't talk if you're close enough for me to smell. The blood I need to think is ending up in the wrong place."

"Okay." Greg backed away from the bedroom and gave me a perplexed look as I closed the door. "How far do I need to go?"

"The lobby?" I took a wild guess. It had to be far enough away that I couldn't get my hands on him.

"For fuck's sake," he grumbled. "Okay."

I wrapped my arms around myself to keep from chasing him. Greg was right; the idea of us was laughable on paper. Thinking about it for too long made me want to laugh and cry. Only after I heard the main door close and the elevator doors open did I fish out my cock and jack off. A raging hard-on would not help us have the conversation Greg clearly needed. My relief was short-lived as I cleaned myself up and waited for Greg to call.

ALIGNMENT

GREGOR

I put myself back together on the ride down to the lobby and called Xavior the minute the doors to the elevator opened. Then I remembered I had left my coffee, wallet, and badge upstairs. So far as plans go, this one was falling apart spectacularly on both sides. I'd only grabbed my phone out of sheer determination to have a conversation.

He was right. I wanted the conversation badly. But it took everything I had not to have him right there in the doorway, and he knew it too. So now he was caged in his rented penthouse suite while I was stuck in the lobby on my phone. Though considering what he said about his biological connection to me, I'm somewhat glad we stopped. My libido, however, did not agree.

Xavior answered, finally. "Is this better?" I asked. I found an out-of-the-way spot to sit and tried not to sound annoyed. It was audio only, thankfully. I'm not sure I could look at him without wanting to run back upstairs and tackle him to the bed.

"No, not really, but it's what you wanted," Xavior replied.

"Not exactly, but if this is how we have a conversation instead of, well, not a conversation, then I'll deal with it."

"Good. So, you broke up with Keith?" He sounded more relaxed now, maybe a bit peeved, but certainly more in control of himself than he was a few minutes ago.

"Yes." I wasn't ready to tell him the truth. For whatever reason, it embarrassed me.

"Why didn't you tell me?"

"It hasn't been all that long, and I wasn't ready to. I needed time to think." I wished I had my coffee. The silence that followed my admission seemed to stretch on until finally Xavior spoke. It was so quiet, I almost didn't hear him.

"I'm used to being in control. My fate has been my own for a long time. Meeting you was. . . unexpected."

I didn't like the hurt in his voice. I didn't like that I had inadvertently hurt him or led him on. That's not who I am. Or at least, I didn't think that was me. Still, his honesty was good to hear.

Xavior sighed and continued. "I've learned to trust you as a partner and a friend. Along the way, that grew into something more. My biological instincts have forced me to reckon with things I think we've both ignored for a while. Even with dragon biology mixed up in this, I care about you, Greg. That won't change, whatever you decide."

I cleared my throat and tried my best to be honest, too, even though it was difficult. "I know I've literally sent you mixed signals. You're headstrong and caring. Funny at times. You're attractive as hell, and there are moments I wish things were different. I. . . I'm not capable of being in an open relationship. Even if it's one by willful ignorance." I took a breath, then continued.

"You flirt with everybody, schedule sex like it's a dinner reservation, and your parties are nothing short of drug-fueled orgies. I'm lawful good, and you're chaotic neutral. The whole idea of us doesn't make any sense," I said, then stared up at the ceiling, imagining him pacing the bedroom.

"Did you just use D&D alignments to negate the possibility of us being in a relationship?" There was a hint of amusement in his voice.

"Maybe." I heard him laugh, and that sound reverberated in my chest and dropped lower, making me fidget in the chair I was occupying.

"Listen, your very adorable nerdiness aside, I'm willing to wait."

Had I imagined what he'd said? "Seriously?"

"Gregor, I'm three-hundred-seventy-four years old. You've been the only person in that entire time that I've been drawn to instinctively, and not only because I'm attracted to you. Because let's face it, I'm attracted to nearly everyone."

I tried to muffle my groan.

"I heard that. I'm trying to be honest here."

"I appreciate that."

"Okay. Then what you need is a show of faith, trust, or maybe both."

"Xavior. . ." He cut me off before I could tell him that I knew he trusted me. If he hadn't, he wouldn't have taken me on as his partner, not with my ability.

"My point is, we'll keep working together, and I'll wait."

We made a good team, but our attraction to each other definitely affected our working relationship. "What about mixed signals?"

"I'll deal with it."

"You sure?"

"No, but I'm chaotic neutral, remember? I'm up for the challenge." The words were playful, but his tone was serious.

"Okay, so how do we do this? How do we keep working together, given the situation?" I tapped my foot on the ground, anxious for an answer. I knew I was asking a lot of him. Things he'd have to change. After Keith, I wasn't interested in compromising myself any further.

"Well, first off, I'm going to clear my calendar. No more extracurriculars without you involved."

"Are you going to survive that?" I had my doubts. If I knew him at all, his extracurriculars were how he coped with things and distracted himself from his feelings. For me, it was ignoring Keith's behavior and lying to myself about my feelings for Xavior. It wasn't the best situation to start a relationship.

"If I can't survive it, then there isn't a point to this, and you'd be right."

The sincerity in his voice threatened to break me. I wanted him to know that I cared about him too, but I couldn't let myself make the same mistake again. I was lured in by a moment of sincerity and kindness before. My gut told me it wasn't just a moment with Xavior. I pulled the phone away from my head. "Fuck, please, please be everything I think you are trying to be, please," I whispered, begging the universe in general.

When I put the phone back to my ear, I heard Xavior ask softly, "Greg, are you okay?"

"I don't want to be right. I want you to prove me wrong." He was silent again, and I was worried I'd said too much. "Xavior?"

He cleared his throat. "Still here. Um, can you come back up to the room?"

"Would that help?"

"At this point, yes, it might," he said with a soft sigh.

"Okay." I hung up and stared at the phone in my hand for a minute.

Is this what I wanted? Was I willing to risk my heart again so soon? There was so much I kept from Xavior already. I've dreamed about him since we met. If he had touched me that night at his birthday party, I would have done anything he wanted. When we drifted apart, I feared I had hurt him worse than I ever could have with my ability.

Our charged connection was so much more than I'd ever had with anyone else, and I should have told him. I desperately wanted this idea of us with all my heart. I could only hope that it was worth all the confusion and hurt we'd put ourselves through to get to this point.

THREE POINTS

XAVIOR

I was nervous, but I needed to reassure myself that this was what I wanted as much as he did. I needed patience, that's all, and about twelve feet of space.

There was a click, and the door opened. I was in the living room with clothes on. Greg picked up his wallet, badge, and coffee, and sat on a couch far enough from me to keep out of arm's reach. "I had to stop at the desk and get another key." He tossed the keycard on the coffee table.

I nodded. "Okay, so. Let's break this down like we would any problem. One, I'm apparently in an aging cycle. Two, we still want to work together."

Greg shrugged. "Three," he said, "we might want to date."

"Regardless of everything involved, the point is, I like you, Greg."

Greg leaned toward me. I thought he would affirm what he felt; instead, he brought up another question. "What happens to you if we break up?"

"Honestly, I don't know. Dragons mate for life or for the life of their partner. As things stand, it would be difficult for me, but not impossible." Once the connection was permanent, a separation for an extended period early in the relationship resulted in withdrawal, which usually led to the dragon's demise. For a non-dragon, a similar physiological addiction could happen. It was usually less severe, and they had a better chance of surviving the withdrawal. My family had examples of survivors, but the individuals weren't all that stable afterward.

He looked at me for a moment, then gave me a slight nod. "Keith dumped me. Left me a note with dinner that said thanks for the good times and all that."

Greg's nonchalant manner about Keith was a counterpoint to the hurt and betrayal I smelled. "You deserved more than a note. I'm sorry he did that to you." I watched as he wiped his face. His lips were tight as he gave me another nod. When we were on the phone, he let me believe he'd broken it off. I knew it was hard for him to trust people with matters from his personal life. Maybe this change was a good sign. It brought out an urge in me to comfort him, wrap him in my arms and let him cry, but we needed some ground rules.

"What's happening to me right now isn't permanent yet. If we decided not to date or work together, I might complete my cycle without lasting effects." I was guessing, and by his facial expression, Greg didn't think my statement was all that accurate either.

Greg played with his coffee cup. "This wouldn't be dating as usual, then. We'd have to take precautions, at least in the beginning."

The relief of his words sank in, and I nearly cried, but maintained my composure. "The pheromones are a concern. Once we've been intimate, it initiates a connection. Some call it mating, but it's a little more than that. It's a physiological addiction. If we were both dragons, we'd mark each other. It's somewhat of a territorial thing. A kind of biological throwback to when we vied for mates." Never mind that I'd already started marking him months ago.

Greg chuckled. "You haven't found a way around it?"

"Well, we've found ways to slow it down, like not staying with any particular person for a long duration or avoiding intimacy in an aging cycle. There's even a protocol that increases the chance that someone can survive a separation, but none of it's foolproof. Biology wins out most of the time."

"By separation, you mean death," Greg said rather bluntly.

"Mostly, yes. Short-term separations are possible. My sister and her partner and my parents are examples of that. We don't have to be together every hour of the day, but the more we're apart, the more my instincts will drive me to find you." Or my body starts shutting down, but I didn't want to scare him with that part if he didn't know it already.

"We've experienced some of that already, so that makes sense. What about slowing down the connection?"

I couldn't tell if Greg asked these questions because he wanted the information or he was trying to keep us distracted. If I knew him at all, it was likely both. "Keeping our clothes on is a good start. Minimal skin-to-skin contact. Then there's abstinence."

The face Greg made was nearly comical. "Wait, do we need to avoid intercourse, or are you talking about complete abstinence?"

"Abstinence means abstinence. Kissing seems to be the exception. I don't know that anyone has initiated a connection via kissing alone."

"What about barriers?"

"Condoms handle fluids, but skin contact is the other half of it." I wiped my hand across my face. I had no idea if it was red, but I felt hot. After clearing my throat, I tried to bring the conversation back to the less sexual side of the problem. "Since the connection would be mostly one-way, your pheromones would become enhanced for me, and you could develop a need for mine over time. We might develop instincts toward each other. We could sense each other more as the connection develops."

"That much I knew already." Greg visibly shivered, as if he remembered something he didn't like. I didn't want to ask. I guessed it might have something to do with his training. He took a deep breath, then stood up.

Greg took a few steps toward me. "Here's what we'll do. I'm going back to work. You're going to take the rest of the day off, meditate, or whatever. Then tonight, you'll call me to set up a quiet date for tomorrow. A simple, no-frills date. Agreed?" I pretended I was rooted to the spot and nodded.

He closed the distance and placed the lightest of kisses on my cheek. The full force of his scent settled around me like a familiar blanket. Greg smelled strongly of dominance and desire. The way he laid out how our first date would go with an air of calm and a hint of excitement made my skin literally heat. I hoped I didn't melt the fabric of the couch under me. He wanted me just as much as I wanted him. It took every gram of willpower I had to keep my hands to myself and not grab him as he moved away.

I tracked his movements like a sunflower and soaked up everything he gave me. His kind smile was the last thing I saw. "See you tomorrow, Xavior."

I gave a small wave, which he returned as he closed the door behind him. I covered my face and groaned, not knowing whether I should laugh or cry about the whole situation. Greg was right. We should take this slow, and a date was a good start. If we couldn't manage that, any talk of connections and continuing to work together was useless.

DATE NIGHT

GREGOR

The requirement of a boring date, plus the lack of any kind of sex, made me think Xavior would back out. Instead, he called and told me he'd pick me up at 7:30 p.m. I agreed. As we said goodnight, it sank in that he'd taken me seriously.

There was no flashy or automated vehicle evident when Xavior drove up to my parent's place. Instead, it was a vehicle designed for rough terrain, and it made me wonder where we were going precisely.

Xavior's face was freaking priceless when the door opened, and instead of me, he saw my dad. My parents never really got the chance to meet someone I was dating when I was younger.

It was the only thing I could control when I was around my mother, Narissa, with her constant matchmaking. I claimed studying was more important and refused to date anyone, never mind that I wasn't attracted to anyone she pushed at me. By the time I wasn't under her influence any longer, I was in college, playing basketball, and too busy to date anyone seriously. I had to admit; it warmed my heart that they were protective of me after what happened with Keith.

"Ah, you must be Xavior. I'm Philip, Greg's father." They shook hands, and I covered my mouth to keep from laughing.

"Greg talked about you a bit. Please come in. Jennifer, my partner, is in the kitchen grabbing a few snacks. You can take a seat."

Xavior looked great. He was in nice jeans and a polo shirt, with a pair of sneakers that looked comfortable. I wore cargo pants, Chucks, and one of my geeky t-shirts that had a lightbulb with horns and a tail and a speech bubble that said, "I'm a bad idea."

Xavior came over to sit next to me on the couch. "Was that a test of some sort?" he said quietly.

"No, I just like watching you squirm in awkward situations," I admitted, though he was doing fine with my dad. "But if it was, you passed." There was a moment I wanted to kiss him, but my parents reminded me we weren't alone when they came back from the kitchen with lemonade and Jennifer's lemon ginger shortbread cookies.

"Hi Xavior, it's a pleasure to meet you," Jennifer said as she set down the tray of drinks and offered Xavior her hand.

"Pleasure is all mine, I assure you," Xavior said as he shook her hand.

After greeting him, Jennifer gestured at the snacks on the table. "Please help yourself."

Xavior grabbed a glass, then another, and handed it to me. I took it as I watched my parents glance between us. Yes, Mom and Dad, he is definitely not Keith 2.0. I took two cookies and popped one into my mouth.

"Greg, do you plan on leaving any?" Jennifer asked.

"If you want me to stop eating them, then you have to stop making them," I said as I put the other cookie in my mouth.

"So, Xavior, what do you have planned for tonight?" Philip asked. His tone was light, but had a playful bit of fatherly authority. I tried not to choke on my cookie.

"Well, sir," I could tell he paused for effect, not because he was really nervous. "I planned a drive to the beach to watch the sunset," Xavior said, then took a bite of a cookie. His face changed to a look of surprise. "These are pretty awesome. What are they?"

"Shortbread cookies. They are an old family recipe that calls for lemon juice and either fine ground ginger or ginger powder. They are one of my favorites," Jennifer said.

"They're delicious," he said, as he took another.

He was particular about food, so I was slightly suspicious of his intentions. I drank half of my glass of lemonade to quench the dry mouth I had from the cookies and the heat I felt creeping up my neck.

I stood, set down my glass, and grabbed one more cookie before I took a step toward the door. "We need to get going if we are planning to watch the sunset," I said. Xavior followed my lead. We said our goodbyes as we left my parents sitting in the living room.

"Have him back no later than midnight!" Philip shouted in our direction as I closed the door behind us.

I heard a muffled squeak of "Philip!" It made me grin as we walked toward Xavior's vehicle.

Xavior sprinted ahead and opened the door on the passenger side. I gave him a quick kiss and smiled before I got in. He jogged to the other side of the vehicle, hopped in, and took off down the road as if he owned it.

"I really like your parents. They care about you a lot."

"Did you get that from how they smelled?" I wondered how much he would actually tell me now that we were trying to learn about each other on a more personal level.

"I got that from their actions, but if you want details, they are proud of you. Protective. Loving. They also have a fairly healthy sex life." Xavior grinned as he drove.

"Oh, fuck, I did not need to know that last part." I laughed. "I know they love each other. Their relationship is much healthier than Dad and Mother's. Jennifer was good for both of us. She was my mom when my mother didn't care to be a parent."

Xavior nodded. "I picked up on that. They're good people."

"You're seriously going for all the brownie points tonight, aren't you?"

"If brownie points can be turned in later for a reward, then yes." He chuckled. "Though I want to see if your mom would give me the recipe for her shortbread cookies. Those were great."

"You liked them? That wasn't for show?" I tried to keep the surprise out of my voice, though I knew my scent would be stamped with it.

He shook his head, his lips curved up slightly. "I'd love to figure out how to make those myself."

"Don't you have a small army of people to do that?"

"They work at the estate. I'm only there for visitors or events and rent the place out a lot. I eat out or cook at my place in town."

"Oh, so that whole place is more like an investment?"

"Well, yeah." Xavior shrugged. "It's why we have security and keycards, though I should have it upgraded to a thumbprint entry. The dance hall and gallery make the most money. I've had ceremonies of all kinds there, and for extra, my staff caters. Which they love, because that money is theirs besides what I pay them."

"Why do you have a job again?" I joked.

"Because mysteries are the spice of life, and I can't live without them."

"Right. Your obsession." I smiled.

"Are you going to tell me you don't have an obsession, Greg?"

"Well, I don't know if it counts, but if I had an obsession, maybe helping people or doing things for people would be it. It's why I became a public safety officer." I saw Xavior glance at me, then grin. I wanted to ask what he was thinking, but he turned off the main road onto a dirt road, then came to a stop in a small clearing.

"We're here. It's a bit of a hike, but worth it. Don't worry, I brought supplies," he said.

I laughed. "Okay."

Xavior's spot was a secluded beach populated by surfers. A couple were still catching waves just as the sun was going down. We found a spot and set out a blanket.

As we settled in and admired the view, Xavior opened the bag of supplies. He pulled out two beers and a bag of chips, then did some trick with his thumbnail and popped the caps off like they were foil. He handed me one, and we tapped the bottles together like we usually did when we went out after work.

"Why this spot?" I asked after I had taken a drink. The beer was a craft brew that we both liked. They didn't bottle it as far as I knew, so Xavior had pulled some strings after all. I'd said no frills, but it was excellent beer, so I didn't gripe.

"Less crowded, and the view is spectacular."

"By that you mean eye candy out there surfing."

"Yeah," he said with a grin. "I mean, it doesn't hurt."

"No, no, it doesn't," I chuckled.

"Though tonight, it's kinda boring."

"Why's that?"

"Because the only person I'm interested in is sitting next to me," Xavior said.

I held it in for about five seconds, then laughed. When he joined me, I was relieved. "Oh Christ, Xavior, that was one of the best executed, cheesiest pickup lines ever."

"I have more where that came from," he quipped.

"That's not hard to believe at all." I leaned toward him.

We gazed into each other's eyes for a moment. I took in the emerald green I'd dreamed about. My eyes drifted to his lips, the set of his jaw, the light splash of freckles that you could only see if you were close enough to his face. Xavior leaned forward slightly, and we inhaled each other's breath. My heart raced like Xavior drove his vehicle. When he spoke, it was barely above the sound of the waves crashing.

"Can I kiss you, Gregor?" It was so formal and oddly fitting. The way my name fell from Xavior's lips made me lightheaded. I couldn't remember the last time someone had called me Gregor and made it sound so fucking sexy.

"Please," I said with barely a breath before his lips met mine. His hand slipped to the back of my neck, and I didn't want him to let go. My hands fisted in his polo, and a conflict warred within me to pull him closer or push him away. I wanted more than a kiss, more than making out on a beach at sunset, more than this one perfect moment. And yet, I was scared.

I think Xavior smelled it and pulled away first. We pressed our foreheads together and looked at each other. I shivered as the wind picked up a little. He pulled back a little more.

"You're cold."

"I'm fine." I shivered again and couldn't tell if it was from the cool breeze or not. My face felt like it was on fire, and any of the blood my body could have used to keep warm was likely going to my dick.

Xavior shook his head and took our beers and anchored them in the sand, moved the bag off the blanket, then said, "Come here." He took me by the arm and guided me to sit between his legs, my back to his chest. He pulled the blanket around us. It helped, but I was still shivering.

I felt Xavior take a deep breath, hold it, then blow smoke downwind. When his chest radiated warmth, I moved to snuggle back into him as he chuckled. He wrapped his arms and the blanket tighter around us. "Not cold, huh?"

"Shut it." He laughed, and I felt it vibrate through my chest.

We watched as the light faded, and the stars came out. Xavior's hand wandered. "Are you looking for something?"

"Maybe." Xavior kissed the top of my head. His left hand tugged my shirt up a little. When it slid up my stomach to my chest and found my nipple, I shook my head. His mouth found my right ear. I tried to move away, but stopped when he tightened his arms around me.

"Just relax, Greg, please?" The plea in his voice taunted me, and the contradiction of my own emotions annoyed me. I wanted him, but if what we felt wasn't real or didn't last, we could end up killing each other. The stakes were too high to be reckless.

He kissed my ear as I leaned back into his embrace. "You're so tense. I get that you're scared. I'm scared too. Sometimes, I want you so badly it frightens me." Xavior buried his nose in my neck and inhaled, then gently kissed his way back to my ear. I shivered again, but it wasn't from the evening breeze.

"I've never wanted anyone as badly as I do you. Greg, I want you, mind, body, and soul. I want to give that to you in return. Until we're ready, we can draw lines."

"Lines?" I said with a breathy voice that surprised me.

"Yes." He kissed my neck again. "Rules, I guess, that we follow until both of us are sure we want more. There's too much at stake not to take things a little slower, right?"

I nodded. "Are you. . ." I stopped talking for a moment. Xavior wouldn't have suggested it if he wasn't prepared for the consequences. "Okay, then, I have some ideas."

Xavior kept me warm the whole time we talked. He also touched me in a way that was somewhere between affectionate and seductive. By the time we ran out of words, I was relaxed and nearly asleep in his arms.

I felt a kiss on my temple before he spoke. "Let's get you home," he whispered in my ear. I turned to give him a kiss. He tasted like embers and a spice I couldn't name. As I got to my feet, I immediately missed Xavior's warmth. He quickly wrapped the blanket around me, then packed up. When we got back to his vehicle, he opened the passenger door, and I hopped in. He gave me another quick kiss and shut the door before he went to the driver's side.

The drive back to my parent's house was quiet. We pulled up into the driveway, and I unwrapped myself from the blanket. "Tonight was good, Xav."

He nodded. "When would you like to go out again?"

"Maybe next weekend?"

"That long? But that's so far away." His pout was annoyingly cute.

"We'll do our usual hangouts during the week after work, but the weekends are for fun stuff," I offered.

"Okay. I suppose that works, handsome," Xavior said. I chuckled and grinned like a goofball. He leaned toward me, and I couldn't help but taste his lips one more time. I wasn't sure how long we spent kissing before the porch light shattered the darkness.

We both snickered like teens. "I should probably get going. I didn't realize they were going to take it this far." I opened the door to hop out of the vehicle.

Xavior spoke before I closed the door. "Never underestimate family. See you Monday, Greg."

"Call me to let me know you made it home." Xavior nodded at the request. When he called an hour later, I answered the phone with a smile on my face.

HABIT FORMING

XAVIOR

I called as soon as I walked in the door. When Greg's sleepy face appeared on the screen, I smiled at it.

"Hey, did I wake you?"

"A little, but that's alright."

"I like sleepy Greg. You're absolutely fuckable like that."

"I know." The confidence in Greg's voice set off a flutter of feelings. Like hummingbird wings, they were all too fast to distinguish. If I had to guess what he smelled like, it would be something similar to when we kissed on the beach.

"I'd call you a tease, but I'm pretty sure we're tormenting each other at this point."

"For good reasons."

"Yes, for very good reasons," I agreed. We'd made decisions on that beach, which I very much planned to keep.

With Greg's previous relationship coloring things a little too much, along with my aging cycle, we decided that sex was definitely off the table for now. We wanted to make sure this was the right thing to do, not something we were compelled to do.

Kissing and touching above the beltline was allowed. Which was probably good because I don't think either of us could stop touching each other. The only restriction to that was during work hours. The phone call was one of Greg's ideas to help take the edge off.

Sex for me has always been an in-person act. I'm not naïve about phone sex, but I hadn't needed it before. If someone wasn't available, I'd find someone else. That was definitely not an option, and I was desperate for the promised interaction. It might be fleeting, but it kept us both safe. "Believe it or not, I've never done this before. So, what do we do first?"

Greg smiled. "You're going to go upstairs to your room, prop your phone up somewhere, and then talk to me while you undress."

"Okay. You want a tour of my house along the way?" I felt awkward showing him around via my phone. What I really wanted was for him to move in and claim it as his space, too. As desperate as I was to have this work, even I knew it was too soon for that.

"If you'd like," he said with a smirk.

I showed him around the kitchen and the living room. "Why don't you have any furniture?" Greg asked.

"No one comes here, and I didn't have anything moved from the estate."

"We could host some game nights at your house for the detectives."

"We?" I loved that idea, and I liked that Greg already thought of us doing things together in public.

"I'd help," he offered.

If we put one together, I'd hold him to that. Plus, it would give him a reason to be here. The idea of Greg's scent being in my house did things for me. I got to the top of the stairs. "Let's talk about that idea tomorrow, shall we, or do you not want to see my bedroom?"

"Yes, I'd like to see your bedroom." I gave the camera a quick smile and entered. It had a king-size bed with a dozen pillows, a duvet, and a large wooden headboard. The color palette was green and black with gray and light cream accents. A long, thin bar, the holoscreen generator, was mounted on the wall across from the bed. Under that was a dresser, and to the left, I opened another door to show Greg the bathroom. The door to the right of the dresser led to a closet.

"There's a guest bedroom too, but it's empty right now." An interesting look played across Greg's face. I hesitated to ask what he thought, then the moment passed as the silence stretched between us.

"It's a very nice bedroom. Why is everything dark green? Do you like that color?"

"They are the family colors, but yeah, I like them."

"Family colors." Greg paused in thought. "Those are the same colors as the suit you had made for me."

"I told you I was marking you, didn't I?"

He laughed. "You didn't mention that you were literally planting a flag. Shit, Xavior." He sighed. "A lot more makes sense about that weekend."

"Oh?" I tried to sound innocent, but it didn't work.

"You were goading him, weren't you?" That Greg couldn't say his ex's name interested me, but I didn't pry.

"I picked colors I liked. If he took it a certain way, that's not my fault. His suit was of the same quality." I remembered the argument with Keith in my library. Greg's reaction to the information was interesting because it meant that his ex hadn't said a word about our verbal exchange. Then again, neither had I.

"But it was flashy and stylish, and the equivalent of putting him on everyone's radar."

I glanced down, then looked back at the screen. I didn't like where this might lead, so I tried to change the subject. "Wish you were here." I watched as Greg narrowed his eyes slightly.

He recognized the out for that particular conversation and took it. I knew we'd revisit it later. "I do too, but we have rules, right?"

"I know." I propped the phone up on the nightstand next to the bed. "Will that work?"

"Yes." He paused, then took a breath. "Now, strip down to your underwear." Greg's voice was laced with desire, need, and a thread of command. It was that combination of authority and confidence I craved.

I sat down on my bed and made a show of taking off my shirt, then tossed it into the room. "I feel like I should have music for this."

Greg rewarded me with a low chuckle. When he cleared his throat, I looked back at the screen. "Music would only distract from what I have in mind."

"Interesting. What's next?"

"Jeans."

"Right." I stood, popped the top button, and slowly unzipped, then pushed them down and revealed a black pair of boxer briefs straining with a partial erection. I sat down to remove my jeans and tossed them in the same direction as the polo. "Now what?"

"Pick up the phone." I did as Greg asked. "Lie down on your bed."

"Okay." He mirrored my actions. "What now?"

"Close your eyes. Tell me the first thing you see."

"Your face."

"What else?"

"The deep sherry pools you have for eyes, the bridge of your nose, soft lips hidden by facial hair, the small scar over your right eye." I paused and opened my eyes. "How did you get that, anyway?"

"Focus, Xav." Greg's voice held amused warmth as he avoided my question. I would have to ask again later. "What else do you see?" he said.

I closed my eyes again. "The way your mouth curls up when you smile. Your hands."

"What about my hands?"

"The strength they have, and the gentleness. They're large too." I smiled. His confident chuckle tickled my ears.

"Do you like the idea of my hands on you?"

"Yes, without a doubt." I kept my eyes closed, but remembered what it felt like to have him touch me. My skin flushed with heat.

"Show me where you want my hands, Xavior." Oh, now this game made more sense. I touched my fingers to my lips. I gave them a soft kiss, then slid my hand down my neck and to my chest and played with a nipple for a moment.

"You're not too ticklish there?"

I jumped slightly at the sound of his voice. "No."

"Good to know." He went quiet for a moment. "Show me how you like your nipples played with."

I swallowed and couldn't believe my cock was already hard and leaking. I licked my fingers, put them on the nipple I was playing with, and then switched to the other. I'd somewhat forgotten that Greg was watching me or that I was holding my phone. I continued toying with myself until I felt a distinct heaviness of an aching hard-on between my legs.

I hadn't realized I was panting until Greg spoke. "Do you want to come for me?"

"Yes, please." I heard myself speak the words, but I didn't quite believe them.

"Then that's what I want you to do." His voice was thick with need. I didn't hesitate to reach for my dick. I started to move the phone so he could watch. "No, keep it on your face. I want to see your face when you come."

I nodded, even with my eyes closed. My sole focus was on do-ing precisely what Greg asked me to do. The next few moments were me panting, swearing, then squeezing my eyes tighter when I came. When I opened my eyes, Greg smiled at me, and my other hand was full of cum.

"That was. . . different," I said as I looked down my chest at my mess. My face felt hot. I wasn't sure what to do with myself.

"Enjoyable?"

"Yes, but not the same as having you here."

"No, however, I made you come with only my voice and some instructions."

"Oh, well, since you put it like that." We laughed. "What about you?"

"What about me?"

"Did you. . ." My mouth was dry, and I found it hard to swallow. I didn't know why I was suddenly shy about anything sexual. While my partners and I were considerate of each other, this was different. As if the physical act didn't matter. It was a means to an end. What Greg and I wanted was deeper.

"That's tomorrow night." He smiled at the camera. It made my heart ache. "Good night, Xav."

"Good night, Greg."

The call disconnected, and I dropped my phone onto the mattress. I took myself to the bathroom to clean up, then returned to bed naked and slightly sated, with a smile. *Take the edge off, indeed. It felt more like playing with fire.*

I passed out and didn't wake again until the next morning. Sunday flew by as I kept myself occupied with the garden in the back of the brownstone. On Monday, I sprinted through my morning routine and was at my desk, thumbed in, five minutes before Greg showed up.

We exchanged smiles as Greg sat down, picked up the coffee I'd left for him, and took a sip. I took a pastry out of the bag and passed the rest over to him. He took it and fished out a chocolate croissant.

"Sleep well?" he asked.

"Like a whelp in a nest. What about you?"

"Like I didn't have a care in the world."

LITMUS TEST

GREGOR

Things were going well after a month of dating while still working together. We stuck to our rules as if our lives depended on them, which they did. It was my turn to plan a date. We'd spent our time together sharing our favorite places to eat, which leaned toward pubs with good food, pho, curry, and Szechuan places. Xavior liked really spicy food, which I could mostly deal with thanks to Keith, though I kept that to myself.

Movies were a bit of a toss-up. Xavior liked action movies, but I tended toward drama or comedy. Sometimes we could agree on what to watch, but mostly we ended up making out until the credits. Neither of us liked musicals, which was perfectly fine with me. Keith listened to musical soundtracks on repeat, and I'd heard enough of them over the years that I was happy to not be inundated with every popular musical since the beginning of time.

Since I was still staying with my parents, I invited Xavior for our usual family weekend dinner. While I'd had plenty of meals on the go or meals that I had to heat when I got home, the weekend dinner was different.

When Xavior agreed to join us, I highlighted how they worked and that everyone pitched in. I didn't mention how much these meals meant to my family. I didn't want to put undue pressure on him, but I knew this was a litmus test of sorts. My hope was that this would be the first of many he'd spend with us.

I was delightfully surprised when Xavior showed up early with a bottle of wine and a nervous smile on his face.

"Hi." He gave me a quick kiss as he came through the door. "I wasn't sure what else to bring. Jennifer insisted she had everything covered when I talked with her."

"You called Mom?" I was amused and curious.

"Well, yeah. I didn't want to embarrass you." He shrugged. "I wanted to make sure I was prepared, you know?"

I stepped in close and put my hands on his shoulders. "You are far from being an embarrassment." I gave him a proper kiss this time, and he seemed unusually shy about the affection. I saw his eyes dart behind me, and I discovered the reason.

"Hi, Mr. Lyndon," Xavior gave a slight wave to Dad.

I shrugged my shoulders at Dad. It made me wonder if Xavior's family didn't hug or kiss each other openly. I'd have to ask later. "Come on in, Xavior. I'll show you what you'll be doing for your dinner. Hope you like potatoes," Philip said. We followed him into the kitchen.

"Potatoes?" I watched as he glanced at the bottle in his hands, then at me.

"Don't sweat it. Mom likes wine. It'll be fine." He nodded, though he didn't look too sure.

Jennifer greeted us as we walked into the kitchen. "Hello there. You two ready to clean and peel your dinner?" Xavior took the bottle of wine to her.

"Hi, Mrs. Lyndon, this is for you." Xavior handed it over.

"Oh, how lovely. Would you like a glass while you work?" We all chimed in that it sounded like a good idea, and Jennifer poured everyone a glass. Dad resumed his station at the kitchen island, chopping onions.

"Are we making potato soup?" Xavior asked.

Jennifer nodded. "Yep! I have the dough for biscuits proofing now. When's the last time you had potato soup?"

"I can't remember, to be honest." He looked over the sink full of potatoes. "Probably when I traveled more."

"When was that?" Jennifer asked as she passed out glasses of wine.

"A hundred years ago or so, I think." I stared at him. Xavior held his glass and looked at the rest of us. My parents looked a little shocked. "Did I say something wrong?"

I leaned over and said sotto voce, "No. But I forgot to tell them something important." I couldn't turn around to face my parents just yet, so I kept looking at Xavior. His eyes darted to the parental figures behind me as they probably stared holes into my back.

"You didn't tell them?" He half-whispered.

I shook my head.

"What didn't you tell us, Gregor?" Dad sounded annoyed. I only ever heard my full first name if he was upset.

I took a drink, set my glass down, and turned to face them. "Xavior's a dragon." I looked at Xavior, and he put his hand on my arm. Silence settled in the kitchen, and I watched Dad process the information. He went from stoic to amused to outright laughter.

"Oh Christ, Greg, if Narissa knew, she'd have a coronary." He laughed some more, to where tears streamed out of his eyes.

"Does it really warrant all of that, Philip?" Jennifer asked, though she didn't look upset.

"Fuck yes, it does." We all looked at Dad, a little shocked. I couldn't remember him ever swearing like that. To hear it now, even as an adult, was weird. "She had these high-minded ideals. Our children would grow up in accordance with the church. Then, when the church doctrines changed, she changed it to the Order's archaic rules." His eyes went wide, and he looked at me. "Please tell me he knows about the Order, Greg." Dad looked between Xavior and me as he waited for an answer.

"He knows. I told him on the first day we met. He's been rather insistent that it doesn't matter to him." I gave Xavior a smile that he returned as he caressed my arm, then let go.

"Greg's been concerned about my welfare from the beginning. Even offered to transfer if I felt threatened." Xavior glanced between my parents, then back to me. Was that a hint of a blush

I saw on his face? The distinct lack of his confident cockiness was adorable and weird at the same time.

"Good. I'm glad to hear it." Dad smiled and picked up his wineglass. "A toast, if you will." We all raised our glasses. "To new relationships and bright days ahead." We all gave a cheer to that, and then he added, "And to the fall of bigoted assholes like the Order." He drank the rest of his wine, set the glass down, and went out the back door to his shop. I moved to follow, but Mom stopped me.

"Greg, let him cool off. He's worried about you, that's all. Your mother did a number on him."

"He doesn't talk to me about it." I tried to keep the frustration out of my voice. I'd help if he let me.

"He wouldn't. You were a child with enough problems, and he wanted you to have a relationship with her, even if it meant he'd have to work twice as hard to undo what she taught you."

"She did that all on her own when she threw me out." My tone was bitter. Fourteen years had passed since I had spoken to Narissa. It surprised me that I was still angry with my mother for her lack of acceptance and maternal instinct. Though what Narissa lacked, Jennifer made up for in spades.

Jennifer patted my shoulder. "It'll be all right. How about we get back to dinner, hmm? Potatoes won't fix themselves."

Xavior and I both nodded. Then she went out the back door, presumably to talk with Dad.

"You alright?" Xavior touched my face. I leaned into it a little before he dropped his hand.

"Yeah, are you?" He nodded. "I didn't plan for your first meal with us to be so exciting."

Xavior laughed. "You think this is exciting? Compared to meals with my family, this is pretty laid-back. Hopefully, I'll be able to return the favor one day."

I chuckled. "I look forward to it." When he mentioned his family, it occurred to me we might end up playing out the same scenario. "Does your family know?"

He nodded. "I told them when I started working with you."

"Really? Why?" I was curious. He had seemed so casual about it in the beginning.

"The Knights are no joke for dragons. My family has connections. I wanted to make sure I wasn't walking into a trap."

"Wow. Why didn't you tell me this before?"

"I didn't because, by the time I knew you better, if it had been
a trap, it didn't matter."

"It didn't? Why's that?"

"Ask me again later, okay?"

"Okay." Xavior was usually forthcoming. I had to trust that
he'd explain when he was ready.

We went back to work on the potatoes. I shook off the
strangeness of the moment while Xavior peeled and I chopped.
By the time we finished all the potatoes, my parents had come
back inside. Before either of us could say anything, Dad walked
up to Xavior and wrapped his arms around him. He said something I couldn't hear, and Xavior nodded.

Dad stepped away from Xavior and wiped his face with a
kerchief from his back pocket. Mom stepped in quickly. "I have
biscuits to bake, and your dad needs to put the soup together.
Why don't you show Xavior the wood shop, Greg?"

"Yeah, okay. Come on." I held out my hand to Xavior, and he
took it. I led him out to the little shop, and he looked impressed.

"Is this where you made my bookmark?"

"Yeah." I pointed around the shop. "The wood is from various ent families that sell it to help maintain their lands. Dad
even has permission to harvest things from various places." I
watched as Xavior walked around and touched different pieces
of wood.

"This entire shop is worth more than my parent's house, and
my house. It's my inheritance, though I'll probably never sell it.
I'd either use it myself or give it away to other woodworkers to
make things with the stock."

"What does your dad like to build?" Xavior fiddled with a few
loose pieces stacked on the shelves.

"All kinds of things." I smiled as I thought about his process.
"Dad has a ritual with the wood where he asks it what it wants
to be. I don't know if it ever says anything to him. It's kind of
magical to watch him work out here. He's made chairs, chopping
boards, desks, small tables, bowls, all kinds of stuff. My Grandpa

Jack taught him. I grew up watching them work, and over time they taught me a few things."

"That sounds like a nice counterbalance to everything else."

"Yeah. It was. I was young when my parents split up." I turned away from Xavior to look at the half-finished piece on the workbench. "One thing Dad gave me after we left and moved here was a stuffed red-and-gold dragon. My mother would give me weapons and horrific parties for my birthdays, and Dad would give me books and teach me how to make things out of wood. The first time I read a story Dad gave me about a boy dating another boy, I realized that not everyone thought like the Order did. I knew it was Dad's way of saying my mother was mistaken in her beliefs."

Xavior came up and wrapped his arms around me as I played with some shavings on Dad's workbench. The warmth of him steadied me. I was grateful for it. When he spoke, his lips were pressed close to my neck and his words vibrated through my chest as he laid his head on my shoulder.

"I can only imagine what your mother put you through, but I also understand the need for balance. Your family was given an ability, or if you like, a gift for a reason. While, thankfully, things have changed a lot, the balance your family represents is still necessary."

I turned around in his arms. "Your view on the subject is rather charitable. Balance was not what my mother taught." I'd never seen a dragon executed. It wasn't for lack of trying on my mother's part. She wouldn't break the laws. A righteous kill was her ultimate goal.

"All I know, or understand, is that without balance, things can tip wildly. So while I don't condone the speciesism at play, I can appreciate that there is something to keep us in check for nature's sake."

I cleared my throat. "That's an interesting philosophy you have there, Xav. But there are other limiting factors where dragons are concerned." Damn pheromones.

He buried his face in my chest, and I groaned a little. "Yeah, true," he said.

I laughed a little and kissed the top of his head. "What did my dad say to you?"

"He said some very father-like things concerning the care and future welfare of his son."

Dad didn't threaten people, as far as I knew. I was about to prod further when he kissed me.

Eventually, he pulled back a little. "It's all right, Greg. He didn't threaten me. Actually, I think he likes me."

"Oh yeah? Good." I smiled and wrapped Xavior in a tight hug. My parent's approval had always meant a lot to me. Keith never understood that.

"Yeah," Xavior said with a smug smile.

We continued to exchange playful kisses until Dad poked his head in the shop door and told us dinner was ready.

A VOW

XAVIOR

The moment played through my mind multiple times that night.

"If you see his mother, take Greg and run. Don't let her separate you. Do you understand me?"

I nodded because I didn't know what to say.

"I can tell you're a wonderful individual, Xavior. Take care of my son," Philip said as he squeezed me again hard. I hugged him back, then let go.

Philip didn't seem to think any more of it, and I didn't tell Greg because I was afraid it would upset him. I can only imagine why Philip gave me that warning.

Dinner was a pleasant affair with soup, fluffy drop biscuits, and beer. As we cleaned up, Jennifer invited me to stay. "Feel free. Greg has plenty of space in his room, and we don't mind. Philip and I sleep on the opposite side of the house, so don't worry about noise either."

I could smell Greg's embarrassment. When I glanced at him, he had a blush to match. I had to admit that I was a bit chagrined as well. "Thank you, Jennifer. I appreciate that."

"No problem. There are pillows and extra blankets in the hall closet. Greg can show you." She left to join her husband in the living room as Greg and I finished the dishes.

"You don't have to stay if you don't want to," Greg whispered. "They don't know that we aren't, um. . ."

I covered my mouth as a chuckle escaped. "You're adorable. Can't even say the word 'sex' in your parent's house." I leaned over to whisper, "Wouldn't they be surprised about some of our phone calls?"

Greg looked like a red balloon about to burst. "I can. I have." He shrugged and said, "I'm just. . ."

"Nervous?"

He sighed. "I don't want to push things between us, and I also know it's a long drive back to your place in the city, too."

"Do you want me to stay?" If I were honest with myself, I was both hopeful and nervous, too.

I watched as emotions played across Greg's face. He dried the last few dishes while I finished my beer. "I want you to, but I also know we made a promise to each other. It's not fair to push our boundaries when we're not ready."

I took a deep breath. "Do you trust me, Greg?"

"Yes, Xav, I trust you. A lot." He sighed. "But I don't trust myself."

"Oh?" I tried not to let on that his admission excited me. I very much wanted to get my hands on Greg in every way imaginable. And yet, it scared me that I would be connected to him for the rest of my life, at least biologically speaking. I couldn't help feeling trapped.

I moved behind him and put my hands on his waist as he folded a dish towel. "There's a spell I could use."

"Like a magical chastity belt?" Greg's voice was full of incredulity.

"Not exactly, but yes."

Greg turned in my arms. His face was a picture of calm, but his eyes were bright with some kind of emotion. I took a light sniff and realized we were in the same boat. His desire and lust were through the roof. All it would take was one nudge. As it was, I was imagining having sex on his parent's kitchen floor.

"If you're going to do it, do it now."

I nodded and tried to clear my throat. The scent of Greg's desire was thick on my tongue. It took everything I had not to drop to my knees and beg for a taste of him. I could only imagine what would happen when we finally decided we were ready. Instead, I did the only thing that might keep us safe from ourselves for the night.

I put his hand on my heart and placed mine on his. I'd been taught the words, but I didn't know what they meant. The language was older than I was, and they designed the spell for bloodlust, not sexual lust, but in my book, lust was lust. I was willing to try anything.

There was a faint glow as a mark appeared on the back of our hands. Greg blinked. I looked at him. "How do you feel?"

"Like someone banked a fire, but the embers are still there." He rubbed his fingers over the mark.

I nodded. Greg's word choices were interesting but apt. "I feel the same. The spell lasts until I speak the reversal words." He was staring at the mark on his hand, but he acknowledged me with a nod.

"Do you still want me to stay?"

"Yes." He kissed me gently. "Absolutely."

We spent a relaxed evening with his parents, watched a movie, and drank a few more beers. When we went to bed, we stripped down to our boxers and curled up next to each other. The closeness without the additional complications amazed and amused us.

"I feel a kind of reverence," I said, as I gently touched Greg's face. "As if I could spend the rest of the night looking at you." Greg smiled. "I'm pretty sure I'll fall asleep eventually." We laughed softly as we both touched each other's faces, exploring the contours, facial hair, and scars. I ran my finger over the one on his eyebrow. I was still curious about how he'd ended up with it.

"Your little trick gave me a measure of calm. I hadn't realized I'd been missing. Do you have any idea how much willpower I have to exert when I'm around you?"

I tapped my nose. "Some. This hasn't been easy on either of us, has it?"

"No, but it's worth it." He sighed. "This entire year has been a kind of torture. Working with you, being around you, wanting you even though I was with someone else. Watching you with other people. I was jealous." He let out an amused noise. "I hadn't realized that until now. Wow, I was really jealous. I mean, sometimes I knew, but just now, I feel it. Like a brick in my stomach."

"It's alright. This makes sense. If our largest emotion were lust, whatever was underneath wouldn't come to the surface as often. Now that I've quieted one kind of emotion, the others should be clearer."

"Won't that be a bit of a problem? I don't exactly want to shoot daggers at everyone you talk to. Jealousy is a bad look on me."

I laughed. "Who would you say you are jealous of now?"

"Jordan, Naomi, maybe Vanessa, and that hot attendant that handles the vehicle pool at work, the one that wears little pieces of art on their uniform."

"The others, I understand, but why them?"

"Have you seen the way they check you out when you turn in maintenance requisitions?"

"No." Loe seemed nice enough, but I hadn't noticed anything more.

"There's no way they didn't smell like attraction or desire or whatever. They look at you like you're prey. Are you telling me you've never smelled anything from—"

"Loe?"

"Loe! Yes. You even know their name!" His voice held a hint of disbelief. It alarmed me a little.

"Now that you mention it, I don't smell much of anything from them. They always smell like something sweet, like cotton candy."

"Probably because they are thinking about devouring you."

I laughed. "Wow, you really have thought about this."

"Yes, I have." He wrapped his arms around my waist and pulled me closer. He was quiet for a moment. "But not this much. Not like this. It's overwhelming and making me feel sick." He sat up and looked around, then darted for his bathroom.

"Greg?" I followed and found him vomiting into the toilet. "Shit. I didn't expect you to have this kind of reaction. I'm sorry. Let me remove it."

"No!" He pushed me away. I stood there as he retched up dinner. "Remove it tomorrow. I want this, at least tonight. I want to trust myself with you. If you take it away now, we'll be in trouble. You know that as much as I do."

I caressed his back as he sobbed a little. "Greg, are you sure?"

He gave me the slightest nod. "Yes. I'll be alright."

I sat down next to the toilet so I could face him. "I should have realized how much this might affect you. You keep all your emotions so close. You don't show them unless you feel safe enough, even if your smell gives you away at times. But I had no idea how deep your well was or how much we hadn't talked about other things."

"It's a lot. I know it's a lot."

"You need to talk to someone about it."

Greg looked at me, and I smelled anger and saw it light up in his eyes. It died quickly, followed by a kind of remorse. I swallowed past the tightness in my throat and held my tongue.

"You're right," he said, as he propped an elbow on the toilet seat and leaned his head on his palm.

"No, I'm a hypocrite. I may not be having difficulties now, but I've had my fair share over the past year. I should find someone to talk with, too."

He reached a hand toward me, and I took it. We laced our fingers together. "This wasn't exactly what we expected, but I have to admit, I'm glad we're here. I'm glad we are talking about these things."

"Me too." I kissed his forehead, and he sighed softly. We spent the night in the bathroom talking. As Greg's nausea eventually subsided, he fell asleep with his head in my lap. I ran my fingers through his hair. I hadn't realized we both slept until the light came through the small bathroom window.

"How do you feel?" I touched his shoulder lightly. He sat up slowly.

"Cranky. Hungry. Frustrated that we ended up in the bathroom." He made a half-whine, half-chuckle noise. I sympathized and leaned over to kiss his forehead.

"I can't help but wonder if this isn't somewhat my fault."

"How so?" Greg wiped his eyes with the palm of his hand.

"I'm not sure how long I've been marking you. You might be more affected than either of us realizes."

He shook his head. "Even if that's the case, I wouldn't change it."

"Really?" It was my turn to be surprised.

"I knew from the moment I met you, then agreed to be your partner, that you'd change my life." He smiled a little. "Keith and Vanessa both picked up on something."

"Jordan knew too. So did Naomi, for that matter."

"Shit, are you serious?"

I shrugged. "She's damn good at making people talk. I would not want to be opposite an interview table with her." I didn't go into details.

"If I'd been less stubborn. . ."

"Greg, no. Don't do that to yourself."

He shook his head. "I knew way before I met you that Keith and I wouldn't work out. I didn't want to admit it because I was scared. Then you showed up, and it made me feel guilty that I wanted you more than the person I was already with. I felt like I had to prove to him and myself that wasn't the case."

"You're talking about dinner with Vanessa and Keith?"

He sighed. "I don't really remember the meal. I only remember being nauseated by guilt. Then embarrassed that I'd assumed you liked me, then the argument the next day was pretty intense."

"I liked you, Greg. A lot. But where we stood at that moment, neither one of us was ready. We still aren't, or we wouldn't be in your bathroom," I said, with a bit of self-deprecating sarcasm, and we laughed at that. It emphasized how much his previous relationship still weighed on him and how much our working relationship was tangled up in that.

We showered, got dressed, and had a light breakfast with Greg's parents without any issues. Afterward, he walked me to the front door. We hugged each other tightly before I took a step back and gave him a warning. "I'm going to remove the spell now, okay?"

"Yeah." His hands twitched like he wanted to reach for me. Instead, I placed our hands and spoke the reversal words, and we both gasped for air as we took a few steps back from each other. Desires roared to life as a few heated moments passed before Greg stepped back inside his parent's house and shut the screen door. "Xavior, go now, before something happens. I'll call you."

I swallowed as I fought not to break down the door to get to him. "Right. See you tomorrow?"

He nodded and took another step back and closed the door. I practically ran to my vehicle and climbed inside. I was driving without a direction when Greg called.

"Pull over now." The strain in his voice was tangled in the command.

I did as he said, though my knuckles were white from my grip on the steering controls. I was lucky they were reinforced. "Okay, I've stopped."

"Take your dick out and wrap your hand around it."

His words shot through me like electricity. "Greg," I whined. "Please." Spells sometimes had backlashes. I wondered if this resulted from what I'd done.

"It will make it better. If you are anything like me right now, you've been driving for the last few minutes with a hard-on." He was right, and it hurt. "Take yourself out of your pants and come with me."

It didn't take long. We were both grunting and panting on the line in moments. I practically cried with relief as I made a mess.

I heard Greg take a deep breath and let it out. "Tomorrow, we work on signing up for therapy."

"Okay." It made sense. We needed help if we were going to make this work.

"Drive safe, Xav." His voice was the epitome of calm. It amazed me how much his voice calmed me, too.

"I will. Promise." I hung up, cleaned myself off, and drove home.

On Monday, we did precisely as Greg had suggested. The rest of the week, we worked on a few cases and had a beer at our local pub on Friday. We talked about our feelings more, and I felt less desperate and fragile. It seemed to be the same for him, too.

"Would you still want to come by for family dinner?" Greg asked, playing with his beer mug.

"Yes," I said with a smile. "Absolutely."

ANNIVERSARY

GREGOR

Our first work anniversary wasn't a huge deal, but we planned on celebrating with the detective group at Xavior's place by having a game night. He ordered food, bought furniture for his living room, and picked up the latest holo games and half a dozen halo headset controllers. It was a very Xavior party plan, any realistic budget be damned.

We left work early to set things up at Xavior's brownstone. When we arrived, Edward was there too. While I was setting up the console, Edward walked out of the kitchen with trays of snacks.

"Hi, Edward."

He was dressed in a jacket, a button-down shirt, and a tie, with coordinating slacks. It wasn't the uniform I saw at the estate, but it wasn't casual either. "Hello again, Mr. Lyndon. Thank you for your help with the festivities." His white hair and beard would make anyone think he was in his late seventies, but who knew for sure? His skin had a light fawn hue and very few wrinkles. I was extremely curious about him and why he worked for Xavior, but I wasn't brave enough to ask.

"No problem. Glad to help."

"Will you be staying the night?"

"Uh." Xavior and I hadn't talked about that. We'd agreed to make sure everyone got home safe with a vehicle service if needed. I hadn't thought about myself in this equation. We'd been dating for two months, and we weren't public yet. Had it only been two months?

"I will take the sound you made as still considering your options," Edward said, giving a slight nod as he went back to the kitchen. I stood there with my mouth open, a controller headset clasped in my hand. After shaking my head, I went back to setting up the equipment for the evening's party.

Holo game systems were plenty sophisticated these days, but easy to install. You placed sensors in a grid around the play area. When the system starts, it draws boundaries around the players and senses the player's movements via the controller headset. When a player stands inside the boundaries, they see the game environment surrounding them. There were pricier setups with directional floor placements that let you avoid hard barriers like your living room walls, but most of the games we had were fairly stationary, so that wouldn't be a problem tonight. We could also use the same system as an immersive movie experience, or just display a three-dimensional film or show. The holo in Xavior's bedroom that used light to create an opaque display that gave the illusion of three dimensions was ancient compared to this setup.

Xavior surprised me with a kiss on the top of my head as I finished the last few connections to the wireless system. I turned and reached for him before he could escape, so I could give him a proper kiss. He squatted next to me and watched me finish the final setup instructions.

"What do you think we'll end up playing first?" I motioned through the options on the screen.

"Depends if drinking starts before we play games or after. I would bet we start with the sports games, then move on to the dancing or obstacle course games. But we'll see. Davidson is pretty good at tennis, so I wouldn't be surprised if people go for that first."

"There's baseball on there, too. The entire group could play as a team against the computer. Maybe we can start that first. I'll load it as a subtle suggestion."

Xavior stood and chuckled. "Or you could just say that's what we're starting with, Greg. You're too diplomatic sometimes." The house system chimed, indicating there was a visitor at the door.

"If it were my choice, I'd start with the dancing game," I mumbled as Xavior went to answer the door.

"I heard that," Xavior teased. "Pick what you want."

The baseball game turned out to be a great choice as it was cooperative and had everyone in a good mood by the time we lost to the computer. Richards asked about the dancing game as they browsed the options. My eagerness to play it had vanished now that my coworkers were present. I kept quiet on the subject, then nearly choked on my beer when Xavior told on me.

"Lyndon can dance really well. You all have no idea."

Everyone turned to look at me. I held my beer as if I'd have to fend off comments, individuals, or both. I didn't know if I was blushing or dying of embarrassment.

"You have magical feet, do ya now, Lyndon? Why don't you come show us?" Kempton said.

"Ah, um, I don't think that's a good idea," I responded.

The cajoling and general ribbing didn't let up until I agreed. "This is peer pressure of the worst kind. You all have to promise not to laugh."

They all swore to various gods, goddesses, realms, and elements. I hoped lightning would strike Xavior's house and the electricity would go out.

After three rounds with the dance-off loser being switched out for someone else, I felt pretty ballsy. Especially when no one else stepped up. "It's cool. We can declare me the winner and play something else if everyone's done challenging these twinkle toes." That got a few laughs from the group.

Edward walked into the room and quietly talked with Xavior, who nodded, then he stepped forward. "Might I play, Mr. Lyndon?"

"Sure, Edward. Do you know how the controller works?"

"I'm versed in its use." He slipped it onto his head and quickly chose the options. When he set it to the most complicated combinations with the fastest music, I was pretty sure I was cooked.

"Are you ready, Mr. Lyndon?"

"If you're about to wipe out my high score, Edward, you can call me Greg."

"Alright, Greg. Are you ready?" A mixture of guffaws and ohs echoed around the living room. I nodded to Edward, and he motioned for the round to start. Eventually, I stopped playing and watched Edward.

The guy was basically Gene Kelly and Fred Astaire in one, and much older than either of them when they were alive. When he finished with a perfect score, the gathered group congratulated him. I gave him a hug, and he stiffly returned it. I'm not sure Edward ever had so many people notice him before. This was the first time I'd seen him not be the impeccable helper or Xavior's shadow.

"That was amazing, Edward. How long have you been dancing?" I asked.

"A very long time. One might say since Moses was a baby."

I had an intense desire to ask him whether he was joking or serious. The look he gave me indicated he wouldn't have answered. He gave a slight bow to everyone, straightened his jacket, though it was not out of place one centimeter, and walked back to the kitchen.

Other folks started up the tennis game.

"Okay, I'm ready for this. Let's go!" Davidson said as she tied back her natural hair, then stepped up to play.

I sat next to Xavior, barely keeping myself from touching him while he handed me my beer. "Did you know Edward could do that?"

"Ah, no. I'm as surprised as you are. He's never mentioned it as a skill of his."

"He made a joke about dancing since Moses was a baby."

"Really?" Xavior looked a bit surprised.

"Yeah." I finished my beer. "Do you even know how old he is?"

"No, he's never volunteered that information, and I don't ask because it's rude, but I've made guesses."

I nodded. "Well, Edward could be a professional dancer. He has some very classy moves, even for a game."

"So do you, Lyndon."

I gave him a distinct look that said not to flirt with danger, especially in front of our coworkers. He laughed and drank his beer. At some point, he volunteered for a tennis match. I watched as Xavior put up a close score, but he was no match for Davidson.

As folks called it a night, Xavior made sure they had rides home while Edward and I picked up the mess. When Xavior escorted the last few people out, he made a big show of slowly returning to the living room. I glanced at him, and he looked at me like I was a side of replicated prime rib. I ignored him until he came up behind me and wrapped his arms around my waist.

"It was a good night, wasn't it?" Xavior asked.

"Yeah. I had fun. Did you?"

"Mmm hmmm. We can have more fun."

"We could, but I should go home. It's late, and I have a long drive."

"How much have you had to drink?" Xavior asked.

"Two beers in six hours, with exercise and food. I'm pretty sure I'm fine." Xavior rested his head on my back and held me tighter.

I turned in his arms. Which was a mistake, as I instantly felt how much he wanted me. How he hadn't ground his obvious hard-on into my ass was a mystery.

"Xavior," I said, with some combination of amusement and annoyance in my voice. I had done reasonably well as of late, setting boundaries and saying no. Therapy helped a lot, though I had a long way to go before I was ready for the next step. Xavior knew that too.

"I know. I know, but I really need you, Greg. All the smells in the house have me frustrated because I only want yours right now."

He used to apologize for his biological instincts, but he'd also worked on stating what he needed instead of holding back his emotional and physical needs. It was good progress, considering we'd only started dating recently.

Xavior pleaded again. "Tomorrow's a weekend," he said, stating the obvious. "You could stay. We could watch holovids, make out, and fall asleep on the couch."

That idea was really appealing to me. Though I had another that might help us both, but keep our rules intact. "Come here, Xav."

I took his hand and sat on the couch. I guided him to straddle my lap. He immediately looped his arms around my shoulders and gave me an urgent kiss. I pulled back a little and gave him my best playful smile.

"Oh, no, what's that look for?" Xavior's eyes danced with mirth and trepidation. While we had boundaries, on several occasions, one of us would start something at a distance. It was too risky for us to do more than kiss, given his aging cycle. Tonight, I wanted to take a risk.

"You did really well keeping our boundaries in front of the group. Do you want to push one a little?"

"How?" The need and desire in his voice prompted me to continue.

I slid my hands up his back, and he moaned softly. It caused my half-hard dick to spring fully to life. I wanted him as much as he wanted me, maybe more, and I was about to play with fire. I brought my hands to his shoulders. "Keep your hands on my shoulders and don't move them. No touching below the belt. Agreed?"

He smirked and nodded. I kissed him again, then moved my hips. His arms tightened around my shoulders as he caught on and pressed closer. I gripped his shoulders harder to feel him against me. The friction between us was everything and frustrating at the same time. I wanted his skin against mine, but I wouldn't push us that far, not yet.

Xavior moaned and kissed my forehead as I panted into his neck and chest. It was barely enough. This was worse in some ways than making out. Xavior's moans shifted to soft growls as our frustration grew. I started to second-guess my brilliant plan.

"Lie down," Xavior said.

I complied by sliding to my right, and his weight pressed into me. It gave him more leverage when he reached for my hands and put them above our heads. I squeezed his hands as his new position lined us up and made us both groan.

We were a mess of swear words and sloppy, panting kisses. Every line of Xavior's body pressed into mine. I couldn't help but think about how fucking hot it would be to have my dick balls deep in him while he rode me. The thought was enough to take me near the breaking point.

"I want you inside of me, Greg." Xavior's soft words caught my attention. I felt my back bow slightly and saw lights behind my eyelids as I squeezed them shut against the orgasm that curled my toes.

When I caught my breath, Xavior was still grinding himself into what was left of my hard-on. My right hand let go of Xavior's and I wrapped it around the back of his neck. I rolled us slightly and pinned him against the couch while I kept moving my hips against his. I whispered in his ear. "Your body feels so right against mine. You made me come so hard, Xav. Come for me."

I kissed and licked his lips. Nuzzled into his neck and sucked at his flushed skin. I heard him whimper and felt his abdomen constrict against me. "That's it. Fuck, I love the noises you make." I moved my hand from his neck to his hair and pulled slightly. Xavior grabbed onto me and held me tight as he came. I held him to me as he shivered through his orgasm.

We were dazed and sated for the moment. We looked at each other and laughed softly between heavy breaths. I kissed Xavior hard, then lifted myself off him. As I watched him sit up on the couch, I remembered we had an audience.

"Oh shit, Xavior. I didn't think about Edward."

Xavior waved me off. "He's heard way worse and dealt with people in way less clothing. Knowing him, he's likely in his room."

"He has a room here?"

"Yeah, why wouldn't he?"

I shook my head. There was no way that I'd get used to that, but that was a topic for later.

"I'll call you when I get home." I leaned down and kissed him again. Xavior made a noise between a grunt and a "what?" sound, and I chuckled. "I've done enough damage to our boundaries for the night. Trust me, I have enough energy to drive home."

He sighed. "I know you're right, but I don't want to let you go." He stood and walked me to the coat closet. When I turned around, we both noticed the substantial wet spot over my crotch. He moved his hand toward me to spell it clean.

I stopped him before he cast the spell. "No, that's mine. I don't want it to disappear yet." It sounded possessive even to my ears, but it was a reminder of what we shared. I wasn't ready to give it up.

"Aren't worried that people will notice?"

I pulled my hoodie out of the coat closet, tied it around my waist, and let the sleeves drop in front of my crotch. "Nope." I kissed him one more time before I made my escape. As I got into my vehicle and turned it on, a message came up on the console.

I can tell you about the blood bank theft.

Press the button to return the call

I called the number.

The voice was low, sounded like gravel, and they had a slight cough as the call connected. "Meet me tomorrow at Café Fairplay. I'll have everything you need."

They hung up.

"Shit."

INFORMER

GREGOR

Café Fairplay was a known Hargrove Coven business. It operated as a tourist trap because it was a well-known hookup spot for those with a vampire fetish. Xavior and I arrived after full dark as the café opened for the night. A few other patrons followed us inside and took seats. We sat next to each other, away from the windows and toward the back of the seating area. When the waitstaff came by, we ordered a pot of coffee.

We'd talked with Captain Lang about the mysterious contact. He didn't like it, but he let us go ahead with the meeting since it was in public. How they had managed to get the contact info for my private vehicle was cause for concern. The covens had resources, though to what extent and how large they were was always a mystery to anyone outside the organization. No one was sure if they would find anything, even though CSI and central tech were looking into it.

"Why wouldn't the coven take care of this themselves? It's weird that they would give us information to go after some of their own, don't you think?" The coffee sucked, and I wondered how long this informant would make us wait.

"I've never known covens to give up information willingly. Sometimes they've done things for favors or to keep the peace.

Maybe this is one of those times." Xavior took a sip of his coffee. I could feel his eyes on me. "Have I mentioned lately that I think your self-control is amazing?"

"No. Why would you say that?"

"Because you're outwardly calm, but everything I'm picking up from you says otherwise."

"Thanks, I think." I gave him a smile and tried to steer things back toward the case. "The break-in happened almost a year ago. So why would they offer information now?"

"That's the problem when dealing with the covens; you never know," Xavior said with a sigh that spoke of volumes he'd yet to share.

An ill-fitting suit that seemed to nearly swallow the person wearing it walked into the café and made eye contact. As the suit walked toward us, I noticed it wasn't only the suit that didn't fit. His skin hung off him, too. The monochromatic nature of the guy put my instincts on alert. While he wasn't a vampire, he looked pallid, with gray eyes and hair that nearly matched the suit he wore. The only distinct differences were his shoes, which were a dark gray that matched the circles under his eyes.

"Detectives, I'm Larry Jackson. I represent the Hargrove Coven."

Xavior stayed seated while I stood and shook Jackson's clammy hand. I barely kept from wiping it on my slacks as we took a seat at the table. I glanced at Xavior and wondered what he picked up from Jackson.

"Coffee?" Xavior offered.

"No, thank you." Jackson set his briefcase on the chair next to him, put his elbows on the table, and laced his fingers together.

We sat and stared at each other until I couldn't handle it any longer. "You said you had information for us?"

We watched as he pulled out his phone and flipped on the small holo display. "These are your people of interest. I know where they are located." Jackson flipped through several pictures that detailed three individuals. "They are pledges, so you should take precautions accordingly."

"This seems fairly convenient. Is there any evidence to corroborate your allegations?" Xavior asked.

Jackson opened his briefcase and pulled out a sealed bag with a blood bag inside that had a label from the blood bank. "You'll find that all three individuals of interest have finger-prints on this. We also know more evidence is at the residence. This was not their first theft."

"Why is the coven giving up pledges?" I asked.

"We do not condone their methods. The bad press and attention are unwanted. If we were to let them complete the pledging process, then it would signal to other pledges and covens that we condone their behavior." Jackson hit a button on his phone and shut down the holo.

I glanced at Xavior, then back at Jackson. "You can send the files here." I made a gesture with my phone that sent a digital copy of my contact information to his device. "We'll take the evidence, but the most we can likely get with any of this is a door knock. This is all circumstantial."

"Is it enough to have you investigate?" Jackson asked.

"It's enough to ask questions," Xavior said.

"Well then, gentlemen, I'll leave you to ask your questions. Good day." Jackson closed his briefcase, stood, and walked out of the café without a backward glance. I moved to take his place so I could look at Xavior. He traced a silence spell onto the table and activated it. It created a dead spot in the area's acoustics. It's pronounced when someone uses one because of the change in sound, but it was so common for people to use them it was likely no one would care or notice.

"What did you pick up?" I asked.

"Well, he was telling us what he knew. Which reads about the same as the truth in his smell. They gave him specific instruc-tions, and he only gave us the information we asked for. I get that he's a lawyer, but that was a little too clean. He smelled too clean, too."

"What do you mean?"

"The guy's hair was greasy, his nails showed he smokes to-bacco or something, his teeth were yellow, and he had stains on his clothes."

"Yeah, I noticed that too."

"All I smelled was the truth from him. That's it. He had no body odor, tobacco, or shampoo. There wasn't even a whiff of food from the stains. They spelled him to give off one scent."

"Which means they know you're a dragon."

"Yeah." Xavior sighed and finished his coffee.

"We need to talk to Lang. This is suspicious as fuck, and while I want to chase down this lead, it doesn't feel quite right."

"I agree, but this is the first lead we've had. Plus, if we can get a provisional order based on what I smelled, it'll give us the chance to search the property based on the information Jackson gave us."

"Your sense of smell is also circumstantial. There isn't any way to corroborate it."

Xavior used a napkin to pick up the evidence bag Jackson left. "Wanna see if there's magical residue on this to corroborate my nose?"

"Fuck, I really want to kiss you right now."

"Pay the tab and wait until we get to the vehicle." He broke the spell when we got up from the table.

I thumbed for the bill and walked outside as Xavior sealed the evidence in one of our evidence bags, napkins and all. "You don't think your magic will contaminate it, or your pheromones?" I asked as I walked up.

"Shouldn't, but I'll make a note of it in case it comes up. I would wager that whatever Jackson used to mask his scent was on the bag, too. Because you know what else I didn't smell that was clearly evident?"

Fuck. "Blood."

"Yes." Xavior smiled. "Have I ever said how sexy you are when you're working a case?" He closed the storage area and ushered me toward the passenger door.

"No, I don't think so." My mouth was dry, and my brain hadn't entirely caught up to where our relationship was sometimes. After work, it was all I could do to keep from acting on every instinct or idea that went through my head.

"No?" He stepped toward me. I took a step back until my back hit our vehicle. Xavior took advantage and pressed into me.

"Um, technically still working," I warned him.

"Technically." Xavior made the slightest movement, and I groaned. "And technically, you're the one who mentioned kissing first."

"I did." It was a moment of weakness, but I didn't regret it.

"So, get in the vehicle, Lyndon. Unless you want to kiss out here where everyone can see."

I opened the passenger door as Xavior went to the driver's side. Once inside, our hands searched for any bit of bare skin available while we kissed. The windows were completely fogged over before we stopped.

I pulled away first and stated the obvious. "We need to take our evidence to the lab and put it under a stasis seal until they can get to it in the morning."

"You're right. It's late." Xavior recovered a bit as he shifted away from me and started the vehicle. "Are you going to drive back to your parent's house tonight?"

I hadn't thought about that. "I'm still working on the house, so I can sleep there."

Xavior narrowed his eyes at me. "You know I have an enormous bed, and I'm willing to share." He backed out of the parking space and drove us toward headquarters.

"I know." I'd seen it enough times via our video chats.

The rest of the drive was quiet. We finished up what we needed to process the evidence. By that time, it was nearly three in the morning. As I headed for the garage, Xavior stopped me.

"Greg, you shouldn't drive home so late."

"What am I going to do for a change of clothes?"

"I have that figured out. You can crash at my place. I would feel better, especially after someone messed with your vehicle." When I didn't say anything, he said, "Please?" with a bit more concern in his voice.

I wavered. It was another push on our boundaries, and that worried me as much as driving home. While the captain had allowed me to borrow an unmarked vehicle, we didn't know if they had followed Xavior or me.

"It's been a long day, and my house is a short walk from here. I'd rather not worry about you tonight, please?"

I looked at my shoes, then back at him. "No rule-breaking?"

He took a deep breath and let it out. "Promise."

The look on his face was full of hope, and those damn emerald eyes of his. Fuck. "Okay."

I didn't remember the walk to his place. We talked mostly about work. When Xavior unlocked the door and invited me inside, I had an odd sense of being home, which was strange since my first time at his place was the previous night.

"Do you want something to drink?" Xavior asked.

"Water would be good." I stood in the living room while he went to the kitchen and returned with a glass.

He motioned us forward, and I followed him up the stairs. He hesitated a moment, then walked further down the hallway, past his bedroom to what I assumed was the guest room he'd told me about.

"I have something I want to show you," he said. He clenched his hands slightly and took a breath before he opened the door. It revealed a queen-size bed, complete with sheets and a duvet, and a single long box sitting on top. I glanced at him, and he gave me a nervous smile.

"That's for you." He nodded toward the box, then glanced around the room. "This is all for you. I wanted you to have a place to stay if you needed it. If you had stayed last night, I would have shown you then, but I didn't want to push after you insisted on driving home." He leaned on the doorjamb as I walked into the room.

I walked over to the bed, set my glass down on the nightstand, and opened the box. Inside was a complete set of clothes, including boxer briefs and socks. "This is too much." I turned to look at him. His face was lit up with pure delight, as I felt self-conscious about the gift.

"You're my boyfriend. It means I can buy you things and give you choices. I can easily pay for a vehicle service to take you home. If that's what you want." It was my turn to take a deep breath.

"Xavior, I'm not. . ."

"I know. That's okay, too. You can stay here in this room. Or share my bed. It's up to you. Even if you slept with me and all you wanted to do was sleep, I would manage. I'd probably have to take care of myself in the shower first. Nevertheless, I'll manage."

We stood there awkwardly for a moment, then Xavior pushed himself away from the door, back into the hall. "Okay, then, I'll leave you to get cleaned up. Yell if you need me."

"Alright. Thank you."

"Anytime." He closed the door behind him without so much as a kiss blown in my direction. He was serious and scared. Admittedly, so was I.

Last night was terrific, but I definitely wanted to catch my breath and think about our next step. Xavior obviously knew what he wanted, which was clear in the care he'd taken with the room and clothes.

He'd mentioned last night how all the smells bothered him, and he only wanted mine. I shook my head and groaned when I realized what he had done by putting me in this room. It's very typical dragon behavior to capture a scent in a contained space. I'd be very flattered if the biological implications weren't staring me in the face. Xavior was much further along in the aging cycle than he wanted to admit. It all meant I needed to decide soon.

I tried not to think about that as I used the ensuite to take a shower. While I dried off and slipped on the new boxers he'd bought me, I noticed the robe on the back of the bedroom door and shook my head again.

Over the last few weeks, therapy had helped us understand ourselves better. It enabled us to better control the biological drives that affected us. Xavior still visited for family dinners, but we hadn't risked another overnight stay until now.

As I lay in bed and stared at the ceiling, all the what-ifs and various scenarios ran through my head. The truth was, I'd made my decision a long time ago. The risk of not only my metaphorical heart, but possibly our lives, held me back.

I sat up and scrubbed a hand over my face, got out of bed, took the robe down, and threw it on, determined to have a conversation. Before I could knock on Xav's door, his voice came through it like a soft caress.

"Come in, Greg."

My eyes adjusted to the darkness in Xavior's room as I closed the door behind me. He was in bed. I stood there a moment to gather my wits. But instead of talking, I took off my robe and hung it on the door next to his.

"Can I stay here tonight?" I wasn't sure it was the smart thing, but I didn't exactly care at the moment.

Xavior moved the covers on the other side of him and patted the bed. "Sure."

I got into bed and pulled the covers up. Before I was aware of it, I moved toward Xavior as he turned to his side, facing away from me. I wrapped my arms around him and sighed. The heat of him felt delicious against my skin. To hold him like this settled my brain faster than any conversation.

"Better?" Xavior asked.

"Yes. Is this alright?"

"Yes. It's absolutely all right." I was the big spoon, with one leg draped over his and his left arm covering mine, circling his waist. I snuck my right arm under his pillow so his head would rest on the bend of my elbow. "Night, Greg."

"Night, Xav." I kissed his ear, and the tension went out of his body. If he hadn't wanted me this close, he could certainly move. I wondered how well he slept without me for him to be this relaxed in my arms.

As Xavior rhythmic breathing soothed my nerves and lulled me into a relaxed state. All the doubts and worst-case scenarios faded away while we slept.

THE KNIGHT OF SAINT GEORGE

XAVIOR

It took three weeks to obtain the provisional order we needed to approach the house and the persons of interest. While much of the evidence we had from the lawyer was suspect, the blood bag, the magic residue, and the report Greg and I gave were enough for a judge. They granted us an order for a night entry to look for more evidence. They sent a notice to the coven of the impending order in accordance with vampire interaction laws. The coven didn't respond, which was extremely unusual. They almost always preferred a representative on hand when someone entered a property they owned.

Once we arrived, I noted the condition of the house. "This looks nice for a pledge house. I don't think I've seen one this good in a while."

"Yeah, it's old and needs some paint, but whoever lives here is taking care of it. Even the lawn is maintained." Greg shut the driver-side door and came around to my side of the vehicle.

"They boarded the windows up from the inside. We should do a walk around while we wait for full dark." Something didn't sit right with me. Since there were only three individuals of interest, we didn't think it would take more than Greg and me to serve the provisional order. At Lang's insistence, we had extra mobile units in the area, just in case.

Greg took one side of the house, and I took the other. Once we reached the back, we compared notes. "It's a slab house. So at least we don't have to deal with a basement," I said. Even the backyard was neat. The place gave me weird vibes the longer I looked at it.

"There's an attic, but the vents look clear, so my bet is that they sleep in a bathroom or closet. I only saw one window that looked like a bathroom toward the front of the house." Greg rechecked his vest pockets. It's something he did when he was concerned.

"It's almost time. Should we call for a unit?" I thought we could still handle it, but Greg's instincts erred toward caution when mine didn't.

He sighed and shrugged. "It's quiet. They don't seem to have a day watcher, or someone would have come out and told us off already." Greg put his hands on his hips and looked up at the house again. "I think we can handle it. If they are in there, they'll probably take off out the back door once they realize we're here. Once they do that, we can call in CSI for evidence."

"Makes sense. I'll message the patrols that we're about to knock." Greg nodded, and we walked back to the front door. I tossed an imager into the air to follow us through the entire process. I nodded to Greg, and he knocked.

"Yeah?" a voice on the other side of the door replied. Greg and I looked at each other. We hadn't expected a swift response.

"It's JPS. We're following up on an investigation. Would you be willing to talk with us and answer a few questions?" No answer was forthcoming. Greg shrugged as he glanced at me. "We have a provisional order that allows us to search the premises. Could you please open the door?"

Either it was a vampire, or they had a day watcher, which meant that these pledges were more important than the coven let on. Still, we expected them to head out the back door. The last thing we wanted to do was tangle with three vampires after they woke up.

Greg continued with the warnings, per protocol. "You are failing to follow a request. Unless you comply, we are allowed to enter the premises without permission. Can you please open the door?" We waited a few more minutes for anyone inside to respond.

"On three?" Greg nodded. I gave him my best, reassuring smile. I'd be lying if I wasn't thinking of making out with him later. Apparently, he could tell because he smacked my shoulder.

"Focus, Brantley. On three," he repeated, as he adjusted his projectile armor. I wore mine because Greg insisted, but I wasn't happy about it. I didn't have to give the door more than one good shove before we walked into the living room with stop-goo in hand.

The imager above us generated a red-filtered light as it moved into the space, but I could see in the dark without it. Different organizations had tried night-vision spells. They discovered the spells wore off at the wrong time or were often overpowered by a bright light, which could cause blindness if the species couldn't handle it.

We cleared the living room, the kitchen, a spare bedroom, and a closet big enough to hold a person near the front door.

"The back door in the kitchen is locked. I don't think they left." Greg whispered.

"Shit." I took a whiff as we approached the main bedroom. I held up three fingers and pointed at my nose, then at the door.

Greg nodded. "It's JPS. Could you please comply with the order as we've requested?" They didn't answer. We couldn't call in CSI if we didn't clear the house. I hoped that we'd find them incapacitated from lack of blood, but I had my doubts.

I shrugged and caught Greg's attention, then counted down silently. When I shouldered the door, I heard boards burst. They had barricaded it. It was the first thing that made sense since we had entered the house.

It was quiet for a moment as Greg and I entered the room. I kicked a few busted boards out of the way. He looked right at me, and I noticed his eyes widen in surprise. I turned in time to see three vampires rush out of another door to our left. Greg and I both threw our goo packs to stop their forward motion. I recognized the flash of goo neutralizer as the packs hit and dissipated quickly.

One vampire went for Greg. A magical light flared as Greg activated his shield. It left me with the other two, who decided I was a better target. I pivoted and slammed the first one into the wall across from me.

The second, with blond hair, showed their fangs as they tried to grapple me. I twisted and kicked. Blondie went down. The first vampire, taller than Greg by a couple of inches, came back from the wall stunner. I used the tall vamp's momentum to spin them back into the wall again. The tall vamp went through it and stuck there in a mass of splintered wood.

I was about to throw another stop-goo pack at the new wall ornament when the blond one came up off the floor and tackled me. I took the brunt of the move. In retaliation, they tried to sink their fangs into my arm. I heard a tooth snap and a howl of pain as they realized their mistake. I swiped their legs out from under them and hit them with the goo pack in my hand. This time, it stuck. Either they didn't have another charge to dispel the goo, or they couldn't reach it, which worked for me. I tossed another pack on the vamp-turned-wall-art, then looked for Greg.

Greg's shield was holding up under the sheer onslaught of blows the black-haired vampire delivered. I got into Greg's line of sight as he maneuvered the vamp so I'd have a clear shot at disabling them with a goo pack. I tossed it at their feet, which missed as they flipped out of the way, then turned to face us with a knife drawn.

One look between us, and Greg nodded. I moved forward as Greg shifted back toward the door to cut off the exit and signal our backup. We'd practiced things like this at least a hundred times in the gym during training. A knife wasn't a threat to me, so I took the lead.

I waited for them to move. The vampire's lunge was sloppy. I grabbed their wrist and trapped the knife against my leg, then pulled them into a neck lock. It seemed like a contest of strength they were losing until they twisted in a way that seemed impossible and broke my grapple by flipping us both to the floor. The unexpected move knocked the wind out of me. They recovered, and to my surprise, rushed Greg.

The vamp slammed into Greg's shield, even as he called for them to stop. They both spun back into the room just as I got to my feet. Something felt off. The vampires should have run, but they didn't. This one had a clear exit now and instead went for Greg. I waited to engage the vampire without impeding Greg's maneuverability as he blocked blow after blow with his shield.

Greg was maneuvering the vamp for me to disable when his shield suddenly failed. He caught the next lunge from the vampire as he dropped his shield, performing a trapping maneuver by pulling the knife toward himself and locking the vamp's wrist against his hip. As I watched for an opening to help, I had a moment to be impressed with Greg.

The vampire twisted and pushed with their better-than-human strength against Greg's hold. Even with that, he seemed to have it handled. Greg moved in a way that spoke of a lot of muscle memory and training. Training that wasn't provided by public safety departments. The knife flashed between them as Greg took a more aggressive tactic, driving the assailant into a wall, twisting the knife to his advantage. While they taught public safety officers to disable or remove a weapon, Greg was clearly aiming to retaliate and use the assailant's weapon against its wielder.

The movements were lightning-fast, and as I watched, I realized I had moved too close. I was all too confident in my invulnerability to keep a perimeter, which gave the vampire an opening. The knife slid through the projectile fabric, pierced my skin, then slipped through my scales. The flash of heat, light, and pain made me gasp as the vamp realized they had penetrated my gut.

We collectively froze for a moment. The vamp leveraged the advantage and pressed the knife in, then up. I heard the pained noise Greg made and saw the fucked-up, bloody, fanged grin of the asshole that stabbed me. I looked at Greg's dark brown eyes, which were too wide with shock at what happened as the vampire let go of us, finally running and leaving their housemates behind.

"NO! No, no, no. Xavior. . ." Greg yelled as we dropped to the floor together. He kept his eyes on me as he fumbled for his phone to call central. "Officer down. Need assistance. Two individuals detained, one fled." He dropped his phone, still connected to central. I could hear them talk about EMS and patrols.

"Don't you fucking die on me, you asshole. Do you hear me?" Greg leaned over me. I noticed the blood on my hand when I reached for his face.

"I don't think we have a choice here, Greg." There was blood on him, on his hands, on me. I saw the knife still stuck obscenely in my guts. The view made me groan as a wave of cold went through my limbs. The pain faded, which probably wasn't a good sign.

"Fuck!" I reached up to touch Greg's face as he yelled. "Please, Xavior, Xav. . . please." Tears mixed with blood as I traced his cheek with my thumb. Greg frantically ripped at his shirt to wrap the knife and stop my bleeding out.

The cold I felt had to be from Greg's ability. This was his magic. The brutality and swiftness of the effect felt like poison, but that was barely an apt comparison because it moved much faster than my bloodstream could have carried it.

I felt Greg tapping my face as I closed my eyes for a moment. "Xav, wake up. Stay with me. Hear the sirens? They're almost here."

I felt my body jerk as Greg dissolved into a litany of no's again. Something kicked in and fought back the cold. A warmth spread through me like I'd held my breath. Instead, it was my entire body.

"Greg. . ."

"Yeah, Xav?" His face swam in and out of view.

"Did I mention my mum is a phoenix?"

THE PHOENIX DRAGON

GREGOR

"No, Xavior, you didn't tell me."

This moment was a living nightmare I couldn't escape. Even with his last breath, Xavior tried to reassure me. He exhaled, and the light went out of his eyes. Logically, that was it, but I couldn't let him go. I'd stopped the bleeding with my shirt and the compression from his projectile armor. I hoped that would be enough, or at least not make it worse.

"Fuck, don't do this to me, please," I begged as I started CPR. The sirens grew louder. I was so focused on trying to get Xavior to breathe that I fought the medics when they showed up until an officer waded into the situation, pulling me out of the way.

"We got him. Let us help," someone said. I tried to stay out of the way while I watched as they used their equipment and continued the same compressions.

Light flooded the room from a portable setup, and I shielded my eyes, then noticed my hands. All I saw was Xavior's blood. I felt numb as the dance of evidence collection and lifesaving measures went on around me. Other people removed the de-

tained vampires. Imagers floated above us and recorded all of
it.

The paramedic seemed troubled by a reading. "This isn't
right. It looks like his body temp is going up, but the rest of his
vitals aren't there." The medic hit the monitoring device. It let
out a warbled beep as they touched buttons and tried to take
another reading.

The other medic tried to adjust a sensor on Xavior's chest
and pulled back their hand like they'd been burned. "He's heat-
ing up."

What Xavior said suddenly clicked. "Phoenix," I said. Or at
least I think I did. "HEY!" I yelled, and people stopped to look
at me. "He's half-phoenix!"

"Oh, shit!" The medic near me jumped up, clearly in panic.
"Get everyone out! Clear the house. Grab anything you can and
go! Now!" People rushed around as Xavior glowed, then the
floor around him burst into flames.

I scooted back as he became a physical ember. "Shit!" Someone grabbed me by my armpits, hauled me up, and shoved me
toward an exit.

Everyone was clear of the structure by the time fire response
vehicles showed up to contain the blaze. The room we'd been in
moments before was engulfed in flames, and the house quickly
followed. Someone had sent word that there was a phoenix
inside.

While the fire crews worked to make sure other houses
weren't affected, the rest of us watched for signs of life. Finally,
something shot up into the night sky and spread its wings as
the fire reached its peak.

The air stirred as the dragon flew low over the neighborhood.
He was slightly bigger than an elephant and had formidable
claws with a mouth full of teeth. People yelled, terrified, as he
soared above us and screamed into the night.

Xavior's beauty staggered me. He was primarily green, and
his wings and tail were covered in shiny feathers swirled with
green, blue, and red. He had a double set of horns, four limbs,
and claws on his wings. I'd seen this dragon in my dreams
dozens of times. I knew it was him.

I watched as he circled a few more times, then slowly landed on the street about a block up from the decimated house. I ran toward him as he roared. Several medics backed up and yelled at me not to go near him.

"It's alright. He's my partner!" Bystanders and the emergency crew backed off as I waved my badge at them. I hoped with everything I had that he recognized me as I tried to project calm while I walked toward him. "Xavior, it's me, Gregor." I shoved my badge into my pocket and held up my blood-covered hands.

He moved his head like he was trying to figure out what had happened. He shook his head again and stilled as I walked closer. I could feel the heat of his breath on my bare chest. When his snout bumped into my hand, it took my breath away. His scales were smooth like a snake's , but had raised edges in some places. I wondered what he would look like in the sun. Even in the dim light of the fire and the streetlamps, he was magnificent.

"Xavior, you scared the shit out of me." He let me come closer and made a soft rumble of what I could only imagine was amusement as he nuzzled, and I caressed him. People were staring, and others came out of their houses.

"Um, you probably need to change back or take off. We're drawing a crowd." He made a small huff that ruffled my hair as he shifted. I noticed a medic holding a blanket, and I waved them over. I took the blanket and wrapped it around Xavior as he regained his human form, then we hurried to the EMS bus and got inside.

The medic focused on Xavior's vitals while I watched. We'd been lucky that I hadn't murdered him. I grew angry as I realized he was safe. Someone else threw me a shirt, and I put it on.

"You could have fucking told. . ." His lips pressed against mine and cut off the angry tirade. We kissed as if nothing else mattered. My anger subsided with each urgent kiss we shared. I didn't care if there would be consequences. At that moment, he was safe, and that's all that mattered.

The medic shut off the monitors that blared warnings at her. Our foreheads touched as he smiled at me. "Hey, you," Xavior said.

"Hey," I replied, so fucking happy to see him, I kissed him again.

Someone cleared their throat, and we both turned to see Captain Lang at the entrance to the bus. I'm sure I was beet red from my neck to my ears, while Xavior sat wrapped in a blanket with a smug smile on his face.

"I'm glad to see you're both alive and well." Lang waved his hand back toward the house. "However, as this is still an active crime scene and the two of you are. . . indisposed, I think it might be good to let the bus take you both to the hospital to be checked out."

"Captain, I. . ."

"Lyndon, save it. You two aren't the first partners to become involved, and you won't be the last. Though right now, that bit of information needs to stay in this bus, if possible." Lang gave the medic a pointed look. She nodded and got up to talk to her driver in the front. "You're both on leave starting now." Lang smiled. "Use it wisely."

Lang closed the doors of the bus and banged on the side. The bus moved and Xavior swayed into me. I caught him around the middle as he put his head on my shoulder.

"Any ideas?" I asked.

I could feel Xavior smile. "I've got a few."

IMPORTANT EVENTS IN HISTORY

MAGICAL SPECIES PACT OF 1452

As trade and expansion became more prevalent, territorial wars and colonization became more commonplace. While harvesting parts of magical beings had always been unseemly, the trade and expansion of different empires pushed it into high gear. It was at this point that the Council of Elders, the wisest and oldest magical beings in Europe, came together to create the Magical Species Pact to protect magical beings or anyone who used magic. The pact made magical beings inert or non-magical upon death. If any part of the being was magical, it would render any magic that part or person carried inert. It effectively enforced tolerance between species that shared the same continent.

What they did not understand at the time was how this would affect beings with regenerative powers, such as phoenixes. Magical species that go through a cycle of renewal, such as phoenixes, have a duality of power, as their death generates magic that causes a rebirth, allowing the individual to keep their magical abilities, whatever those were. There's been some side effects attributed to the pact, as phoenixes have reported issues with memory loss since its enactment.

Nor was death magic taken into account. Of the number of elders that were represented by the council, very few had any dominion over the dead or undead. This was the loophole that allowed Joseph Florentine to thrive.

NECROMANTIC WAR: 1873 TO 1878 (THE NECRO WAR)

The major theater of war was in Europe and the Prussian Empire, though it spilled over into parts of the Russian Empire as well. Joseph Florentine had been an exceptional necromancer who rose to power in the mid-1800s. His platform centered on allowing magic users the rights and freedoms to use magic as they pleased. He and his followers wanted to abolish the Magical Species Pact created by the Council of Elders to protect magic users. Florentine considered it the height of hubris that one of the most powerful groups of magical beings in Europe had forced magic users on that continent into the pact.

It took many magical species, including necromancers, vampires, and non-magical species (mostly humans) to fight off Florentine's forces.

AUTHOR'S NOTE

If protagonists have origin stories, writers do as well. Mine was somewhat of a reboot. A dear friend of mine, Elizabeth, encouraged me to attend a writer's conference in 2019. What followed has been nothing short of a dream come to life.

The Saint George Chronicles has come a long, long way since its initial inception in March 2020. Originally, it started as a serialized flash fiction I published on my blog. I thank Kharma K. for that idea. They gave me a way forward when I was stuck on another project that was frustrating the shit out of me. They are officially Gregor and Xavior's godparent, as neither character would exist without them.

Since those first dozen flash fictions, this story has evolved a lot. At first, I'd leaned into all the copaganda that I had grown up with, though with less violence. I wasn't looking for the good guys necessarily, but I was still idolizing a system that has brutalized so many people, and continues to do so.

Another writer, Skye K. who read one of the worst drafts of this book, pointed out that my characters didn't have to be part of the current policing system. She waved at the literal fantasy world in front of me and asked what could I do differently instead of continuing to perpetuate the same glorification and idolization of copaganda I grew up with.

Little did she know that it not only spurred me on to rewrite the book but also create a universe where things could be better, so like the Crononauts card game, I made a slightly altered timeline, then made an open magical world where myths and legends exist. Today it even has a name: the Mythical Desires Universe.

As with all endeavors, a lot of folks supported this one. First off, I want to thank Kharma K. and their group: Inclusive Romance Project. I've found a lot of support in their group and appreciate absolutely everything they have done to build an inclusive place for anyone interested in writing romance.

I'd like to thank my steadfast crit group. You made this dream a reality, supported and vetted my odd tangents, and encouraged me to write bigger and better. I published this book in large part because of you all and I won't ever forget that.

To my editor, Tori, who kept encouraging me even though I had a lot to learn about craft and my bad writing habits.

To my beta readers — Gonzo, Johnna, Kristy, and Shawn—thank you for jumping in and giving me excellent feedback. Some, if not all, of your suggestions ended up in the book.

A shout-out to the Tapas readers who commented and liked this story as I was figuring things out. Your support and encouragement kept me posting the next chapter to see what you all would say next.

Stories need visuals, and two artists have done so much to bring Greg, Xavior, and the world around them to life. Joanne and Marty, thank you so much for taking my words and making them lines and color that come alive. Your visuals continue to inspire me, and I hope they will inspire others too.

And finally, to my stalwart writing buddy, my first beta reader, and dear friend, Sam B. You read every chapter before I posted it, as I worked through what was next and even helped me get to the next plot point. I don't think this book would be as coherent if it wasn't for our constant conversations about characters and motivations. Thank you for being as excited about this story as I am.

To anyone I missed, know that somewhere in this long process over the last two years your contributions were appreciated, positive or critical, as I wouldn't be the person I am now, writing this story, and putting it out there for everyone to enjoy.

Much Love,
M.L. Eaden

About the Author

M.L.(Mel) Eaden works by day in the tech industry, but at night, she reads books, writes stories, and is an avid board gamer. Originally from the sunflower state, she migrated to one with a lone star for work and sunshine. She has indie-published several books and short stories from the same queer-centric universe. She's also published several contemporary short stories in anthologies.

There are more great things to find at mleaden.com—blogs, reviews, and her latest newsletter.
Sign up today at mleaden.com and receive a free downloadable short story!

ALSO BY M.L. EADEN

You can find more books from the
Mythical Desires Universe at:
mleaden.com/books

Or sign up for the newsletter:
mleaden.substack.com

9 781962 655026